The Law of Quiet

J.M. Barrows

Magic Chicken Press

For: My parents.
This came out of me, so it counts as a grandbaby!

Contents

Chapter One

What Was Wrong

Yet another traffic light decided to turn red as Lauren approached. All she wanted after a crappy day at work was a cold beer and a hot shower. But no. All the traffic lights in the city apparently had a meeting about turning red as soon as she approached. She glared at the latest taunting red glow until her phone sang out a text notification.

Sorry everyone else bailed. No fun if it's just us two. I'm gonna buy a new laptop.

Grace. Her roommate and last possible ski trip buddy.

"Dammit!" She slammed her phone back into the cup holder. She'd been saving and looking forward to this trip for months! Killing herself with finding, fixing, and selling all those janky cars to save enough for a couple weeks of luxurious fun. Fun! She deserved it. Some adrenaline, some friends, some time away from her everyday troubles. Was it so wrong t-

Beep! Beeeeep! The car behind her was already blaring its horn about the light being green. Flipping them off, she sped forward.

Last Saturday, a scant six weeks from their scheduled departure from dull, dreary Iowa was when the first pair had bailed – a married couple with two young kids. Adventurous kids, who had decided that the living room of their apartment needed a fireplace for Santa to travel down at Christmas. While their babysitter had been stoned out of her mind on the couch, the kids used hammers on a wall to carve out space. Aluminum foil was glued to a shoebox and shoved in place. Toilet paper rolls served as a chimney out the window.

Naturally, they'd needed to test the fireplace.

The one stroke of luck they'd had was that when the "chimney" caught fire, the oldest kid thought maybe their idea wasn't great and ran next door to get a neighbor. It didn't save the apartment. The neighbor did manage to pull the babysitter out after calling 911. He also banged on doors and got several neighbors out of the small building in which the cheapskate landlord had neglected the fire alarms. Not one had sounded a warning.

The day after hearing that story, Lauren had tested her own fire alarms, bought three fire extinguishers for house, garage, and car, and checked her renter's insurance to make sure it covered accidental fires started by curious little kids. She didn't begrudge the beleaguered parents dropping out of the ski trip. That another friend canceled to repair their car made sense too.

Lauren did mind it when two others didn't want to be the only couple on the trip and decided to go to Florida by themselves. After their flakey departure, another friend went back to usual winter plans of visiting family in Boston, and *another* stopped answering texts. Now Grace.

"Fuck them." Lauren muttered to the steering wheel of her car. "I'll go by myself."

Actually, it might be better this way. She could sneak in a flight or two up in the mountains without having to make up reasons about why she ducked away from friends at night. Frustration, anger, and the teasing hope of flight simmering under her skin, Lauren raced home, forgoing the cold beer and hot shower to fidget in front of her laptop, clicking through ski instructor bios and training packages and lodge prices and reviews.

```
"Lernt to ski with Bear and he's grate! Super glad
I took Nona's advise and pict him on my 2nd trip
out there. He's pashent and fun and never made me
feel stupid."
```

Lauren finished reading the glowing review about Bear and scrolled on. Another reviewer with better grammar mentioned how glad they were that they'd gone with Nona's advice about Bear. Curiosity had Lauren hunting for more information on this Nona and why her advice should be followed. Apparently, Nona Hummel was a resident of the area. A guide for hire. She'd take any level of hiker on a customized trip through the mountains.

Anything from a guided day hike to a two-week adventure was on the table. There were hike-thrus from a drop-off point to a pickup. Or get dropped off at a base camp with daily adventures around the area. Or cross-country skiing. The hiker or backpacker had to provide their own basic essentials. Almost everything else could be rented from the local lodge or Nona herself. Groups were preferred, yet she would take a solo hiker who paid extra fees.

Her Facebook page was full of glowing reviews and pictures from people who'd hired her. The woman was white, tall and lean, and looked like a professional tree hugger. But it was the mountains and expanses of raw nature that pulled Lauren's attention.

It would be easy to get lost up there. And sneak in a few midnight flights.

"Oh hell yea." Lauren grinned.

The price was comparable to a ski package, and the small group scheduled for Lauren's time frame was open to solo hikers joining them. Even if the group dropped out, the price was within budget. Not that a couple hundred bucks more would deter her now. She kept reading.

The guide had years of experience and training with survival skills, CPR, first-aid, and backpacking in the Colorado mountains. Local forest rangers endorsed her expertise. In fact, she was a regular assistant and teacher in the survival skill programs that the rangers offered every season. She assisted in rescue operations after storms and avalanches, when people went missing.

More research found some crazy reviews about how Nona was a fake and not to be trusted. The venom in their messages made Lauren pause. One comment right after a particularly vicious review argued about how Nona was one of the most professional, knowledgeable guides they'd ever met. Anyone saying things that mean about her was probably refused sex. That reviewer, along with many other of the positive ones, were well-traveled people. Members of the backcountry website. They were legitimate, with heaps of adventuring under their belts.

Lauren shrugged. If the guide was really that bad, she'd get her money back. Or leave the bitch somewhere on the trail. Either way, there was flying in her future. She started an application to hire the guide.

"You're seriously going to go by yourself?" Amber's voice rose with surprise, tilting sideways into digital as the video connection fuzzed. Best friends shouldn't live so far away. They definitely shouldn't have boiling hatred for all things winter, *especially* when it was Lauren's favorite season! But no, Amber had refused to even consider the idea of joining Lauren in the snowy mountains, didn't even let Lauren finish asking the question during the BBQ party last Memorial Day weekend. She sure as balls couldn't be convinced last minute.

"Yea." Lauren shrugged.

Amber muttered something off camera to her spouse, followed by said spouse popping his face into the screen, squinting at Lauren's declaration of solo travel. "You're going alone?" Royce asked.

"I'm a big girl." Lauren muttered. "I can do things by myself."

It was Amber who rolled her eyes and started laughing first. "I know. You're also a group activity kind of girl. When's the last time you did something other than grocery shopping by yourself?"

"Yea, well." Ego soothed, Lauren agreed. "I need to get out of this town for a while. I'll make some friends in the lodge or the bar or something."

Amber snorted, "Flipping extroverts."

"We do enjoy making new friends." Royce snickered. "Go get 'em, Ren!"

<hr>

"She looks Polynesian." Lyleigh said.

Nona shrugged at the comment. If reddish-brown skin, thick black eyebrows, and big, brown eyes were Polynesian, then sure. Whatever. Client pictures were for an idea of who to look for when they met for the first time, not to ogle.

"Think she speaks any Polynesian? Is that a language too? Or maybe she's Samoan. Samoans have big shoulders and pretty black hair like that."

"She paid her deposit and listed as fluent in English. I don't need to know about her genetics." Nona grumbled at her sister's obvious attempts to point out...

"She's really cute."

That. "I don't date clients, Lyleigh." How many times did she have to repeat it?

"Doesn't mean you can't look, Frizz-head. Nothing wrong with looking and enjoying what you see."

Nona glared at her little sister's irritating nickname and incessant pushing. "There's a lot wrong with ogling a client. Puts me in a mindset that I don't want to be in. Not to mention, what if there was something between us? Half my clients live in completely different time zones. I'm not looking for a long-distance relationship. And what if that chemistry gets noticed by other clients? They leave reviews! I don't need that kind of complication in my already complicated life!"

Lyleigh was quiet for a moment. "We live in a small town. How else you going to meet someone new?"

"A small vacation town. I could meet some other tourist that hasn't hired me."

"Right," snorted out. "When you are in town, you avoid tourists like the plague. When you can't, you're the professional, who puts on her customer service smile and pretends to not notice the nice people flirting with you."

True. Unpleasant to hear, but true.

"Makes me wonder if you still aren't over Duncan or if you're just that afraid of trying again with someone new."

Nona was long past being stuck on her ex-husband, but she also wasn't ready to trust someone else with her heart. She didn't want to admit to being that afraid though. Who ever wanted to admit to being afraid? "The thought of getting back together with Duncan makes me more than a little nauseous. Don't ever insinuate that again."

Lyleigh's steady gaze didn't blink. "Okay," she finally said. "I won't insinuate that again if you go on a date with my buddy Fernando next week."

"He's short!" was her first reaction. So short. His eyes were at level with her breasts.

"He's charming, really cute, and has a degree in software engineering with a really good job." Lyleigh shot back.

"He leaves the house about twice a year."

Eyes narrowed at her. "He works from home."

"He's afraid of heights," Nona vaguely remembered a conversation from a few months ago about why Fernando never went skiing.

Lyleigh huffed. "The man goes to the gym five days a week. He's ripped. You will drool when he takes his shirt off. So what if he doesn't like all the things you do? Differences make for interesting relationships. You'd hate it if you could never go on hikes or ski trips alone occasionally."

Out of arguments, Nona sighed. "Fine. One date."

Her sister cheered, already thumbing at her phone, and within ten minutes, Nona had a date for Thursday. It came despite her dread and annoyance. And went much better than expected. Nona would never admit it, but she was glad that Lyleigh had manipulated her into that date. One, Fernando was extremely attractive and charming. Two, she enjoyed herself thoroughly. Three, there was zero romantic chemistry between them. Four, Lyleigh would stay off her case for at least a few weeks. What was wrong with being single anyway?

She sighed. What was wrong was that she didn't want to be single. She also didn't want her heart ripped out again.

Chapter Two

Flannel

Authentic, crackling fire caged in a hearth behind her, Laurn sat people watching. The occasional employee went by in their color coded uniforms and worn shoes, but the place was mostly filled with privileged snow bunnies wearing expensive labels and brand-new ski boots. They bragged about time on the slopes, the cost of their trip, and how long they waited in line for the lift.

The scents of expensive coffee and hot cocoa mingled with fresh pine. Snow melted on wood floors. Pictures of semi-famous people hung on the walls.

Lauren grinned. It was everything the movies made these places out to be. Only thing missing was a murder mystery or monster in the woods.

"You're Lauren?" a voice asked from behind her.

Coffee sloshed with her jerk of surprise. She cursed and wiped her burning hand on a napkin.

"I didn't mean to scare you," was both amused and concerned. "Are you okay?"

Above Lauren was a tall woman decked out in winter gear like all the others, but it lacked their pretentious air, looked practical and durable instead of pretty and single use. Her boots were rugged, scuffed things unsuitable for skiing. She must be the backcountry guide.

"Yea. It wasn't that hot." Lauren shrugged, her voice tight. She cleared her throat. "I'm Lauren. You're the guide?"

A hand, long-fingered and pale pink, was held out. "I'm Nona." Her smile was gently crooked. Disarming. It brought out a dimple on her left cheek. It almost distracted from the thick scarring along her right jaw.

Looked like she'd been in a bad car wreck or something had tried to claw her face off once. Probably the latter, given her profession.

Lauren grasped the hand, felt dry skin and calluses and a firm grip. Nona didn't wear makeup to cover her weathered skin, kept her wispy blonde curls in a simple tail, and had a wide, confident stance. At home, she probably lived in flannel. Not the hipster-lesbian kind of flannel that filled coffee shops. The practical kind that probably smelled like pine-wood cabin and campfire and hard work. This wasn't a pretty city girl. Not a girl at all. Nona looked several years older than Lauren.

Absolutely not Lauren's type.

Relief swept through her. How long had it been since she'd really taken notice of a woman who didn't remind her of Whitney? Too long. Maybe it would be okay to flirt with Nona. Just for fun.

"I got them when I fell down a mountain." Nona broke Lauren's reverie. "A rutting bull elk charged and scared me off my feet."

"Huh?"

Nona dropped Lauren's hand to gesture upwards. "The scars. You've been staring."

"Oh." Guess she had been staring at them, even if she hadn't been looking. "Sorry. They're impressive." She lifted her gaze to Nona's eyes. Her extremely pretty, intensely green eyes. "Oh," she breathed. "Wow."

Eyebrows lifted. "What?"

Lauren's cheeks heated, and she found purple snowpants to distract herself. Maybe Nona was a little girly. "Um."

"You can't suddenly say 'wow' like that and not tell me why." Hand to hip, Nona huffed.

Well, now was as good a time as any to make sure the guide wasn't homophobic. That'd be almost as bad as Nona reminding her of Whitney for the entire trip. Lauren sucked in a breath. "Your eyes are really pretty." Lame. Ugh. Even when she wasn't trying to flirt, she sounded like an idiot. She braced herself for Nona's response.

When a minute of quiet went by, Lauren darted her gaze up to Nona's.

Those eyes seemed to be even greener, spring leaves poking through snow, bright and delicate and sparkling in the light. "Thank you."

Lauren released the breath.

"I'd better get this out in the open now. Yes, I'm single. No, I don't get involved with clients. If you came up here hoping for more than a hiking trip, I'll give back your deposit and we can part ways now." Nona spoke firmly, unwavering.

"No." Lauren shook her head, abruptly remembering the venomous reviews. Scorned suitors?

Nona's brow arched.

"Um. I came up here to hike," squeaked out.

"Good. Okay," Nona sat in the chair across from her. "You got the list I sent and checked everything off?"

Lauren nodded. "Yes."

From a plain manila folder that Lauren hadn't noticed her carrying, a piece of paper was pulled out. "I'd like you to go over it now, as a precaution before we head out."

The paper was the same list of essential supplies. "That's cool."

Mentally, she went through what was on her person and in her backpack. She stalled on the knife. Had she brought the knife? Geez. Carrying a mundane blade was redundant. She bent and dug into her pack, touching fuel and food and matches and yep, the knife. Camera? Nah. She'd stowed her phone, wallet, and car keys in one of the lodge's secure lockers just in case her car got broken into. She wasn't the kind to take a lot of pictures anyway. Her parents would give her shit about not having any nice pictures to share, but whatever. She wasn't risking her phone on this trip. And she hadn't thought to hunt down a disposable camera. Who developed film anymore anyway? Maybe Nona would take some pictures.

"Got it all."

"Fantastic. These," more papers, "Are basic liability waivers. Basically, they say you've provided yourself with survival essentials, you understand the risks of the trip, and if you take any unnecessary risks, you won't sue me for your stupidity."

Lauren chuckled. "I take full responsibility for my own stupidity."

Soft laughter joined hers. "Good. I'm happy to hear that, and that you're laughing. Cheese, when people can't laugh at that, I know it'll be a long, quiet trip."

"Cheese?" she demanded.

"Cheese." The dimple returned. "I use food as alternatives to swearing."

What a dork. Feeling good about the trip, about the company she'd be with, Lauren grinned and signed the forms.

Nona reviewed them, added her own signatures, and stuffed them back in the folder. She stood. "Any last questions?"

Lauren stood as well, noted that she still had to look up to meet Nona's eye. "Am I the only one going?" She'd been certain a group was joining the adventure.

Weathered features tightened slightly. "Yes. The group I mentioned in the email made other plans." Was business bad? Why the face? "Looks like it's only us. Price is the same since it's not your fault. Your application said you were fine with a solo trip."

That sounded like a question. Lauren shrugged. Maybe it would be better this way. A group of friends could've made Lauren an outsider at camp. This way, it would simply be two strangers on the same social footing. Maybe it'd be easier to get in some flying. "Yea. I'm not afraid of being out there alone with you, even if you are way taller than me."

Nona laughed. "You aren't used to being the shorter woman, are you?"

"No. Five-nine isn't exactly short."

"It is when I'm six-foot-one."

"Is this what short women feel like when they're around me?"

"Okay. If you don't have anything besides comments on my height, I suggest that you use the restroom one last time before we head out." Nona waited expectantly.

Lauren refrained from a Bigfoot joke and shook her head.

"While you do that, I'm going to drop these papers off in my office." A pause. "Want me to take your gear with me?"

"Yea. Thanks." Lauren didn't think to question if Nona could handle the impressive weight of the pack until after she'd handed it over.

"Meet me out front. I'll be in the brown truck parked on the right." And she turned away, moving smoothly, as though she didn't have over 40 pounds of gear on her back. Cool. It was easy to forget how strong normal humans could be.

Nona sat waiting in her old, beat up SUV for her latest client. She had mixed feelings about this one. The ragged mop of ebony hair, with its shock of vivid blue highlights, and the tattoo poking up from Lauren's sweater said she was probably immature, or at least rebellious with a load of personal issues. And she was clearly attracted to women. And definitely cute. And new to the backcountry.

She glanced at the 'about me' section of the client application. Lauren went jogging regularly, did a little weightlifting, but otherwise wasn't athletic. Car mechanic by trade. Twenty-four years old. Her likes included adrenaline, coffee, movies, and cars. She hadn't been camping since high school and never primitive camping. Few survival skills.

This trip could be a lot of fun or a complete disaster. She'd planned an easy hike. No peaks. After she'd had a chance to evaluate, there were intermediate trails with a couple harder ones or much easier ones. She wished that group hadn't backed out. They would've been a nice buffer between herself and Lauren. With just the two of them, they'd be sharing a tent to conserve pack weight and what little body heat they could accumulate at night. So much intimacy could lead to arguments or worse, sexual tension.

"Fuck you, Duncan," hissed out of her. Why couldn't her ex-husband stop interfering in her business? Was his endgame full custody of their child? It must be. He avoided her and anything to do with her, including having ditched all of their mutual friends. Their son was all he wanted. Trevor would be the only reason Duncan would continue to pay attention to Nona's business and livelihood.

She normally wouldn't take anything less than a three-person group on a trip like this in deep winter, especially not at the discounted rate she'd given Lauren, but she was getting low on funds. Duncan's interference had cost her two good groups already this season.

Knocking on the window made her banish the scowl that had formed. "It's unlocked!" she called out.

The door groaned slightly at opening. The door hinge that Duncan had bent during their last fight as a married couple. How was that only three years ago?

"How did you manage to bend a door hinge?" Lauren chuckled as she slid in the cab.

Nona blinked at her. That it was bent wasn't obvious, and Lauren couldn't have done more than glance at it. "How..."

The paper in her hands was tapped. "Car mechanic. It's the kind of thing I'm paid to notice."

Right. "A drunk guy happened."

"Ah."

"How are you doing in the altitude?" Nona asked.

Lauren grinned, a self-satisfied smile that seemed a bit too eager. "I love it."

"You aren't feeling lightheaded? Headache? It's perfectly normal for someone who's just come from a low altitude like Iowa. I don't want to take you out there if y-"

"Altitude doesn't bother me," interrupted her. Lauren's eager smile shifted to strangely serious. "I promise. I've spent a lot of time at high altitudes in my life. No issues."

Didn't mean they couldn't crop up. Nona frowned.

"Look, if I feel like I can't keep up or any symptoms of altitude sickness, I'll be sure to let you know." Lauren shrugged. "As long as you don't use your giant legs to run and leave me behind, I don't foresee any issues."

"Giant legs?" she demanded.

"Exceedingly long legs. Like those of a giant," was said straight-faced.

Cute and a good sense of humor. Nona felt a smile creep up. "Shrimp."

Lauren's face looked like her tongue swallowed itself.

Nona fell into laughter and put the truck in gear. Never mind her earlier thoughts. This was going to be a good trip.

Chapter Three

Complicated

"This," huffed out of Nona's rookie client, "is hard." Lauren stalled to rub her thighs and glare at her snowshoes.

They were still two miles away from where Nona planned their first campsite. She glanced up at the sun. Three hours at best. Her watch confirmed it. Could Lauren be safely prodded forward to get to the campsite before sunset? Or should they aim for an alternate site?

Lauren moved forward, and Nona followed. "It's awkward now, but it'll get easier, I promise."

A glare was tossed back at her. Lauren showed no sign of altitude sickness and had reasonable stamina, handled the weight of her gear well. She was simply slow. Slow and not used to long trips. She'd probably get the hang of the snowshoes right as they switched to crampons for the sections of dense ice. "If I'd just shut up and stop whining, it'd get easier faster," sounded an awful lot like she was quoting someone.

"Have a sports coach tell you that often?"

"Yea." Lauren's tone had an odd quality to it. "I heard it a lot."

Sports hadn't been mentioned on Lauren's profile. Most people were eager to list every single athletic thing they'd ever done. Intrigued, Nona asked, "What'd you play?"

Lauren didn't immediately answer, and she was quiet long enough that Nona wondered if she'd been heard. She waited a minute before opening her mouth to repeat the question.

"I didn't play sports." Lauren replied in a way that suggested this was a bad topic.

Accepting that, Nona didn't press further, and allowed the hike to continue in quiet. She engaged herself with watching the terrain. The profile of the mountains was sharp and bright and familiar. Change only happened along the slopes, to the forests and streams, to the paths and snow fields. A fire had gone through a decade ago along the eastern ridge; its scar remained, black stumps and ragged, dead trees barely hidden by the winter snows.

The rest was full of fat evergreens, their boughs weighed down with sparkling white cloaks, tree wells hidden under their lowest branches, dangerous, murderous things that she'd been trapped in once. One of the most terrifying experiences of her life. If her good friend Bear hadn't been right on her heels on that skiing disaster, her body might still be wrapped around that tree's trunk. She made sure to carry a whistle about her neck and a...

"I did martial arts."

Nona blinked out of memory to focus on Lauren. "Martial arts?"

"Yea. My trainers were really intense, but I never got really good. Not after..." She stopped. "Not as good as I wanted to be. My best friend Amber, she's the epitome of badass. She's always winning tournaments and kicking ass. If it wasn't for her pushing me and cheering me on, I'd never have gotten as far as I did." Her voice trailed off on a wistful note.

"Why did you stop?"

Lauren's feet slowed, and her neck bent, tilting her face to the sky. "For some really complicated reasons." Snowshoes crunched onward. "I make sure to practice some basic stuff, keep up for when Amber visits and makes me spar, but without trainers to constantly push me, I've gotten pretty soft."

A concept that Nona understood well. If she didn't have Trevor to provide for, if she didn't need to be in good shape to do her job, if she wasn't an outdoor guide, she'd spend a lot less hours at the gym and on the trail. On the thought of stamina, she noted that she should take over as trail-breaker soon. Tiring Lauren out too early was a bad idea. Most of her muscle was in her broad shoulders. Must be a mechanic thing. "What kind of martial arts was it? Karate? Kung-fu?"

Low and short, chuckles came from Lauren. "Nothing like that."

"Capoeira?"

"What?"

"Brazilian martial arts. It looks more like dancing than fighting." For their first anniversary, Duncan had gotten them a couple months worth of classes. It'd been fun. And exhausting. Then Nona had gotten pregnant, and she'd never gone back. Maybe she should. Or some other defense training.

Lauren shook her head. "No."

She waited patiently for an explanation that never came. Lauren shifted the conversation to their surroundings, asking about the mountains and the forests and the animals that lived among them. Nona took over breaking trail and talked about the dangers of elk. She was moving on to cougars when she caught sight of movement among the trees about a hundred yards out. She stopped, pulled out binoculars, and smiled.

"Mule deer." Nona said quietly and held out the binoculars.

Lauren searched them out, watched for a minute, passed the binoculars back. "Cool." A moment later, she announced, "There's a cat behind them."

A cougar? This close? Nona scanned the trees, not seeing anything, started to wonder if Lauren was toying with her or allowing her imagination to run wild. She went back to the deer that were nibbling at tree bark. It was a lucky thing to see them this close. The light breeze was blowing from the deer's direction toward the humans, keeping their scent and sounds away from the animals.

How could Lauren have seen a cougar without binoculars? Nona could barely see the deer with her naked eye let alone...

The deer leapt into motion, a tawny blur on their tails. Both were quickly lost from sight in the shadows of trees and folds of the land.

"What a show for your first day in the backcountry." Nona shook her head at the wonder of it.

Lauren was sporting a wide, toothy display of excitement. "Cool."

———◆———

Nona eyed the woman staring up at the local fourteener, awe and wonder plastered across her features. When her gaze dropped and found Nona, there was a hunger in them, one she was more used to seeing in the eyes of lifelong mountaineers eyeing a challenging climb.

"Can we go up there?" Lauren asked.

That peak was far beyond what she had contemplated for this trip. Nona eyed the bright cap of snow. "We don't have the gear for that kind of terrain." Not to mention that the weather up there was dangerously unpredictable at this time of year. She didn't want to be caught in it with a rookie.

"You've been up there?"

"A few times."

Lauren sighed as she returned to staring.

"If it was summer, I'd consider taking you partway up, but it's too dangerous in the winter, especially for a first trip." She reached to touch Lauren's shoulder, smiled at the woman when she turned to her. "Even if you do handle the altitude as promised."

Slowly, a small grin lifted. "Bet you don't meet a lot of lowlanders who breathe like mountainfolk, huh?"

She laughed. "No. Don't get many who talk like they live in a Tolkien book either."

The grin became a toothy smile. "Not all those who wander are lost."

With that, the conversation devolved to *Lord of the Rings* movie quotes and terrible impersonations. Or really good. Lauren's Galadriel impression was horrifying.

"So," Nona giggled. "You the only adventuring hobbit in your family? Or are your siblings as bad as you?"

"Nah. Only child, and I was more than enough trouble for my parents. When I was twelve, I wanted to learn how to drive a car, but, you know, everyone told me I was too young. I found books at the library and stuff online to learn as much as I could, and I watched mom and dad drive really, really carefully. Mom came down with the flu one weekend. Dad was at work, and I wanted to go to the grocery store to get stuff to make Mom soup, so I grabbed her keys, got in the car, and drove myself there."

Nona gaped. "Seriously?"

Laughing, "Yea. I got what I wanted with money I'd earned doing chores and drove home. I was two blocks away when a cop pulled me over for a broken taillight. He nearly pissed himself when he found me behind the wheel. He was expecting some little old lady driving as slow as I was."

"Cheese!" She laughed with her. "What happened?"

"Well, he got me and the groceries in his cruiser, drove me home and was surprised to find my mom as sick as I'd said she was. He walked back to Mom's car and brought it home. He helped make dinner too." Nostalgia was bright in Lauren's eyes. "Mom and Dad punished me by making me learn basic car maintenance. I was changing oil and checking belts like an old pro by my thirteenth birthday. I saved up to buy a junk heap of a car the year I got a driving permit. I had it fixed up and painted and ready to rock by the time I could drive by myself."

Wow. Talk about a strong-willed, independent kid. Nona could picture her little sister doing something that brash. Never herself. She'd been too mild-mannered. Still was. "And now you're a mechanic."

"Now I'm a mechanic," agreed with her. "What about you? What kind of kid were you?"

"Quiet," was her easy answer. "Always reading or running off to the woods. Dad was a survivalist. He loved nature and made his living teaching and sharing his backcountry skills. He was my hero. I went hiking and camping with him every chance I got."

Lauren's features pinched. "Was?"

She suffered the familiar ache of loss as she explained that her father had died of cancer when she was 22. That was five years ago, yet her heart twisted at the fresh thought of never talking with him or going on another trip with him ever again.

"I bet he'd be proud of you."

At Lauren's sincere words, her vision went hot and blurry, and her throat tightened. "I hope so," came out cracked and ragged.

"If the guy loved teaching others about nature, how could he not be proud of his kid for doing the same thing?"

Nona brushed at her damp eyes. "Yea." Her heart warmed as the idea grew on her. "Yea. I guess so." She looked at her rookie companion and found a smile waiting for her.

"Anyone who can convince me that there's something good about snowshoes is someone to be proud of." Lauren mock-scowled at her footwear.

"Oh? And what did I convince you is good about them?"

The scowled flashed back to a smile. "They're a hell of a lot easier to walk in than trying to wade through hip-deep snow."

It wasn't much, but it was something. Lauren kept going, her reassurances quickly becoming silly jokes intended to make Nona smile and laugh and forget how much she missed her dad, to goad them back to a lighthearted banter as they resumed their trek. Their snowshoes scuffed through fluffy powder, and a light wind teased their faces. Beautiful day. Good company. Nona's heart shook free of the dark blanket of memory to relish the present.

She was doing what she loved, what her dad had taught her to love, being out in nature and sharing it with another. He *would* be proud of her. She tucked that realization safely away before finding a way to tease Lauren about her silly blue hair.

Chapter Four

The Freedom it Teased

"Fudge," spat Nona.

Instantly curious about the angry tone, Lauren brought her attention down from the thin slice of crescent moon and the expanse of twinkling stars. "Something wrong?"

An oblong, red thing about the size of a soda can was held up. Cracks were obvious on its plastic surface. "My weather radio is broken. The forecast is pretty clear for the rest of the week, so that's not a big deal. I'm just irritated about the dead weight. It was fine last trip. I must have dropped some heavy gear on it when I wasn't paying attention." She sighed and stuffed the thing in her pack. "Oh well."

Lauren shrugged. Whatever. Even if the weather changed, a little more snow wouldn't hurt them. Lauren was perfectly comfortable in her fleece despite the dropping temperature of nightfall. She smiled at the crackling fire, the happy dance it made as Nona fed it. Tonight Lauren was going to take a flight. She'd tested Nona the past two nights by announcing late-night walks and going on them.

The guide had merely given her reminders of the mountains' dangers, made sure she had flashlight, whistle, and survival kit, and demanded a return time. One hour. A minute after, and Nona would suspect the worst. Lauren had set a timer on her watch and set forth despite the ache of sore muscles.

It would be worth it. She hadn't gotten to fly in months. Months! Up here, it would be incredible. The chances of being seen were minuscule, and there wasn't a nearby airport with pesky radar to pick her up. Best of all, Nona didn't question Lauren's need for alone time.

Perfect.

"That's an awfully happy smile." Nona said, eyes sparkling with firelight.

"It's glorious being away from civilization." Lauren gushed. She rose and gestured at the vast expanse of darkness around them. "No screaming neighbors or barking dogs or cars or roommates."

"I didn't think mechanics minded the sounds of cars."

Giddy and childish, Lauren stuck her tongue out. "I like being a rebel."

"You're such a kid," chuckled at her.

Despite the joking tone, and the nice way Nona was looking at her, Lauren felt a pang of hurt. Being enthusiastic and silly as opposed to serious and brooding didn't mean she wasn't a fucking adult.

Was she ever going to get over Whitney's parting words? The urge to fly high and far above her troubles swelled in her chest. She glanced up and back at Nona. Okay, maybe some of the urge was because of Nona's smile. Lauren liked it too much. She needed distance.

"I think I'll take my walk before dinner." Lauren said.

Lines formed between blonde eyebrows. "You've got the energy? You aren't cold?"

If she wasn't a guide, she'd sound like such a fucking mom. "I'm good. I had a nut bar an hour ago."

Seriousness overtook amusement. "How are your toes?"

"Wiggly and snug."

"Headache?"

"Nah."

A long minute passed while Nona contemplated her. "Dinner will be ready in an hour." Green light glowed from her watch face. "Enjoy your walk."

Headlamp and survival kit were grabbed, snowshoes strapped back on. She plunged into the forest until the campfire was a vague thing. Nona would never be able to see Lauren's little red headlamp from the small clearing where she stopped. There were at least twenty feet between trees, enough room for her wings to fully spread. She set her pack on the ground, unstrapped her snowshoes, turned off the headlamp and pulled out a flashlight. The little cone of aluminum she'd prepared earlier was settled around the light, the whole thing pointed skyward. Nearly invisible from the ground. Highly visible from the air. It would guide her return to the pack.

Giddy, she released her wings, stretched and gloried in the rush of magic.

She gave a few experimental flaps before committing herself to the sky. A good jump and downward stroke, and she was airborne. She barely contained her whoop of joy as she plowed through the thin air. Some few hundred feet up, she let it loose, calling out to the stars as the world stretched out beneath her. Nona's fire was a bright spark in the night, the flashlight another.

No other sign of human life in the small valley. Perfect.

To the peak of the highest mountain, Lauren rose before circling and diving and playing and acting as much like a kid as she wanted to. She was exhausted too quickly. Feeling cheated by the short recess, she alighted on an overhang where she could admire the view and catch her bearings. The campfire was easy enough to find. Enthused by the flight, rebellion wanted to fly right to it, land not ten feet from Nona, and scare the crap out of her.

As fast as it had swept in, the impulse passed. The consequences of breaking the law were clear, and Lauren didn't want to see Nona hurt. She reigned herself in and looked for the flashlight. There. Goal found, she dropped off the edge and glided to it.

Gear retrieved, she looked at the distant fire, then her watch. Her hour was up and then some. Shit. "Dammit. It's so much farther by foot." Her thighs and back and calves burned from the day's overexertion, but she pushed herself to get back to the fire before Nona freaked out.

"Lauren!" yelled out from the shadows, nearly scaring the skin off her back. A beam of light preceded Nona's running form.

"Balls! Where the fuck you come from?" Lauren squawked. And how the hell could she run in snowshoes?

"I was following your trail." Nona gestured at the trees. A couple yards away was Lauren's previous path. "I waited an extra ten minutes before looking for you." She was calm, but anger simmered under her cold-pinked cheeks. "It's been over an hour and a half. I was terrified a cougar had gotten you or you'd fallen into a tree well or you'd gotten frostbite or something!"

"Sorry."

"I'm glad you're okay," seethed at her. "But don't make me worry like that again." teaNona spun around and stomped back to camp. Her anger boiled under quick glances and sharp words for the rest of the evening. In lieu of the usual post-dinner chat about the day and what awaited them tomorrow, the guide pulled out a book and ignored Lauren until she went to bed.

Guiltily, Lauren hummed to herself. "Worth it."

Flying had been awesome. And angry Nona was much easier for Lauren's fragile psyche to deal with. Angry people didn't encourage attraction or attachment. Lauren leaned back to admire the night sky, reliving her glorious freedom, plotting the next night's escape.

"Lauren," prodded her.

She grunted, content in the darkness.

"Lauren. Get up. It's too cold to sleep in the open."

No it wasn't. "I'm comfy. Go away." She grouched at the annoying voice.

A grip on her shoulder shook her. Gentle at first, harder when Lauren grumbled about being left alone. Her eyelids peeled apart to glare up at, "Nona?"

"Get up." Irritation barked at her. "You need to go to bed."

Oh yea. Nona was angry with her about staying away from camp for too long. Lauren fought her protesting, clenching muscles to sit upright. "I'm up." She rolled from butt to knees to start crawling to the tent.

Nona stopped her. "Look at me."

"But you just told me to go to bed." Lauren griped.

"I know. I'm sorry." Nona's tone lost its sharpness. "I need to make sure you're okay."

Curious, Lauren peered at her. She was squatting and wearing the fuzzy thermals she liked to sleep in instead of her bulky coat. Her breath puffed in big white plumes under the starlight.

"I'm sorry I was so rude with you tonight. I didn't think you'd stay outside because of it."

Now she was confused. "What?"

Nona's expression was hard to read and not just because it was dark out. "I was angry because you made me worry. These mountains are dangerous, especially at night, *especially* in the winter. And I know you don't seem to mind the cold as much as most people, but it's better not to push your body. We have several days ahead of us, even if you want to cut the trip short."

Cut it short? Walk away from more flying so soon? "No!" Lauren barked. "No way. Balls, woman, I just fell asleep out here. You aren't that scary."

Nona paused. Her gaze shifted over Lauren. "Then you won't mind letting me inspect your toes and hands and check your pulse and listen to your lungs?"

"Why?" That seemed excessive. "I don't have frostbite." She frowned at her boot-covered toes. What would it take for her to get that? A few days without boots up here? A week?

Lips thinned at her. "Relieve yourself if you need to and get in the tent." Nona rose and returned to it.

Lauren gaped after her, stunned at the commanding tone. She found herself obeying, using the cathole she'd dug earlier to pee in, covering it with some snow, and following Nona inside. She didn't even argue when Nona gestured for Lauren's appendages and thoroughly inspected them under a bright lamp.

"Deep breaths." Nona leaned close, ear to Lauren's mouth, fingers on a pulse point and listened closely.

Her hair stank a little, was the first thought Lauren managed to conjure.

Nona stopped listening to her breath. "What's two plus four plus seven?"

Math? "Uh." She counted. "Thirteen."

"What color do you get if you mix yellow and red?"

"Orange."

Nona sat back. Her fingers remained on Lauren's pulse as their gazes locked. "When's your birthday?"

"June sixth."

Quiet ensued, Nona watching her, Lauren growing increasingly more uncomfortable. Her gaze drifted down to where Nona was no longer feeling for a pulse, yet kept Lauren's hand in her own. There was a gentle squeeze.

"You're fine." Nona said softly. "Good, healthy digits. No sign of altitude sickness. Let's keep it that way, okay? If you want to take a longer walk, just let me know beforehand. I'm responsible for your safety." A crooked grin appeared. "Even if you signed a waiver about your stupidity."

Lauren snorted. "Yea."

Nona's dimple appeared. "You're really comfortable out here, aren't you? I thought you said you grew up in the Midwest?"

"You do know that Iowa winters are cold as balls, right?"

"I've also heard that the only thing in Iowa is endless cornfields." Nona challenged.

"Des Moines isn't tiny. The metro has over half a million people. Omaha's even bigger." Stubborn pride defended her homeland from non-Midwesterner ignorance. "And don't forget Chicago and Cleveland and Kansas City and..."

Nona laughed. "Down, big city girl. I get it. Not everything is cornfields and small towns."

Good humor and chuckles saw them back in their sleeping bags and closing their eyes. At least, Lauren's did until she felt a prickle go down her spine. She thought she saw Nona staring, yet when she focused, Nona's eyes were closed. She shook her head and retreated to sleep.

⊷◆⊶

Eyes strained, brain numb, everything else aching, Lauren puffed and stopped, closing her eyes and stretching her back.

"Need a break?" Nona called.

Lauren opened her eyes to glare at the guide who didn't seem bothered by anything the trail had thrown at them. Not the rocks that threatened to twist their ankles or the steep incline or the glaring snow. "I'm tired of staring at the ground." She growled.

Bright sunlight glinted on sunglasses. "It's hard to not watch where your feet are going when the ground isn't flat."

Why was she putting herself through this nonsense? Lauren scanned the sky, the freedom it teased.

Last night's flight soared in her mind, and she smiled. "Oh. Yea."

"Doesn't take much to make you smile, does it?"

Lauren shook her head. "I'm a simple creature."

"Somehow I doubt that, but being able to smile like that is a gift. I've had more than a few clients who got to day four of cold nights and hard trails with dangerously sour attitudes."

"I bet they didn't take walks after making camp."

Walks, she snorted. "No." Chuckles popped out. "No, they didn't."

Chapter Five

Frigid, Arctic Kiss

On their last day, they had barely crested the high point of the rise between valleys when Nona caught sight of an approaching storm. Mutely cursing, she studied the clouds and wind while her client was bent over catching her breath. The barometer readings on her watch agreed with what her eyes were seeing. That storm would kick their butts in a couple of hours. She cursed her broken weather radio for not being able to warn them.

"Oh. Damn," puffed out of Lauren.

Nona was careful to put a pleasant expression on before turning. "View was worth it, right?"

Lauren frowned. "Those are storm clouds. Not the view I was hoping for."

Cheese! She'd already noticed? Nona started to frame a calm response, but chose to delay the topic. "Let's take a picture." She pulled out her camera and set it up with the background of the bright, sunny terrain. Time delay was pressed. She got up, threw an arm over Lauren's shoulder, used an old joke to get them both smiling.

Nona checked that it turned out well enough, showed Lauren, asked a question to both distract Lauren and reassure herself. "How's your breathing?"

"Lungs are great. Now, my calves and ass on the other hand, those are burning like a hillbilly flashlight."

Snorting laughter, "Hillbilly what?"

"Something my mom always says." Lauren smiled as she waved the question off. She unbuckled her pack and slid her butt to the ground with a sigh. "She's got cousins in Kentucky she likes to make fun of."

At the mention of family, her worry went to Trevor and Lyleigh. Her poor sister would be fielding his questions for hours if Nona got trapped in this storm. Nona sent her gaze to the clouds and watched as they thickened and grew, darkening much too fast for comfort. The storm was definitely heading their way, and it was going to be a beast.

She smiled gently to soften the blow of her next words. "Lauren, looks like we have a little change in plans."

"That storm's going to be bad, isn't it?" sounded resigned. Better than scared or anxious.

"There's a ranger shelter we can head to. We'll be fine, riding out the storm there in five star comfort."

"You don't think we can make it to the truck." Lauren interpreted.

Nona took a moment to weigh Lauren's possible responses to the naked truth before going with it. "No. I don't. We have enough supplies to extend the trip an extra day and wait out the storm. If it lasts a little longer, the cabin should be well stocked."

The truck was only half a day's hike away, less if she pushed Lauren hard. But that storm probably wouldn't even wait until they reached the valley. By the way Lauren's sight was tracing the horizon and the approaching front, how her expression hardened, it was obvious she wasn't fooled by Nona's understated reply. Nona braced for an argument, but Lauren silently nodded. She paid careful attention when Nona brought out her map and showed her where the cabin was. Just in case. Blizzard conditions could separate even the best prepared.

Barely a mile down the slope, and the wind slapped them with a frigid, arctic kiss. Nona hissed in displeasure. Ahead of her, Lauren paused, completely stopped. She didn't zip up her coat or adjust her hat or anything. The ridiculous woman turned her face into the wind. Her coat's hood and loose edges billowed wildly, threatened to rip their seams and escape her coat. The reprimand that jumped to the tip of her tongue stalled. Lauren didn't seem fazed in the slightest by the abrupt drop in temperature or the way the wind was trying to shove them off the mountain. Her body was casually angled into the gusts, her feet spread and knees bent as though she did this all the time.

Her eyes closed, and she seemed like she was tasting the wind, calmly taking its measure in a way that Nona had once watched the captain of a sailboat do at the faintest hint of gray on the horizon. When he'd opened his eyes, he'd sent his small crew scurrying to prep the ship for a wicked squall that tried to capsize and kill them all. His weather sense had saved them all. His ship, crew, and passengers made up of a pre-teen Nona, younger Lyleigh, and their parents. Nona had been terrified of open water since.

She wished she'd had half his weather sense. Maybe she could have used the hours spent climbing the ridge to build a snow cave or find a natural cave where a fire had a chance. Or better yet, cut the trip short a day. Get her client safely back to civilization before the storm hit.

Hopefully Lyleigh would do a good job distracting Trevor so he wouldn't be sitting at home worrying about his mom being out in this weather.

"Have you turned on your emergency transmitter?" Lauren pulled her from reverie.

Right before following Lauren down. Bear would be watching for a radio signal to pop up. He'd know right away that Nona was taking shelter. He would inform the rangers, and if rescue became necessary, they'd know where to start looking.

"Yes. Bear will figure out what's going on. Let's get out of this wind!"

But the woman didn't move right away. Her gaze tracked to the sky, that same unreadable expression etched across her.

Nona glanced up as well and did not like what she saw. Or smelled. Or felt. The wind wasn't simply frigid, it was heavy with the threat of snow. Deliberate movements below returned her attention to Lauren. Quick yet careful strides were taking her down. Shaking her head, Nona followed.

An hour's time found them struggling with blowing, stinging snow. Visibility had dropped to a few hundred feet. The sun was a vague idea behind the wall of clouds, would soon be lost altogether, and leave them to a frigid void. Time was not on their side. It was already bitterly, dangerously, *painfully* cold. Nona cursed her broken weather radio almost as much as she cursed the storm itself. The first time she misplaced her footing because she could barely see, Nona used a light rope to tie her and Lauren together and exchanged a hiking pole for her ice axe. She worried that she couldn't suggest Lauren do the same. The woman didn't have an axe. Why hadn't Nona put that on the must-have list? Next time. If there was a next time. This could be the clincher for Nona's mountain guide days. She might have to suck up her pride and get a job at McDonald's just to keep food on the table.

Powerful wind gusts battered her until one caught her mid-stride, stole her balance, sent her tumbling. Her axe-arm hit the ground and she lost her grip on the tool. Then she was airborne, sailing the bitter wind that abruptly lost interest and dumped her. Hard impact stole her breath and she wheezed.

She did a quick mental check of her body, decided that nothing was broken. Distantly, she heard Lauren's yells, but didn't have the breath to call back against the wind. Poor woman. How much did it suck for this disaster to happen on her first backwoods trip? Lauren would probably give up hiking because of it. A damn shame. Too many gave up on nature because of one bad experience. It was...

The ground under her shifted, was accompanied by the distinct sound of ice cracking.

"Oh, shit." She scrambled to her knees, one of which shrieked at the pressure. Too bad! She yelled back at it, in pain, in fear, in desperation. The sounds of more cracks were skittering all around her. She'd fallen on a frozen river. Not a big one, but big enough. If the ice gave and she went under, she wouldn't come back up.

"No. No. No!" punctuated each desperate movement toward the vague tree line.

The ice opened, and rushing water grabbed at her legs. Somehow, she managed to get her axe in hand and swing, lodge the pick into stable ice, and keep herself from being dragged under. Her shoulder howled at the sudden jolt and refused her efforts to drag herself out. Frigid water jumped and slapped her in the face, climbed into her mouth, tried to drown her anyway.

She was fighting against too much. Something had to give. Her pack. Everything in it was replaceable. Her free hand fumbled for the catches. She got the chest one free and was groping for the waist when the ice holding her axe shivered and gave way.

Nona screamed.

Water rushed down her throat, over her head, dragging her under, laughing, roaring with triumph. She was going to die. She was going to leave Trevor without a mother. Duncan would get custody of him. Her little boy would grow up with that jerk, under the influence of Duncan's batshit crazy mother, probably cut off from Nona's family completely. All her dreams and aspirations for Trevor shattered. Panic flailed. Her hands caught on something. Yes!

Her head burst out of the water, and she coughed up water, sucked in burning air. The river hissed at losing her, tried to yank her back to its murderous depths, but Nona crawled up and out of the grasping current, off the ice, to the solid ground between trees.

"Nona! You okay?" yelled into her ear.

No. Nona hadn't dragged herself. Someone else had.

"Nona!"

Lauren. Her client. Rescued by the rookie. That was a first. Nona coughed and spit and generally tried to breathe.

"Nona, are you hurt?"

Was she? Her head was spinning, body shivering, lungs spasming. "I-I..."

"Nona?" Hands were on her face, lifting it to panicked eyes.

"I-I'm g-good." Nona managed to get out. She remembered her arm and knee hitting the ground too hard, but there wasn't blood, so other priorities were rearing up. They had to get out of the wind. She was going to freeze if she didn't get out of her wet clothes. Frozen hair whipped around her face. Swirling snow obliterated the landscape. Her rattled brain tried to place where they were against the map in her head and failed. They could be half a mile away or two.

She groaned. First things first. Get out of the wet clothes. Then head to where she thought the cabin was. If they couldn't find it within an hour, they'd set up the tent and hunker down in their sleeping bags. Sweet peaches and cream, she wanted nothing more than to huddle in front of the cabin's wood stove with hot chocolate and a thick blanket. Or in the lodge's hot tub. Yea. That.

"I h-have to g-g-get out of these c-clothes. T-Then we'll k-k-keep going." Teeth chattered as she tried to open her pack. Lauren had to brush her numb hands aside and open the clasps, reach inside.

"Everything here's wet," was groaned.

No. She always packed spare thermals in a waterproof bag, like her dad had taught her. "T-There's a-another bag-g-g inside."

Lauren found and wrestled it out while Nona battled with her sodden clothes. Ice had already started forming on her coat and pants, and it shattered as she shed them. When her layers came off, the wind managed to surprise her with how painfully it burned. Lauren did her best to shield Nona from it with her coat spread. But it came at her from all directions. All the poor woman really managed to do for Nona was act as a sturdy rock to balance against and respect Nona's dignity by closing her eyes.

Spare thermals and fleece jacket were struggled into. Dry socks were pouted at, stuffed back into the plastic, and sodden boots were pulled on over her soaked socks. They were wool and would retain some insulation, enough to keep frostbite at bay until they found shelter.

"I-I'm dressed!" she yelled into Lauren's ear. She shivered violently. How the hell could Lauren be standing in this wind with her coat open? Even if she was dry? Cheese, what Nona wouldn't do for a coat right now!

Lauren's eyes opened and fell on Nona. What was that expression? Frustration? Anger? Sadness? All perfectly understandable emotions that could get them into trouble if left unchecked. She needed to nip that in the bud. Moving would help.

"We n-need to k-k-keep moving!" Nona yelled.

The lack of immediate response had her wondering if Lauren had heard or if the wind had taken her words the moment they'd left her mouth. She gaped when Lauren started unbuckling her own pack.

"W-What are you doi-i-ing?" Nona yelled into the wind.

Lauren's answer was to shrug out of her coat and push it at her. "Put it on."

She balked as much as she was touched by the noble gesture. "I'm fine. L-"

"You aren't fine," yelled over her. "Put the damn thing on!"

Teeth chattering, shivers running up her spine, and Lauren looking as comfortable in this blizzard as she had all trip derailed her argument. The night Nona had insisted on checking Lauren's feet for frostbite rushed through her mind. She'd been terrified when she woke up in the dead of night and discovered that Lauren had stayed outside of the tent, slept on the snow without insulating pad or sleeping bag for protection, but had been totally comfortable, snug even, without hint of frostbite or hypothermia or altitude sickness.

The woman just wasn't normal.

"Take it!" Lauren shoved the coat into her chest, nearly knocking her over.

Nona gave in. She eagerly bundled into the coat, cooing as the harsh wind was blocked from her torso. A hat was shoved over her stinging ears. Lauren pulled the coat's hood up, tugged the drawstring until Nona's face was almost entirely covered, then transferred gloves.

Lauren stood back, sans coat and hat and gloves and *still* didn't appear affected by the arctic weather. Frozen gear was shoved into Nona's pack. The rope was tied back around Nona's waist and Lauren waited expectantly for her to take the lead. Heart in her throat, Nona hoped for the best and headed away from the river.

Another half hour's trudge through the blistering wind, Nona gave up on finding the cabin. Her knee was bleating its need for rest. The sun was going down. She had no idea where they were. Only sheer luck would put the two of them in front of the cabin, more luck would have them actually see the thing. She grabbed Lauren's arm to get her attention and yelled that they needed to set up the tent. Lauren's eyes bulged.

"How the hell we going to set it up in this wind?" was demanded.

"Carefully!"

Lauren groaned and dropped her pack. Nona dropped her own, her knee sighing in relief. It was probably the size of a grapefruit now after walking on it after that fall. Must have twisted or banged it, maybe cracked it.

The two of them packed down snow into an even, stable square and managed to wrangle the tent from Nona's pack, anchor it, set the poles up. The fly was even more difficult. Wildly flapping guy lines snapped Nona in the face twice. There was a line of frozen blood on Lauren's cheek. A lot of cursing and shouting finally got the thing attached to the tent, the guy lines anchored to sticks, then buried in the snow. Even the blizzard winds shouldn't be able to yank those out. Hopefully the tent seams would hold.

What energy they had left was spent building a snow wall around the tent to break some of the wind. It was all they could do. Nona convinced Lauren to empty her bladder beside a tree, followed her own advice, and swore heavily when the wind blew her own urine on her legs. Ugh! At least it froze immediately and brushed off. Mostly. Intimate parts tingling from exposure, she ushered Lauren into the tent as the sun completely vanished, secured the vestibule behind them.

Being out of the wind was an immediate relief. Nona shivered as the tent snapped and danced around them. They slapped the snow off each other, did their best to gather it up and toss it to the vestibule before unpacking sleeping bags and fluffing the down insulation. Boots were removed and placed in the vestibule. Thick, dry socks were exchanged for the ones they'd been wearing.

Nona set out her little stove and kettle, dropped snow into it, and set it to melt. While opening the vent of the vestibule, she warned Lauren that this wasn't a safe practice, but that wind wouldn't let them use the stove outside. Nona rolled eyes at herself. Always in teaching-mom mode.

Hot tea was made. Trembling, Nona sipped gratefully while she prepared their evening meal, her breath puffing in the light of her headlamp.

"H-How are you?" Nona asked.

Lauren's response was an enormous yawn. "My everything aches."

"I brought Ibuprofen if you want." She gestured with a shaking hand to her pack. "Top zipper. I'll take a couple too."

"You're shaking," frowned at her.

And you aren't, she didn't say to the coat-less woman with frozen hair. "Tea's helping. Don't worry. A hot dinner in my belly and stuffed in my sleeping bag, I'll be fine." Hopefully, she'd be able to feel her feet soon.

Lauren's frown didn't ease as she turned away to dig for the painkillers while Nona poured boiling water into the bag of freeze-dried spaghetti. Sealed and shaken, it was set aside. She boiled more water to pour into thermoses that were tossed into sleeping bags every night. They helped keep body temps up and provided warm liquid through morning. And who didn't like pressing cold feet to something warm in the middle of the night?

The stove's flame was shut off, the stove piece disconnected from the fuel, and the whole rig left in the vestibule. Nona closed the vent, zipped up the door, and tucked her lower half into her sleeping bag, pressing her toes to the warm bottle. Oh that felt good. She moaned.

Shortly after, the spaghetti got split between their bowls and quickly shoved into hungry mouths. It was bland and sweet, but was otherwise amazingly hot, wonderful, and filling. Nona's shivers let up. Her toes tingled. Finally.

"If the storm lasts more than a day, what will we do?" came softly from Lauren.

Nona deliberately chewed her bite of dinner.

"We don't have much fuel left."

Her dinner had already lost most of its heat, and her breath continued to cloud. Seriously too damn cold. If the temp stayed like this, and they remained trapped out here longer than two days, they were in serious trouble. Without fuel to melt snow...

"A storm big enough to last more than a day would've made it into the forecast, Lauren. We'll be okay. This is just a surprise bluster."

Two days later, Nona glared through the plastic window of the vestibule. Going out into the wind to relieve herself simply wasn't an option. No. Not in the least. She'd have to go against her usual rules. She sighed, wishing she'd found a career where she didn't have to think about poop every day and dug two catholes in the vestibule. One for liquid, the other she lined with a plastic bag for the solids they'd pack out. The same frigid temps that were turning her into an icicle would at least keep the smell down. She did her business and dove back into the main tent, shivering like a mad thing, wishing there was fuel to make hot tea.

That was the only thing they had in abundance. Tea bags. They were out of everything else. She scowled at the yellow roof. Snow and clouds continued to obscure the weak sun and showed no signs of letting up.

Two days. It had been blowing and snowing like mad cats for two days.

Nona's teeth chattered. She'd be lucky to last another day at this rate. Her eyes went to Lauren, who wasn't shivering, whose teeth weren't chattering, who never showed any sign of being cold. Was she even human? Or was that little layer of pudge she had enough to insulate her?

Tense brown eyes slid from their study of the tent's flexing seams, landed on Nona. "Any fuel left?"

"N-no. How are you d-doing?"

"I'm hungry," was Lauren's dull response. She tucked her hands in her armpits.

Maybe she was cold, was simply inhumanly good at hiding it. She did seem a bit ashen. "I'm s-sor-ry."

"Storm isn't your fault, Nona. Don't apologize." Hard, cutting anger laced her tone. She sucked in a breath. "Don't apologize," was repeated, anger gone from her voice, though it remained in her eyes. "You did everything you could to keep us safe."

Lauren's words warmed her. In a proverbial kind of way. Her teeth continued chattering even as she smiled. "F-Feel free to keep flatt-tering me."

"If anything, it's my fault we're in this situation," came out dark and angry.

That self-hatred wouldn't do. "You c-c-couldn't have known."

Lauren went back to staring at the seams, and Nona sighed, tried to rebuild some body heat in the confines of her sleeping bag. There wasn't room for anything more than situps and leg lifts or she'd be doing squats and jumping jacks too. Well, if her knee didn't still hurt like the dickens. After twenty minutes, she sat up and snuggled into Lauren for shared warmth. Lauren flinched at the contact, but eventually slung an arm around Nona's waist. Neither spoke for the rest of the afternoon.

Dinnertime came and went. The sun gave up its weak effort and plunged them into bone-chilling darkness. Nona tried getting Lauren to talk about anything and failed miserably. The woman was too busy staring angrily at the door. Nona spent what little energy she had to do a few exercises at a final bid for warmth before tucking close to Lauren and saying a prayer to any deity that might listen for the storm to finish come morning.

Lauren scowled at her companion as the meager glow of daylight made its way into the tent. If the storm didn't let up today, Nona wouldn't survive. She was getting too tired to even shiver properly.

"I gotta stretch my legs." Lauren announced.

Nona insisted that Lauren put on her coat, hat, and gloves before allowing her out with, "Don't go far."

Outside, hidden by tent wall and snow, she made one of the craziest decisions of her life and brought her wings out. A promise was focused on a single feather, then it was plucked. Pain lanced from wing to heart. She muffled her cry in a sleeve, breathed heavily to calm herself. A drop of frozen blood glistened on the shaft, and the promise of the call pulsed within it. She closed her fist around it and ducked back into the tent with the excuse that she'd forgotten her snowshoes.

Nona shook her head, not seeing the feather that Lauren stashed next to her. "I don't know how you're not cold, but don't overdo it out there and burn off your good luck. Or get lost."

"Sure," was the easy promise. Not like a little blizzard could keep her down. Almost happily, she escaped the tent and faced the white world. She checked the compass and set off in the direction that the ranger shelter should be. A minute more, she brought her wings out for the sheer fact that her second eyelids came with them. Tiny bits of frozen ice pelting her eyeballs with hurricane force freaking hurt!

Three hours of useless trudging saw her returning to a frantic Nona. "What the hell happened? I went out looking for you two hours ago! Are you okay?"

Shit. Nona had gone outside? She looked even colder. How was that possible? "Sorry. I lost track of time."

"You took a walk in this weather? I know you signed a waiver about getting yourself killed from your own stupidity, but damn that is really taking the cake!"

"I was looking for the cabin." Cowed by the outburst, Lauren ducked her head. "Sorry."

Blue lips thinned at her. "You're lucky to have found your way back."

Lauren's eyes flit to where she could feel the hidden feather. It was as easy to find as a raging mosquito bite. She could distract herself from it, yet a brief thought would bring the insistent thing to stark attention. "I'm going to try again in a couple hours."

"Lauren, t-"

"I won't sit here and watch you freeze," cut her off.

"Look," fierce determination locked gazes with her. "I appreciate the sentiment. However, I'll feel worse if you get lost or hurt out there wandering around blind."

Lauren held her tongue.

Shortly before noon, when Nona was half-asleep, Lauren slipped out. She escaped and returned four more times.

The shelter with its fireplace and warmth couldn't be found. Shame held Lauren outside the tent, staring at it until exhaustion finally induced shivering. The blizzard had been raging for three full days now. She hadn't had food or water since the night before. Her patience and hope were thin. Lauren fretted that Nona wouldn't survive much longer, that she might already be dead and stiff.

No. She shook herself. Nona couldn't be dead.

Lauren would know, because the feather she'd left behind was tied to Nona, even if the woman was ignorant of it. Damn the law. Damn it! Lauren's magic, her weirdly warm wings could keep them both comfortable in this frigid weather. If only the secrecy law had a loophole for survival situations where non-family was involved.

"L-lauren?" called from inside. "Are y-y-you out-t-t there?"

Her emotions twisted further. She could hear the numb exhaustion in Nona's stuttered words. "F-fuck," was her own stuttered curse. Cold had finally found its way under her skin. A tremble buzzed through her, and she swore viciously. Angry motions turned off her headlamp, sent her into the vestibule, shook off snow, and unzipped the tent. "I'm back."

Tired eyes greeted her, watched her, laughed. "S-so. You d-d-do get cold-d."

Lauren stilled. "Yea." Hands curled into impotent fists. "I'm only human."

"W-was that in d-doub-t-t?" Despite being well on her way to dead, Nona conjured a gentle smile, the one she used to soothe nerves and instill confidence.How could Lauren let someone like her die because of some stupid law? Nona was sweet and patient and compassionate and simply a good human being. Lauren ground her teeth in frustration. Hot anger pooled in her stomach, pushed at the chill that had settled in over the day of fighting the blizzard.

"I won't let you die."

"L-lauren, d-don't b-beat yours-self up-p-p."

"No!" Lauren barked. "I can do more."

There was a low sigh. "Lik-ke y-you said." Nona reached out, set a hand on her arm. "You're only-y h-human."

Reflex had said that. It wasn't true. She was lokref. "No."

"Laur-ren?"

"I'm more."

She gave the law a proverbial middle finger and brought her wings out. Keeping the small confines of the tent in mind, her wings curled as they appeared, taking up what little space was left. Inhuman warmth rolled off them. They wouldn't heat the tent air much, but if she could wrap them around Nona, they'd bring her body temperature back to normal.

And her own. Lauren revelled in the warmth even as she felt the magic taking its toll on her slacking energy. She needed to eat and drink and sleep. She pulled the water bottle she'd hidden under her coat and smiled at the sound of sloshing water. Nona didn't have the body heat to spare to melt snow, and Lauren had let her think the same of herself. Damn, it was nice to quit lying. It'd be nice not to eat snow in lieu of drinking water too. She took a sip of pure relief.

"Here," was presented to Nona. "Drink."

Terror was staring at her.

"It's okay. I promise I'm not a demon here to take your soul." Lauren tried a joke.Frightened silence was the only response.Her wings drooped, feathers scraping the tent floor. "I'm sorry. I didn't mean to scare you." She wished she was anywhere but there right now, lowered the bottle, and plucked at the seam of her pants. "They're warm, Nona. They'll keep you alive."

Dilated green eyes were darting between wings.

Lauren flailed for something to calm the unexpected terror. "I didn't really go for walks all these nights."

Nona's eyes locked on hers.

"I went flying. It's not something I get to do very often."

"What-t-t are y-you?" Nona finally asked.

"Human. Just," she sighed, "More. We're called lokref. People with magic in our blood." She retracted her wings as best she could, folding them around herself, hoping the retreat of the huge things would calm Nona some. "I'm sorry." She hung her head. "It wasn't supposed to go this way."

What felt like hours later, she jerked at the feel of fingers sliding along her feathers. Tingles raced from the touch. She squeaked.

"I'm s-sorry!" Nona snatched her hand back. "D-d-did I hurt y-you?"

Lauren forced startled muscles to relax. "No. You just, um, scared me a little." She sucked in a breath. "No one's ever touched them before. Except my mom and dad, but they don't count. They're my parents, you know?"

"Oh."

"It's okay." Hesitantly, like a little kid trying to tempt a squirrel with nuts, Lauren shifted her wing closer until the knuckle brushed Nona's hand, slid under it, lifted it a little.

Blown pupils fixated on their touching parts. They glinted in the hanging lamplight. "Oh my cheese."

Lauren held her breath for Nona's reaction.

"So w-warm." Nona's entire frame was listing toward the wing.

Yea. They were. Her weird wings. Not only were they black, but they were freaking space heaters, like pavement in summertime. It wasn't an entirely unique feature to Lauren. A few lokref had wings that exuded heat or cold. Not common enough for Lauren to have ever met one, only heard about them from secondhand sources.

Nona's other hand joined the first, then her cheek. Fingers dug into the small coverts and soft down underneath. This time, Lauren was ready for the crazy tingles that buzzed from the intimate touch. Almost. It was... wow. Her body twitched. She distracted herself by reaching for the water and drinking.

The last of her spiced jerky was scrounged up, stuffed into her face in between sips of tepid water, under Nona's sharp attention. She accepted some when it was offered. They shared a silent meal, the food and water mellowing them both.

"Food is good," Lauren hummed.

Something like a smile appeared on Nona. "C-can..." she bit her blue lip. Fingers stroked the wing that she hadn't released. "Can you sleep with them out?" was spit out as a single rushed word.

It took Lauren a few seconds to translate in her head, to decide that Nona was asking to cuddle. Well, cuddle with Lauren's space heater wings at least. Hopefully. "You want a wing blanket?"

Teeth kept a tight hold on that blue lip as Nona nodded assent.

"Yea." Relief hummed. "Yea. Totally. Let me stuff more snow in the bottle to melt." She pulled away only because she knew they both needed to be hydrated, nearly jumping through the vestibule to outside for fresh snow and back. Her heart was booming in her chest as she slid into her sleeping bag and arranged herself. Her upper half remained out so one wing could be laid on. It wasn't comfortable. Didn't matter. It would get Nona warmer faster.

If Nona would ever scoot over.

Lauren fretted. Had Nona chickened out already? Was there anything that could be said to...

Nona and her sleeping bag were abruptly wiggling over with the speedy determination of someone getting a scary task over with as quickly as possible. The woman plopped herself in Lauren's embrace with closed eyes. Lauren's wing smarted from the impact, and she clenched her teeth. Worth it, she had to remind herself.

Gentle consideration slowly draped her other wing over Nona's form. Lauren's arm stayed on her own hip. The rest of their bodies didn't make contact. It was a thousand times more awkward than last night's snuggling.

But...

"S-so warm," hummed happily

Worth it. Lauren stayed awake until Nona stopped shivering. She almost cried in relief when she felt the healthy return of stillness. That knowledge allowed her to fully relax, knowing that upon waking Nona would be alive and well, instead of the terrifying alternative.

Chapter Six

Small-Minded Assholes

Amber swore at the elbow she got to the mouth as she wrestled with the drunk lokref. White hot pain flashed through her skull, loosened her grip, almost set the rogue free. Screw this job! The acrid taste of blood spurring her anger, she yanked arms into place and latched nullen cuffs around wrists. Furious epithets slurred up at her as she rose. The creep even spit on her leg. Nasty.

A ragged poster on the wall caught her eye. *See the world, join the Navy.* If only. As a kid, she'd dreamed about backpacking across Europe, then Asia and Australia. Her life had gotten sidetracked in college when her magic had been awakened in a dorm fire and she'd had to spend a couple years learning to control it. Then she'd gotten roped into joining the Gierdes and gotten stuck.

She wanted to go back to college, study fashion and marketing, intern in Paris, Milan, and NYC, open her own clothing line in America. Travel the world selling it.

"You're a fucking disgrace! You're as bad as a skugg, being friends with one! Both of you should be branded! I sh–" cloth was shoved in the open mouth.

"Thank you." Amber smiled her appreciation at her work partner.

Brian shrugged. "I didn't want to listen to her either. What the hell is a skugg anyway?"

She scowled at the poster. "It's old lokref myth. Traitors in league with the shadows."

Consideration crossed his face. "Because Lauren has black wings?" He frowned. "Stupid, but I get it." He hauled the cuffed woman up. "Speaking of Lauren, ever been to Hawaii?"

Angry sounds puffed through the cloth gag. The stench of rancid gin made its way through as well.

"It's on my bucket list." A bucket list that she rarely got to check items off of. Too much time watching her back, watching Lauren's back. She'd gone to Gierdes training because she wanted to learn. She'd needed to understand how the system worked before chasing her dreams.

She knew now. She didn't like it. She didn't trust it.

Staying a knight meant she couldn't chase her dreams how she wanted, that she spent more time tracking down dumb as rocks lokref than designing outfits, that she grew more afraid of Meisenger and what he was capable of, that she became more determined to change the Gierdes.

If she became Commandant, she could see Meisenger in jail. She'd be on the Gierdes Council. And then…

"Amber."

She blinked out of her thoughts. Her mouth started to throb. Her tongue probed the injury, found a cut in her cheek and a loose tooth. Damn drunk. She resisted the immediate urge to kick her. "What?"

"Help me get her in the car? There's a crowd outside."

A crowd? Super. Amber made herself meet the woman's eye. "Mouthing off about Gierdes at the bar got me at your doorstep. Doing it on YouTube will have Commandant Meisenger skipping your trial and going right to branding." Fear widened bloodshot eyes. Good.

She checked her appearance in the cracked hallway mirror. The trousers and blazer were as fashionably forward as she dared and only took a little tugging and smoothing to be presentable. Her wool peacoat was buttoned back up against the winter cold. Okay. She looked like a normal law enforcement agent with swollen, bloody lips.

She went to open the front door and paused. With a sigh, she removed the gag, tried to ignore the demeaning slurs that vomited out after it, and made her way to the waiting car.

Somehow, the awful woman didn't speak a word about lokref until she was safely caged in the car's backseat. Brian turned on the radio and cranked it to deafening as soon as they rolled away from the crowd.

Amber watched the drunk's face turn purple and smiled, enjoying what she could of the situation.

They passed an ice cream shop, its front walk freshly shoveled from the afternoon snowstorm. Amber's smile faded. Ren was stuck in that blizzard in Colorado. Any lokref could weather a bad storm, Ren better than others, yet… Amber still worried.

She'd been having such a great month too! Easy assignments. A vacation to the Florida Keys to look forward to next month. No news about Meisenger or Tibbits making lokref vanish. In general, a distinct lack of small-minded assholes. It'd all come crashing down yesterday.

The news about the blizzard in Colorado. The assignment to collect this dumb drunk. The tip that yet another dark-winged lokref had gone missing in Nevada.

Amber scowled at the falling snow. Hopefully, Royce was cooking a hot, tasty dinner at home. God, she loved that man. He was gorgeous, loving, incredible at everything he did, including cooking. And sex. She flicked a glare at the backseat passenger. She could absolutely use a good dinner, great wine, and amazing sex after this awful day.

Maybe someday, Ren would find that kind of special someone too. If she lived long enough. No. Not if. She would.

She would! Amber slammed fist to dashboard.

Brian looked up from the report he was already preparing. His brow rose at the cracked plastic.

Rage clenched her trembling fist. Slowly, she regained control, forced her fist open, splayed her fingers until they stopped shaking. Brian eyed her until the hand settled calmly on the center console.

She almost blurted out her thoughts. Brian was a great partner. He didn't hold any love for Meisenger. She trusted him. Yet…

She wasn't one hundred percent about him. Not after only a year working together. She couldn't be too careful. Meisenger had eyes and ears everywhere. He'd made it damn difficult for Amber to climb the ranks, to gain any sort of clout or voice among her peers while she remained friends with Ren. And that was why she was certain that when he made another attempt on Ren, he would try to make Amber disappear as well. Unfortunately for him, she was ready.

Her fist clenched again, this time with fear. She *was* ready. If she got word in time. If Tibbits hadn't sniffed out Amber's inside man. If a thousand other random events didn't play against her.

Chapter Seven

Terrae Cura

Morning was a vague idea, a gradual brightening through the persistent blizzard. The two women discovered that they had rolled together overnight. It was warm and cozy, and distinctly uncomfortable. They separated slowly, silently, stiffly.

Nothing but melted snow to put in their bellies and stifling tension to weigh them down sent Lauren out into the storm one last time. A miracle sent her dashing back to the tent as fast as she could, yelling at the top of her lungs, "I found it! Nona, I found the cabin!"

The zipper was frozen again, and she shrieked her impatience, only barely keeping herself from ripping the damn thing apart. She dove into the tent, took a breath, closed the zipper, and grunted when she faced another zipper. This one smiled open, and she could yell right in Nona's face. "I found it!"

Nona jolted upright. Hope put a little color on her face. "You found it?"

Lauren handed boots over. "Get up."

In a bluster of movement, they left most everything in the frozen tent and followed Lauren's instincts to the shelter. The short mile felt like a dozen in the howling storm. Nona's bum knee gave out twice before Lauren scooped her up and covered her with wings, their unnatural warmth dispelling her weak protests. Thanking her lokref strength, Lauren got them to the cabin and deposited a weak Nona on her butt while she dug a path. A car's worth of snow moved, and the door wrestled open, Nona was heaved inside.

Exhaustion fled the woman as her eyes fell on the dark woodstove. A ferocious zeal lifted her from Lauren, dropped her on a low stool, and started shoveling old ashes out. Within minutes, little flames were dancing under expert hands.

They started to cheer. Smoke choked their lungs, made them cough, and swat at the air.

"Chimney's probably buried." Nona coughed. She looked up. "Think you can get up there?"

"Yea." Despite her flagging energy and sore body, Lauren marshalled the strength to once again face the storm and scramble up the sharply angled roof.

She immediately fell off.

For her second effort, she rummaged in the pack Nona had insisted they bring. Crampons and Nona's ice axe. She leaped at the roof and actually stuck this time. Teeth grit, curses spitting through them, she crawled across the roof, the wind trying to shove her off with every forward motion. A frozen eternity later, she made it to the smoke stack, managed to clear the base and top, and sat panting while fresh snow started to pile on top despite the hot smoke puffing out. She gave it a murderous glare before contemplating her descent. Jump or slide?

Easier to slide. She should land safely in the snow drift below. With a squeal, she released her grip and slid sideways off the roof. Cold snow punched the air from her lungs, tried to bury her alive, made her flail and curse her way back upright. Fuck this weather!

She shook her fist at the sky before turning her angry energy to useful motions. The remaining snow keeping the door from fully opening was kicked at until she thought to summon her shield and use it as an impromptu shovel. Something like a snow-free porch was cleared and a shed was discovered. She excavated the little door and discovered a trove of firewood and maintenance supplies.

She went back in as Nona was happily raiding a plastic tote of its edible contents. Lauren's stomach hollered eagerly, letting her know that it wanted whatever Nona was going to cook, that Lauren needed to help make it cook faster. She said and did as much. Steaming soup was filling their growling stomachs within half an hour.

Hope and hot food soothed frayed nerves enough for conversation to make its reappearance. It started with the cobwebs in the corner of the cabin. Then the cabin itself. Nona explained how the local community maintained it.

Rangers, guides, frequent trail users, they all found ways to support it. Most helped with donations for the emergency supplies stored within and the yearly maintenance. Keeping it clean and tidy and telling rangers when it was in need of resupply or repair was everyone's job. About the only thing not stocked there was batteries. They wouldn't hold a charge in winter.

There was a weather radio powered by a hand crank that told them the storm should be ending sometime today or tonight. Rescue parties were prepped and ready to head out as soon as the weather cleared.

"Are your wings what keep you warm?" Nona abruptly asked. Her eyes were on the empty space behind Lauren.

Last bite of soup finished, Lauren lowered her spoon and gaze to the empty bowl. She'd been waiting for the questions about her wings. "The magic, you mean? Yea." Before an uncomfortable quiet could descend, Lauren rose. "I'm going back to get our stuff."

"It can wait until the blizzard's done."

It could. She eyed the exit.

"Please, stay."

Her chest tightened. Nona was going to ask more questions, and Lauren didn't want to have to explain, about her magic, about how Nona was now in danger, because of some ancient, stupid law. She didn't want to have to lie either.

"I want to apologize," pulled Lauren's gaze back. Nona offered a little smile, showing off healthy pink lips that were almost startling what with them having been blue only yesterday. "And to thank you for saving my life."

Lauren picked at a loose string on her sweater. "No problem."

"That's an outright lie. Saving me was a lot of trouble for you."

She shrugged.

"I haven't been fair to you at all. I'm sorry. You didn't deserve me being scared of you and your wonderful wings. You do deserve to know why." Her hands lifted, slapped her knees. "My gramps used to tell me horror stories about the *Terrae Cura*."

"What's that?"

"You."

Um. No? "What?"

"*Terrae Cura* is Latin, I believe, though I don't remember what it means. The only credible source we could ever find on you people labeled you that. False angels is what gramps usually called you."

What the hell?

"In his stories, the false angels are the result of tainted blood. They're cruel, powerful beings that prey on humans, would lead humanity into constant war if they got the chance."

No wonder she'd been terrified if this kind of shit was what someone had pounded into her about people with wings.

"He always claimed that one of them beat him, tied him up, had their way with him, and flew away laughing." Her tone was bitter, and she glared down at the table.

Lauren sat under the pressure of the story. "It could be true," her mouth spoke before she could censor herself. She cringed under Nona's intense gaze. "Not the generality that we're all bad. That's like saying all brown people are bad. It's basic ignorance." She bit her tongue on the harsh tone. Not helping your case, she scolded herself. "We're human. Lokref just... we come with a little more."

"Lokref?"

"I've never heard *Ter-Terai Terra?* Whatever. We're lokref. Don't know what language it's originally from. Amber might. I don't really remember the history lessons."

"Amber. Your friend? She has wings too?" Nona leaned forward.

Shit. Stupid mouth. "Look, the less you know, the better. When we get out of here, you're going to have to pretend you never saw my wings, okay?"

Nona balked, straightening, frowning. "What? Do you really think I'll act like gramps and go tell everyone I see that a black-winged angel saved my life?" Insult frowned at Lauren. "Here I thought we'd gotten to know each other better than that."

Lauren's fists balled. "Why do you think you've never heard of lokref?"

"Gramps..."

Fists hit the table, made the dishes jump and wood crackle. "I honestly have no idea how your gramps lived long enough to tell you his stories. The law is explicit. The secrets of lokref are not to be known by humans without protection of blood or bond to lokref. Forgetting about my wings will keep you alive, dammit."

"Someone would kill me for knowing about you?" Nona demanded. "And you? What would happen to you?"

Branding or imprisonment, at best. An old suspicion waved at her, and she expressed the worst. "The commandant already hates me, so probably the same."

"You," she went quiet.

Lauren looked at the exit, wanting to go hit something, maybe a tree, preferably the commandant.

"That's why you kept looking for the shelter. You were trying to avoid this."

Her knuckles were turning white. "Yea. I," she groaned. "I didn't want to save you just to put your life in danger." What was that saying? Out of the frying pan into... the pot?

A loud snap from the woodstove had them both jumping. The logs shifted, and sparks glittered behind tempered glass. Lauren stared, not sure if she still wanted to hit something or simply cry. Air shuddered in and out of her lungs as she struggled for composure.

Nona's hand touched hers. "Thank you. For trying."

Tears won. She brought up her other hand and hid behind it. She hated being lokref. No, a silent growl rumbled, she loved flying too much to hate being lokref. What she hated was the secrecy, the ridiculous hatred of dark feathers, the stress of it all. It was too much already and now this? If she hadn't found the shelter, they'd have had to find a way to explain Nona's survival that wouldn't arouse suspicion. Fuck, that would've been impossible!

The friendship of Nona's hand vanished, and more tears struck at the loss of support. Lauren peeked up at the sound of the shelter's totes being rummaged in. A package of tissues appeared, Nona coming back to the table with them, offering them with a gentle expression. Lauren grabbed one and blew into it, loud and gross. She choked when she felt Nona's arm wrapping her in a hug, and Nona began apologizing, and Lauren had to wave it off, but she was blubbery and her tongue was tangled and suddenly they were both laughing, leaning into the other, releasing the day's worries.

A safe sense of calm suffused Lauren. She sighed at the respite, blew her nose, dried her puffy eyes, watched the fire burn. Warm and out of the wind, she noted that she stank. Nona stank. It wasn't enough to scare her out of the comforting hug, but it was enough to make her self-conscious. She scanned the little cabin's interior. There was the cooking pot they could use to heat water. Well, melt snow into water and then heat that. A bucket in the corner would do while more was heated. Was there soap? A towel?

Was she brave enough to wash her naked butt with another person three feet away?

She gave herself a surreptitious sniff, decided it wasn't too bad. Her armpits started itching. Then her head. Her butt. Her groin. Super nasty.

"I know. I stink." Nona started to retreat.

An involuntary whine left Lauren, and their eyes met. Those pretty green eyes smiled at her. How was it possible for someone to have eyes that damn pretty? Poems could be written about them, comparing them to shiny emeralds or whatever. It was unfair. Distracting. *Rude.*

"Okay. We can keep hugging. I can handle the stink if you can." The teasing tone dispelled the fresh tension. "I'll find some soap later. There's bound to be some somewhere. We can take turns having the place to ourselves to wash up."

Lauren chuckled. "You are such a mom."

There was an agreeing hum, "Yea." A sudden twitch. "How the fudge do your wings not rip your clothes apart when they come out?"

"Um." Lauren shrugged. "Magic."

Nona flicked her on the ear, and they both fell to giggles.

———

Snow was melted, water was heated, and soap was found. So were two towels. Nona stepped out in Lauren's coat and boots to see about more firewood while Lauren luxuriated in scrubbing herself and her hair with the minty soap. She rinsed and toweled down, decided to wash her underwear before putting her stale clothes back on. The silly, bright fabric dangled conspicuously from the nylon line that hung across the room. Whatever.

She'd have several sets of clean, dry underwear later, and she wouldn't begrudge Nona doing the same thing. The wind felt like it was actually starting to let up when she went outside to tell Nona it was her turn and that the second pot of water was nice and hot. Lauren accepted the coat as they traded places. Warm and refreshed and full of lunch, she played with the icicles that her wet hair quickly turned into before investigating the pile of uncut wood behind the cabin. There was a big, flat stump in front of it that Lauren sat on.

There was probably a wood axe somewhere. She thought about the little pile of split wood in the shed. How long would it last? She hadn't a clue, but it'd be polite to restock what was used. Common sense and rules of hospitality told her that. Chopping wood would keep her occupied for a while. She hunted for the axe for a few minutes until deciding that it was probably in the cabin, safe from the elements.

She shrugged. Her spear would probably work. She summoned it, eyed the long, sharp edge that made it more like a glaive than a spear, swung it experimentally a few times. Yea. It would work. A fat log was propped up like she'd seen in TV shows, and she carefully lined up her spear. One quick swipe split the thing in two.

The blade sank deep into the big stump of a table underneath. Shit. She pried it out and frowned at the dilemma. Maybe toss it in the air and then swing? She cut the log every time.

Into weird, awkward pieces that wouldn't stack nicely.

Setting up her spear like a sawmill would work, if she didn't have the issue of it disappearing without her touch after a few seconds. She'd have to hold it and drop the fat log on it. Her hands weren't big enough, her fingers not strong enough to wrangle an eight-inch diameter log with one hand. Ten minutes later, she realized she could just cut the damn thing sideways.

"You dumbass." She muttered at herself before making quick work of five logs.

"Lauren!" called from the door. "Are you chopping..." She gaped. "Cheese and rice."

What? Lauren was a city girl, not helpless. She was insulted until she realized that Nona's gaze was on the spear. Oh.

Shit.

Flustered, Lauren barely managed to banish the weapon. Her mouth fished uselessly.

"I'm done with my bath." Nona eventually said. She blinked a few times before turning and closing the door.

Autopilot kicked in, had Lauren picking up the chopped wood, carrying it inside, and going back out until the pile she'd created was dropped into the box inside. She couldn't look at Nona, who was sitting in the same chair as earlier. Lauren deliberated between sitting or going to bed for a nap. She decided on the chair until her hair defrosted and dried. A wet pillow wasn't appealing.

Nona's chair creaked. "In for a penny, in for a pound."

Lauren frowned at her. "What?"

She leaned on the table. "I already know too much, right? Might as well tell me everything." Her expression was a picture of intense curiosity.

"Nona..."

"Lauren, you won't sleep tonight if you don't tell me." Stubborn self-confidence stared her down.

Her own stubborn nature argued. "I don't have to be in the cabin to sleep."

Nona hesitated, then upped the ante. "What if something happens, like the window breaks, and I can't keep the fire going? You'll let me freeze to death after going through all that trouble to save me? Save me twice, actually."

The guilt trip smacked her like a wet blanket. She cast a glance at the sealed window, the sturdy shutters that were iced over and holding fast. "Seriously?"

"Knowledge is power, Lauren. I'll be better able to take care of myself and avoid trouble if you tell me more about lokref."

"This is a horrible idea."

"I have your email and mailing address. You can't escape my curiosity."

Lauren dropped her face directly to the table. "You're a pain in the ass," was muttered against the wood.

"Show me your axe?"

Affecting her best evil eye, Lauren lifted her head. "It's a fucking spear."

Disbelief challenged. "You chopped wood with a spear?"

Nona's prodding got Lauren to show her spear, shield, armor, wings. Standing in the little cabin in full regalia, Lauren felt stupid. And impressive. Nona's awe was a powerful thing. Her concealing helm must have muffled her gasp when Nona ran fingers through her feathers, because she didn't pull away or ask if it hurt.

"All of this is amazing, beautiful even, but unless you've got some serious science fiction gear in that space helmet of yours, how did you find your way back to the tent all those times?"

Space helmet, she griped. She banished everything. Tried to. Her wings more or less refused to break the connection with Nona. "Magic."

Nona rolled her eyes. "Yes. How very explanatory."

Lauren shouldered her way by, went to Nona's survival pack that had emergency supplies and a black feather. She held it up. Firelight caught the scarlet coloring along the edges, made it glow. "I bound this feather to you and left it."

Curious fingers reached up. "What does that mean?"

The feather fluttered into Nona's hand. "I can feel where it is. If you had called my name, I would have heard it anywhere and come running."

"Really?"

Lauren nodded. "The feather is a magic promise. You could be in China, and I'd hear it. I'd have to find a way to you."

"But I didn't know about the feather. Would it have worked?"

"You were close enough to it." The tiny thing could be easily lost, blown away. Lauren wondered how the first lokref had figured out how to use the promise.

"You used it as a homing beacon. Can you un-summon it? Like you do with your wings?"

"Yes." Lauren left the feather in Nona's hand.

That wasn't lost on her. Her brow twitched. "Can you give a feather to anyone?"

"Technically, yes. Only one at a time though. Bonded lokref can't. Their magic is already tied to their bondmate. Amber and her husband are bonded. They don't need a feather for him to call her, though he usually wears one anyway, because it's pretty and bondmates do that sometimes. The magic is a little flexible."

Long consideration was given the feather before Nona asked more questions. "So, magic. Are there wizards and dragons or fairies and evil curses?"

Lauren would have laughed if these hadn't been questions she'd asked as a teenager fresh to her magic and the existence of lokref. Her parents had asked similar ones when she'd brought them into the fold as well. Understanding kept her response free of patronizing sarcasm. "No dragons, but there are magic weavers."

"Magic weavers?"

"Yea. Never met one." As a rule, weavers and lokref didn't mix unless they happened to come from the same family, which was incredibly rare.

"Are they like spiders?"

Lauren blinked and laughed. "Spiders? No. They're people. Kind of like wizards, I guess."

Nona's eyes couldn't possibly get any wider, could they? "Can they cast spells and ride brooms?"

"Balls, woman. I trained to be Gierdes, not a scholar. I don't know." Weaver magic was a mystery to her and most lokref. Only elite Gierdes dealt with weavers. Even if Lauren had stayed and managed to climb the ranks, she'd never have been accepted into such prestigious company, not with her black feathers.

"Girdus?"

This was going to be a long day. Lauren slumped to her chair, forgot she had wings out, jammed them on the back of the chair, and squealed in pain.

"Sweetie, are you okay?" gasped from Nona.

Irritated, Lauren banished her wings. The pain lingered for a moment before dissipating, and she grunted. "Fine."

The other chair got a butt in it too. Nona stared at the space behind Lauren for a while. "Girdus. What's that?"

"Gierdes," she corrected. "Ghee air dess. Lokref police."

The rest of the afternoon was spent talking about the Gierdes, the command structure, the local asshole commandant, that the Gierdes acted as police for the hundreds of lokref in America. Tens of thousands across the globe. The Gierdes was a global organization, with separate headquarters in different regions. Gierdes regions often ignored political boundaries. They policed more by geography and population density. When they did follow them, they were ancient treaty lines drawn up centuries ago. Commandant Meisenger was in charge of the continental United States, and there were commandants in charge of entire swaths of countries like in Europe.

Nona's questions drifted toward individual magic, asking if all lokref had dark wings and futuristic armor, and she was stunned at the feathered bigotry among lokref. The lighter the feather color, the better. There wasn't a lokref in a position of power who had wings darker than almond brown. Supposedly, there were old legends about dark wings and evil lokref, who betrayed humankind to the shadows, but Lauren had never found anything more than vague allusions.

Armor and weapons were individual. They were as unique as the person, sometimes didn't even look like armor. When Lauren was a cadet, she met a lokref whose armor looked like painted on fish skin. A bright blue tropical fish. Their weapon was a long chain with a spiked ball at the end. They'd been sent to China for training with that thing.

At the mention of training, Nona wanted to know about Lauren first realizing she had magic. Was it apparent as a baby? A kid? Were her parents lokref too? Did the magic run in families? She didn't stop the flood of questions until laughter exploded from Lauren, leaning back and howling until her stomach hurt.

Lokref magic did tend to run in families. The commandant was from a long, unbroken lineage of lokref, going back hundreds of years to the Viking ages. Amber had a grandparent with wings. Lauren's parents weren't, and she didn't know of anyone in her family like her. Magic made itself known in times of extreme duress. Dangerous or frightening situations when the lokref had to protect themselves or someone important to them summoned the armor or weapons or wings, usually only one at the time. It took time and patience to learn how to summon them at will.

Lauren gestured at Nona's scars. "If you didn't sprout wings falling off a mountain, then you're doomed to be boring human."

"I'm doomed?" grinned at her.

"Doomed," was her amused reiteration.

Nona's eyes and dimple smiling at her was heart-stopping. "I guess I'll have to settle for borrowing yours when it gets cold then." She checked on the fire, much to Lauren's relief, mumbled that it was getting low, and rose to put more logs on.

Lauren took the opportunity to get up and stretch. She made noise about needing to pee and dashed outside for fresh air and space from the attractive woman. The memories and pain associated with being in love cooled as Lauren stood in the snow. She was too caught up in the past to immediately notice that the wind had died, the snow was barely falling, the clouds thinned enough for sunset to be more than a lessening glow, and when she did, she ran back to the cabin, yanking the door open.

"Nona! Come look!"

Boots and coat were quickly put on, and Nona joined her. "Holy macaroni. It's over."

Lauren squashed the immediate impulse to sprout feathers and fly back to the tent. She blinked. Why not? With a shit-eating grin at Nona, she set her wings free, and leapt into the air.

A hundred feet up, she smiled at the expansive vista spread beneath her. Miles of snow-covered valley in every direction. If she got high enough could she see the lodge? Would she see the people swarming around like ants, starting the monumental task of clearing snow from sidewalks and parking lots? Would they see her?

Balls. This was why lokref knew better than to fly in daylight. All it took was one stray set of eyes looking up at the birds. Stupid, impulsive *child*! She yelled inside her head.

Disgusted with herself, she pushed away all thoughts of fast dives and barrel rolls. Haste snapped her wings and found the bright yellow fabric despite her eyes darting to every pocket of shadows in the landscape. She went to land, but at the last second, she thought about how deep the snow was. The tent was almost completely buried. Without snowshoes, she might sink to her chest. No thank you.

She finally returned to the cabin where Nona remained outside. "Tent's still there."

"Didn't bother bringing anything back?" was Nona's playful challenge.

Still berating herself for her earlier recklessness, Lauren only shrugged. "Nowhere safe to land."

Nona blinked at her. "Oh."

Lauren shrugged again.

"Okay, well, my boots are dry enough. Let's go get our stuff. I'll grab the snowshoes," was tossed over a shoulder as Nona ducked into the cabin. She quickly returned wearing gloves and hat and snowshoes. Her survival pack and headlamp were strapped on, and she had the snow shovel.

Lauren laced the giant snowshoes on with a grimace. She had a higher opinion of them now than when she'd started, but she still hated them. "You sure your knee can handle this?"

Nona nodded and moved ahead with her obvious limp. Okay. Worst that could happen was Lauren carrying her back to the cabin again. She shrugged and followed.

Despite Nona's limp, they got to the tent without issue and went to work digging up the tent. While Nona fought to unearth a couple stakes with her little ice axe, Lauren used her shield and spear to slice through compacted snow and ice and freed the rest.

"Aren't you just the handy multi-tool?" Nona joked.

Lauren snorted. "That's what dad calls me. Every time I go home, he's got something he wants me to cut open or loosen or fix. Mom has me dust and clean fans and stuff because I'm tall."

"I suppose some people would consider you tall," came the mischievous retort. "Shrimp."

"Beanpole."

"Shortstack."

"Amazon."

"Dwarf."

Cheerfully trading jibes, they stuffed most of the gear into packs. Dusk was turning the sky a thousand shades of purple, orange, and red by the time they finished. Lauren had to carry the ice-encrusted rainfly. Frozen chunks swayed and thumped against her as they made their way back in the dark.

"I was a few inches shorter than dad." Nona smiled. "Mom and my sister are the same height, and I'm a couple inches taller. Since we're only a couple years apart, we got equal share of the horrible chores. Makes me wonder how tall Trevor will be."

"Who's Trevor?" A baby brother?

For the first time, Nona stumbled in her snowshoes. She got this deer in the headlights look, all frozen and wide-eyed and ready to run. What the balls was that about?

"You okay?"

"I..." Nona's expression shifted from scared to shy, maybe wistful. "I have this rule about not talking too much on my personal life with clients, and I never talk about Trevor."

Oh. "Okay." Doing her best to shrug off the hurt, and respect Nona's choice, Lauren kept going.

"But if I can grill you about your wings, it's only fair you get to ask about Trevor."

She turned to Nona, who offered an ask-me-anything face. "Okay. Who's Trevor?"

"He's my son." Warm love and pride beamed from her. "My really smart, adorable, painfully shy little boy."

If Lauren wasn't already standing motionless, she would've stopped. She still kind of swayed. Nona was a mom. Like, actually a mom.

"Trevor is the only reason I don't regret having been married to Duncan."

"Duncan?"

"My ex-husband. Okay, I don't regret having been attracted to that tall, ripped stud, but he turned into such a fucking asshole."

Lauren wasn't sure what she was more surprised by, Nona's personal life or the fact that she'd just cursed. "You do swear!"

Rich laughter filled the growing space between snowflakes. "I do. I just try not to as a professional and as a role model for Trev."

Disappointment over Nona's sexuality darkened Lauren's mood for about five seconds. It vanished when her delicate heart realized this meant there was no chance of Nona being attracted to Lauren, that Nona would never have the power to rip Lauren's heart out and set it on fire like Whitney had. Lauren looked back over the times she thought they'd been flirting on the trail. Must be Nona's good nature and easy attitude and open mind. Awesome! She grinned happily.

Their effortless banter continued on for the rest of the evening. Nona announced that rescue teams would probably show up in the morning, homing in on her radio transmitter. They cemented what their story was for survival. Neither would mention the dip in the stream. There was a lull in the storm that they'd used to risk finding the shelter. They'd spent the rest of the storm in relative comfort. End of story.

Above their heads, the nylon line exchanged their clean, dry underwear for Nona's frozen gear. Dinner was another hearty stew, dumplings, and stale Little Debbie cakes. They sampled from a dusty, half-empty bottle of whiskey. Both crawled into the bed and snuggled under the blankets without reservation. When Lauren woke up to Nona spooning her, long body molded along her back, breath tickling her neck, she felt another stab of disappointment that was harder to dismiss. Oh well. They'd part ways in a few hours and never see each other again. It didn't matter.

She found it hard to leave the bed anyway.

The fire was stoked for breakfast. Their gear was packed. Hot water was prepped for tea. The first people to show up weren't rescue crew, but another guide and his four clients who'd been stuck in the blizzard. His radio had warned them many hours ahead, enough time to hunker down in a tiny cave, not quite enough to make it to the cabin. One of his clients had frostbite on her toes. She hadn't bothered to exchange sweaty socks for dry ones after crawling into their emergency shelter. They'd frozen, along with her toes, and she hadn't told anyone, not until it was too late.

A makeshift sled had been used to drag her to the cabin where Lauren and Nona essentially moved out to give the newcomers the warm sanctuary and its trove of wonders. Not before they saw the bandages get unwrapped, and the wounds checked. Two of the toes were gone. What was left was black and green and...

Lauren dashed around the corner to puke.

"I know how you feel." One of the other clients was standing two feet away. His arms were crossed, and he was staring at the landscape. "I've known her for six years. She's a ballerina. Really good. She's supposed to take up a really prestigious appointment to..." He scratched at the short scruff on his jaw. "She screamed when her toes fell out of her sock. Like twigs. Just... pop. God, she cried for hours."

Her gag reflex triggered again.

"Here." Nona was suddenly next to her and holding out a canteen. Lauren swished and washed out the taste of vomit, and Nona sat nearby on the splitting stump. Thankfully, the guy didn't offer more details, kept them behind his stony mask. Lauren kicked snow over her stomach's mess and joined Nona on the impromptu furniture.

"Thanks," as she handed back the canteen.

"Sure." Nona's gaze darted to the cabin. She lowered her voice to a bare whisper. "Thank you. Again." She didn't have to say that it could've been her in that poor woman's condition. Worse.

Lauren could only nod.

They stayed like that until the rescue teams showed up on snow-mobiles. The frostbitten woman and her companions were taken first. Lauren and Nona were still there when another small group showed up. Nothing worse than empty bellies and minor frostnip among them. Lucky.

Local reporters and such got in their faces and took statements the moment they arrived at the lodge. The former ballerina was already on her way to a hospital. Photographers were everywhere. Lauren ducked away to where the lockers were and retrieved her stuff. When there was a lull in the crowd, she made a dash for the exit.

"Hey." Nona popped out of her office as Lauren tried to scramble past. "I was hoping to get a chance to say goodbye." She rolled her shoulders. "And offer to return your deposit. Seems only fair since my broken weather radio got us into that mess."

Lauren's squeezed bank account wanted her to immediately agree. There were a lot of things she could do with that money. She was sure a single mom could say the same. "Thanks, but it's okay. I knew the risks when I decided to go exploring mountains in winter. Besides, it was totally worth it." She'd flown more the past week than she had in years. "All that freedom."

"You're sure?"

"Yea." She nodded. "I'm good." She stuck her hand out.

Nona bypassed it to hug her. "Happy travels, Lauren."

Words suddenly choked her. She barely managed to mutter, "Happy travels."

Lauren went straight to her car, tried to. It was nowhere to be found. There were only mounds and mounds of snow in the parking lot. A young man pulling skis from his car roof stopped to mention that some cars had been buried by the snowplows. She groaned. Now would be a good time for it to be okay to show her shield in public. It made a great alternative to the snow shovel she didn't have. Dammit.

The clicking of the guy's ski carrier had her glancing his way. He ran up to the lodge without them. A couple minutes later, he was back with another young man and a couple shovels. Half an hour later, they found her car and set it free. They refused to let her buy them coffee, simply grabbed their skis and went to attack the slopes. She stared after the helpful guys.

They hadn't hit on her or expected anything in return. Wow. Were they gay? Or some of those endangered specie of decent human being? Smiling, she got in her running car, turned on some music, and drove slow as honey over barely-plowed roads. She got lucky and found a hotel with a vacancy where she spent the afternoon on her phone. When room service arrived, she used the excuse to tell her parents she loved them, but she needed to eat and take a bath. Spicy noodles kept her company while she luxuriated in a foamy bath and dreamed about flying.

Yep. Worth it.

Chapter Eight

Did You Warn Her

"**M**ommy!" was all the warning Nona got before Trevor was in her arms, driving her backward, nearly knocking her off her feet. Fifty pounds of excited seven-year-old launching himself at her the moment she opened the door was expected. And yet…

Laughing, she swung him around, squeezed tight, and enjoyed the feel of coming home. "I missed you too, pumpkin." Around the kisses she placed to his hair, she saw her sister smile.

"And big sister returns from yet another daring adventure." Lyleigh hid her worry behind sass. "Meet anyone interesting?"

Wings and a brave, selfless woman came to mind. "Cheese and rice, Lee, you act like a blizzard is a big deal," was her airy reply. She tried to imagine what Lauren was like around kids. It was as dangerous a line of thought as reliving how nice it'd been to snuggle in the cabin. Wondering about her meeting Trevor and if they'd get along would only lead to trouble. Nona would never see her again, let alone introduce her to Trevor.

"I was scared, mommy," came Trevor's quiet voice. "They said you got stuck out there, and it was really cold. It snowed a ton!"

She bumped the door closed, taking them completely inside where she turned and shrugged off her pack, let it fall to the couch. Her knee sighed in relief.

"It was pretty cold," came out after another kiss to his cheek. His answering squeeze made her want to reassure him that she'd been perfectly safe the entire time. That she'd had a wonderful guardian who had kept her warm and alive. But she couldn't. She was bursting with all the fascinating things that Lauren had shared. She also distinctly remembered the terror on Lauren's face as she explained lokref law.

The way Nona understood it was that some lokref were guardians, most were like the average person. A normal mix, which meant some could be false angels. Her grandfather's story was suddenly much more frightening when she pictured someone like Stalin with magic like Lauren's.

"Mommy, you're squeezing too hard."

"Sorry." Scolding her muscles, she relaxed and forced a brighter smile. "I just missed you so much! I'm going to make hot chocolate. Want some?"

"Yea!" He cheered and raced her to the kitchen, too busy being excited about cocoa to notice her limp. Lyleigh motioned at it and frowned at Nona's wave off. In the kitchen, she not only put milk in the microwave to heat up, she also pillaged the pantry for dinner makings. Lunch? She didn't care what she called her next meal. Her stomach said she hadn't had nearly enough to eat all week. Maybe she'd make a cake too. And pie. Oooh. Pie.

⋅◆⋅

Trevor tucked in bed, Nona was finally free to take that shower she'd been itching for all day. She popped out her contact lenses and moaned in relief. They were designed to stay in for three weeks. Naturally, she always left them in too long. How old was this pair anyway? An answer didn't come, and she sighed, dropping them in the wastebasket.

Hot water splashed across her face, shoulders, and soaked her hair in the best way. So good. She was fully ready to stand under the spray for the rest of the night, ignoring her angry knee, but a massive yawn split her face. She washed and scrubbed in a blurry rush. Before she could yawn again, she was rinsed and towelling herself dry.

Hair was wrapped in a towel, cozy pajamas were climbed into, and glasses tossed on her face. Habit had her peeking into Trevor's room to make sure he was asleep. No phone or flashlight under the covers. Her knee complained, and she started to retreat, but his little snores were too precious. Five or ten minutes were spent just watching until she yawned to the living room to get her gear and start unpacking. One look at her scuffed pack, and she decided it could wait. She collapsed on the couch with her sister.

Lyleigh set her phone down and looked over. "He's asleep?"

She grunted, sinking into the soft cushions.

"What's up with your knee?"

"Bruised. It looks like an eggplant. I'll make a doc appointment to get it X-rayed tomorrow."

Lyleigh hopped sideways, throwing them into a tight hug. "I'm glad you made it home safe, Nones. You really scared the shit out of me this time. What really happened out there?"

"Got stupid lucky with a side of good luck."

Her little sister snorted into her shoulder. "Don't give me that shit. Bear told me when you turned on your transmitter, where you were, how long you stayed stationary. You can fool anyone but me, and you know it. How the hell did you survive out there?" Concern lowered her voice to a whisper. "Without frostbite or anything."

Lauren's warnings and Gramps' story melded together, reminded her that there were forces in the world she neither understood nor could defend against. Not telling Lyleigh the truth would hurt them, put a wedge in their tight relationship, but telling her could actually kill them. "I love you, Lyleigh," was the only thing she could say. "Thank you for watching Trevor."

"I know it's been three years, but I still can't believe that asshole divorced you." Lyleigh muttered.

She rarely complained about babysitting, and she wouldn't have to so much if Nona was still married or could afford regular daycare. Yet, it was better this way, to know now instead of years down the road, that Duncan hadn't been the one for her. The sneaky thought of what Lauren would think of Trevor waved from the back of her mind. She groaned.

"Sorry, Nones. It's just," Lyleigh tossed her phone to the side table. "Trevor brought him up."

Trev tried hard not to let it show, but the abandonment hurt him too. That she and Duncan had devolved into bitter exes fighting over him didn't help. "Shit."

Lyleigh grabbed one of Nona's hands and held it. "He asked if his dad left because you spend so much time with other people."

"Oh my gravy."

"But then he asked if all men were that insecure."

Nona blinked. "What?"

Giggling, "Not in those words, but that's the gist of it. He didn't understand why Duncan was like that. He knows his mom always comes home to him. Sometimes she gets delayed, but she always comes home and gives him big hugs and kisses and when she's home, she's the best mom ever. Even his friends think so. Other moms and dads leave home for a long time for jobs and they stay together. His dad must be broken."

Tears pricked at her eyes, and she coughed.

Lyleigh sighed. "How'd you manage to turn a spawn of Duncan into the coolest kid ever?"

Somehow, a laugh came out. "He does have an auntie who helps." She dragged her sister into another bone-crushing hug.

"Can we open that bottle of pinot you wouldn't let me drink while you were gone?" Lyleigh grinned.

"Sweet cheese and crackers, I could definitely use some wine."

⋯⋯

The next evening saw Lauren arriving home to a full house. Her house-mates were entertaining Amber in the living room, their laughter cutting short when Lauren stepped inside and the dogs bum-rushed her. There was a smile on Amber's face, and she greeted Lauren with a pleased hug, but there was a tension in her shoulders that said she was hiding something. That she hadn't called or texted Lauren to warn of the visit made her nervous. An hour later, after Grace left for a night shift and Jeff took his dogs for a walk, Amber's smile morphed into a furious scowl.

"What the fuck happened up there?" Amber demanded.

"Um?"

Folded paper was yanked from a pocket and shoved into Lauren's face. "Blizzard Strands Unlucky Hikers For Days", was in bold print across the top.

"'Despite arctic temperatures and whiteout conditions, experienced guide manages to find shelter just in time?'," was Amber's disbelieving snarl as she quoted the article. "Are you trying to get yourself branded?"

"You came all the way from Chicago to yell at me about hiring an experienced guide who knows those mountains?"

"Yes, it's such a surprise that the lokref with heated blankets for wings and her cute guide survived the arctic temperatures." She continued her tirade. "And managed to find shelter in a fucking whiteout."

Lump in her throat, heart thudding against her ribs, Lauren stared at her. The silence between them was thick and alive. It wrapped around her chest and squeezed, made it even harder to draw in air without looking like a terrified rabbit. Lying to Amber about this was stupid. But if Amber didn't know for certain, she couldn't be called an accomplice, couldn't be called a criminal, couldn't be branded or taken away from Royce.

"You don't want to know what happened, Amber." Lauren eventually spoke, her words ragged, barely more than a whisper. "You have Royce to think about."

Amber's eyes narrowed a breath before she softened and breathed, "Oh. Shit."

She nodded.

"What about this guide, did you warn her?"

Another nod.

"And you're not going to contact her again?"

"Never." Lauren promised and carefully omitted the part about having left a feather with Nona. It had been an impulse, a reaction to the thought of what if the commandant found out anyway.

Amber's hands went to her neck and she paced a few times before stopping and staring at Lauren. "Tell me what happened. Tell me all of it."

She hesitated.

"You're family, Ren. To me and Royce. Tell me everything so we can prep for the worst."

Another email was glanced at, deleted. The next could be interesting. Tibbits tagged it for a follow-up. The third made her eyebrow twitch. Lauren Trent's name was in a news article involving a blizzard that had stranded a dozen hikers, killed a few people in their cars, sent more than two dozen to the hospital for various injuries. Frostbite had claimed quite a few toes and fingers.

Trent had been with a guide, a local, who had managed to fight gale-force winds and whiteout for over two miles to locate a cabin where they took shelter. Neither suffered any injuries. There was a quote from Trent about how scared she'd been and how lucky that her guide was experienced enough to have found the cabin. Nona Hummel had a humble quote about experience and luck being on her side.

Tibbits frowned. Her fingers danced as she brought up every related article, blog, and report that she could find or hack into. She studied the blizzard, the area, its people. Agents were sent to get to know Nona Hummel. One was told to get as close as possible, and when they had Hummel's trust, ask about the blizzard, learn anything possible about that trip with Trent.

Weeks passed. Tibbits was studying a lokref astronomer who had theories about interstellar travel. His work was fascinating. She enjoyed reading his papers and following his blog, and it bothered her more than she wanted to admit when she discovered that his pedestrian boyfriend knew about lokref. She wished the astronomer had bonded with the man. He hadn't, and she had to submit her report to Commandant Meisenger.

The astronomer was brought in for interrogation and a trial where he was found guilty of breaking Xuande's Law of Quiet. He was branded with nullen ink, never to summon his magic again. The pedestrian met an unfortunate end while on vacation with his friends in Jamaica.

A shiver passed through Tibbits' lean frame. Branding not only kept the magic locked inside, but it was said to be eternally painful. She pitied the poor man and expected for his interstellar studies to be hindered, if not outright cast aside.

Trent's file was pulled up. Mostly unimpressive save for her talent with the spear and the unique aspects of her wings. Except for the black feathers, she would have been a good knight, smart, willing, strong-willed, brave. Age and experience would have tempered her proclivity for impulsive actions. Lokref would have liked and followed her for her charm and generosity. Privately, Tibbits wasn't sure the legends about dark feathers had enough merit to be acted upon as ruthlessly as the commandant demanded.

She clicked through updates from her agents tailing Trent and Hummel. No change to Hummel's story about the events during the blizzard. Hummel and Trent didn't stay in contact though Hummel admitted she might have liked to be friends with the other woman. She had an ex-husband, a child by him that she almost had full custody of. There were rumors about Hummel's sexuality that the ex had spread when they were first going through divorce. The agents couldn't find anything to corroborate the rumors. Hummel spent her energy pursuing clientele and taking care of her child. There was little chance that Hummel would ever pursue Trent for friendship, even less as a romantic interest.

As for having any knowledge of lokref, she had stories her grandfather had spread. Stories about a false angel that had terrorized him one summer night. The woman put no stock in them. She believed he'd been hurt by a stranger. She didn't believe that stranger was anything but a regular human, and alcohol had probably skewed his recollection, as he'd been known to drink too much. She wasn't religious though she believed in a higher power. Overall, the woman was practical, simple, and domesticated. Not the kind that Trent ever showed interest in.

About Trent, the agent noted no change in her regular habits. She continued her work as a mechanic, staying employed at the garage, buying and fixing cars to sell, tinkering with the car she would race in better weather. Her internet activity showed no interest in returning to Colorado or communicating with Hummel. Monitored phone calls and texts didn't reveal anything pertinent. Neither did Knight Garrett-tt-Mansour's.

Tibbits prepared a small report about Trent as she did every few months for the commandant. She made note of Trent and Hummel's lack of interaction and advised that she saw no evidence of misbehavior or warrant for Hummel's disposal. It made her feel a little lighter to hit send on that email.

Chapter Nine
Randal

Nona's baby boy had been missing for four days. Four excruciating days of crying, screaming, pacing, vomiting, and needing to do something, *anything* to find him! And now, *now* she was learning that it wasn't her asshole of an ex who'd taken him as everyone had first assumed. She couldn't even be angry with him anymore. It was his mentally unstable mother she was furious with. And the idiot she'd hired.

An arrogant prick who thought he was a woodsman, but couldn't light a fire without kerosene or navigate a marked trail without a damn GPS. Randal Williams. Incompetent coward. He'd gotten scared by a ranger on a routine patrol who hadn't had the slightest clue he'd had Trevor, was simply checking to see if Randal had seen anything suspicious. Randal shot the deputy, run into the forest, and probably gotten his dumb ass so lost that he couldn't find his way out what with having left his GPS behind in his panic.

"Your mother." She wished she could bring Trevor back with the rabid glower she was aiming at Duncan. "Hired Randal to steal my son."

"And he didn't deliver my son like he should have two days ago. I didn't know about this, Nona. I would never have agreed to something this idiotic." Duncan spat at her. "My lawyer was sure he could get Trevor from you. Why would I be part of his kidnapping when I was assured his custody?"

Scratch that, she could be angry with him. Furious. Absolutely fucking *livid.*

⸺◈⸺

Investigators, Duncan, and well-wishers gone for the evening, Nona made a choice that definitely wasn't the smartest, but it was what her maternal instincts demanded. She texted her sister and packed her spring weather gear, adding a fresh set of Trevor's clothes, a couple flares and flaregun, three days of rations, a local map, and a two-way radio tuned to the emergency frequency. Pack tossed into the passenger seat of the car, Nona found herself calm. Her worried, angry shaking had stopped. She was focused. She had a plan.

She was going to get her son back.

Instead of parking at the nearest trailhead, Nona pulled off the highway as close as she could get to where Randal had last been seen. She tossed back the last of the coffee in her mug and grabbed her pack, locked the car, flicked on her headlamp. A soft, misty rain pattered on her head and nose. Her breath puffed white. Damn Duncan's mother! Damn Randal! Trevor didn't deserve this!

Angry again, she stomped into the shadows and within an hour, she found the meadow where the deputy had been shot. Randal's initial direction was easily parsed by his and Trevor's footsteps in old mud. But like the police before her, she quickly lost the trail on the rocky slope and had to guess which way he might have fled. It was difficult putting herself in his shoes. She shivered in disgust as she tried to fathom what he'd been thinking, where he'd want to go.

He'd still want to be paid and avoid manslaughter charges, so he'd keep Trevor alive. He'd want to move quickly. There was a tiny airstrip a few miles away. It mostly handled the tourists who could afford aerial tours of the mountains. A couple firefighter helicopters called it home. Randal had a pilot's license. Or used to. Nona was pretty sure he'd lost it for a DUI offense a few years back. That was why he'd turned to land-based guide work. Incompetent jerk.

Destination chosen, she put in a few hours hike uphill. The light mist turned into real rain. What had been an annoyance became a real danger. Slippery rocks and mud threatened her footing more than once. Around midnight, she cursed the weather and pitched her tent. She'd catch a few hours rest, refresh her eyes, and attack the trail with the sun on her side. She set her watch alarm and stuffed herself into her sleeping bag.

Sleep didn't come quickly, nor did it leave her feeling rested. She sprang up eagerly anyway. Her gear was quickly stowed, and she set off for the airstrip. When she thought she was only a couple hours behind Randal, she came across cougar scat under a rocky overhang. It was relatively fresh, with small bones -probably rabbit- gleaming within. Maybe a day or two old. And small. It probably wasn't eating well.

Oh no.

A hungry cat would lick its lips at the sight of a little human. A desperate one would eye an adult man the same way. Nona felt for the reassuring weight of her rock axe and hurried forward.

When she was starting to think about breaking for lunch, she caught a whiff of rotting meat. The wind was bringing it from up ahead. As her heart jumped into panic, she made herself survey the area, put her axe in her hand, ready the little whistle she kept in her vest pocket. Nothing close. She pushed forward.

The stench only got worse. It wasn't quite the puke-inducing odor of trash baking under the summer sun, not in this cool weather, yet it still made her stomach twist. Her breath caught when she saw a boot sticking out from under a pile of pine needles and scrub. She gasped when she saw the blue of a coat too.

Her first thought was Trevor. She flung away the detritus, revealing a shredded coat, ripped open stomach. She coughed and turned, breathing shallowly, blinking rapidly, willing herself not to vomit. The body wasn't Trevor. It wasn't him, but she needed to know who it was. She needed to know if it was Randal or someone else.

She turned back and finished exposing the corpse. Most of it was intact, ignoring the defensive wounds on its arms and legs, the ripped out throat. Randal's features remained recognizable. She whirled about, every sense straining for the vaguest hint of Trevor. She followed the drag marks back to Randal's abused pack. A muddy handgun was nearby. The whole area was scuffed from the fight. No Trevor. Heart thundering at her ribs with fear and hope, Nona screamed. "Trevor!"

Over and over, until her voice was hoarse, she called for him. She circled the area. Nothing. No trace. Buzzing from the radio at her hip reminded her that she could call for help. Hope surged through her.

Three hours later, with a helicopter overhead and Randal's body stuffed in a bag for the morgue, neither Trevor nor his trail could be found on the rocky slopes. Shaking, she screamed again. A wordless, horrible thing that spat her panic, her terror, her hopelessness at the world. The deputies around her shifted and muttered to each other.

One tried to console her, but she shook them off with a violent snarl and stalked off to pace and pull at her hair. What the fuck was she going to do now? It'd been almost a week since her baby was stolen. A week!

Trevor was smart, had lived up here most of his life, had the advantage of it being spring and his mother's constant lessons on survival. The snowpack was melted. Temperatures had been decent. But he was only a boy. It was raining. And a cougar that was willing to attack an adult human could've made short work of...

Crying, tugging at her hair, her fingers caught on a thin braid. A thin leather cord wound through it, decorated on the end with colorful glass beads and two feathers. One a pale ivory, the other ebony and scarlet-tipped. Her thoughts slid sideways. Trembling and panting, she yanked the feathers out, held them up to her eye, dropped the ivory one.

The one in her hand was Lauren's.

Could she help? Nona almost laughed at herself. Her first thoughts weren't of the impossible concept that a woman who she barely knew would hear Nona calling her through a feather. A silly feather! Not at all. Nona wondered if said woman could help find Trevor. Lyleigh would tell her how she really needed some sleep if she was contemplating magical help.

But she hadn't been there to see Lauren's wings or feel their incredible warmth or watch her chop wood with a spear made of magic. Nona held the feather tight in her fist.

"Lauren," she begged. "God, Lauren, please. Help me."

⸻ ✦ ⸻

Gasping at the vise suddenly gripping her chest, trying to crush it, Lauren stumbled mid-stride from her car, falling forward and sprawling across the pavement. She tasted hot iron on her tongue.

"What th-"

Lauren, whispered across her mind.

"Nona?"

The pressure released. Changed. It became an insistent tug, an un-failing compass, in what must be Nona's direction. Okay. Wow. Lauren got to her unsteady feet. Nona was in trouble. She needed help badly enough to actually use the feather. Panic abruptly reared, tried to cloud Lauren's thinking, but she kicked at the fog of emotions and managed clear thought. Call Amber. If she wasn't busy jumping Royce's bones, she'd help.

Hand halfway to her pocket, she remembered she'd dropped her phone last night, watched the screen fuzz to a solid, useless yellow. She'd handed it off an hour ago for repair. "Okay, I'll go back to the house and," foot halfway in that direction, the tug became a hard yank that tried to rip her heart out of her chest.

She turned back to Nona's direction, and the pressure relaxed.

"Holy balls," she wheezed, holding her chest. "Ow."

Help me, was a desperate, searing plea that completely dispelled the idea of wasting time on getting Amber's assistance. Without stopping to think of what would happen if she was seen in broad daylight in the middle of suburbia, Lauren brought out her wings and launched herself skyward.

<hr>

On her knees, clutching the feather, staring up into the rain, Nona finally laughed at herself. "What did I expect? For her to suddenly appear? She can fly, not teleport." She rubbed at her eyes. They felt raw. From crying or having had her contact lenses in too long? Probably both. Lyleigh was always after her to take her contacts out after the prescribed three weeks. Four to five was what usually happened. How long had it been this time?

"Ms. Hummel?"

She allowed the deputy to pull her up, put a cup of hot lemon tea in her, and convince her to get a few hours rest. Only because she was exhausted to the point of stumbling over nothing and having the shred of hope that Lauren's arrival would bring did she crawl into her sleeping bag and close her eyes.

What felt like a moment later, she was jerking awake to the sound of someone calling her name.

She fumbled with the zipper. "How long was I asleep, deputy?" she mumbled around the hand she'd lifted to wipe the sleep from her face.

"Wouldn't know. I just got here," returned a far softer voice than she'd been expecting.

Her head snapped up to blink at a shadow much too large for a person.

"It's me, Nona." The shadow's tone was gentle, worried. "Lauren." A pause. "Lauren Trent."

The shape of her made sense now. Wings. "You came." She threw herself out of the tent at Lauren, clutching tightly to her shoulders, burrowing into her neck. "You came."

"Yea. I came." Hesitantly, Lauren settled her arms around Nona's torso. "Are you okay?"

"No," she managed to cough out. Shadows folded around her, and heat soaked into her bones. Lauren's incredible wings. A double-hug. Her warm, safe, reassuring embrace. It eased the lump in her throat enough to speak. "Trevor was kidnapped."Lauren twitched. "Trevor? Your kid?"

Nona froze. How did Lauren know about Trevor? She never told clients about him. When h- the cabin. A tiny laugh appeared. "Yea. My kid."

Suddenly afraid that Lauren would retreat in anger or disgust or something else emotional and irrational, she clung tighter. "My ex's mother hired a total moron to kidnap him. Randal got himself lost and eaten. I found his body this afternoon, and I, God, I don't know what's happened to Trevor. There's no sign or trail or..."

"I'm so sorry, Nona." Lauren wasn't pushing her away. She was rubbing Nona's back. "Tell me what I can do to help."

A surge of relief swept through her, powerful enough to make her collapse had she not already been in someone's arms. "How's your night vision?"

"It's alright." Lauren shrugged.

The movement lifted Nona's head, pressed bare skin harder against her cheek. What was Lauren wearing? She leaned back to take Lauren in, watched as the wings retreated, allowed moonlight to show slip-on sneakers, tight jeans, and a flimsy tshirt. Not practical clothing for the upper mountains. Lauren might not need it, but she was smart enough to blend in with the average person. Why wasn't she in a long-sleeve shirt and gym pants and shoes at the very least? Nona checked her watch. It couldn't have been more than six hours since she'd remembered the feather. To get here this fast, she must have been close, maybe driving to Nevada for a desert vacation?

"Where did you come from?" Intrigue demanded.

"Iowa."

That was at least a twelve hour drive away. To the western border of the state! Let alone if Lauren had been in Des Moines or someplace farther east. "My God. How fast do you fly?"

She ducked her head, picking at her pockets. "Usually not that fast."

"And you're not tired?" Nona wondered.

Lauren looked at her. "Not tired enough to delay looking for your kid. I can sleep when the sun comes up and puts a damper on black wings in the sky."

At the mention of getting caught, Nona looked for the deputies, discovered soft snores coming from a squat tent. Realizing she could hear snores, she became aware of the clear skies and lack of rain. She was also surprised to notice that Lauren wasn't drenched. How had she managed that? No. Not important. Finding Trevor was what mattered now. She turned to her tent and started packing.

"I'm going to keep going north. They've been flying search patterns in this area all day."

She was shoving her water bottle in an exterior pocket when Lauren's words about flying fast hit her.

"Here." Nona offered the liquid. "You must be thirsty."

The way Lauren tossed it back said she was parched. Nona dug out trail food that she carelessly hadn't removed from her pack before sleeping and handed it over, then looked at the deputies' tent. Where was their food? The ATV? She slunk up to it and eyed the locked metal chest in the cargo space. What else was in there? Extra ammunition? She pulled on the padlock, because why not?

It opened. She silently cheered and removed it, lifted the lid. Yep. Ammunition and other police equipment and food. She pillaged enough to last herself and Lauren two days, which was most of it, and didn't feel an ounce of remorse. The deputies had radios. Their stomachs would be okay. Nona needed Lauren, who had a much better chance than grounded men to find Trevor, to be strong and alert. She quietly sealed the chest, returned to Lauren and the pack, and stashed her stolen goods. It was when she was deliberating which route to take further into the valley that Lauren shocked her.

"Want to take an aerial peek before you go?"

"Aerial? You mean fly?!" squeaked out of her.

Twin shadows buffeted her with a little breeze. "Duh."

Pack strap in one hand, she nodded dumbly.

"You can bring that too so we don't have to come back for it." Lauren gestured at the laden pack.

"It's not light. I brought a lot of emergency supplies in case..."

The wings stopped rustling. "Lokref are naturally strong, and I've been working out more. I can handle you and your pack for a short flight."

As if she needed another reason to be impressed with Lauren. "Okay. Right. How do we do this?"Lauren grabbed the pack with her left hand and held out her right. "It'll be easier for both of us if you jump on and use your legs to, uh, help keep you up."

It was the thought that Trevor was out there that swatted away her nervousness, had her doing exactly what Lauren suggested. She hopped up, wrapping arms around Lauren's neck and legs around her waist. The free arm snugged around her, held her flush to the other woman, who darted into a run down the steep mountainside and jumped. Her great wings cracked downward, and Nona's stomach lurched into her throat.

They were airborne, the night air rushing by, the moonlight full upon Nona's upturned face. She coughed and gulped her stomach back down to where it was supposed to be. "Fudge," creaked out.

"Look down." Lauren called.

She did. Silver lined the mountains, shivered across the forest, danced on a sparkling waterfall. Down in the valley, the lights of her little town twinkled. Home. Where her baby boy should be. She shifted her gaze to scour the area for a freckle of campfire. "Trevor's a smart boy, and I taught him to always carry a pocket knife and lighter. If he has those, then he would have built a fire."

"How old is he?" Lauren tilted their flight into a circle.

"Almost eight. His birthday is in June."

"I begged for a pocket knife when I was a kid, but my mom refused to let me have one until I was thirteen. She said I lived in a city. What kind of city kid needed a pocket knife?"

Nona glanced up from her survey of the ground. "What about your magic?"

"It didn't show up for a few more years. See anything down there?" Lauren's short reply left her full of questions about the magic, but she let the topic go and scanned the darkness for sign of fire or anything that might be Trevor.

"Not yet."

"We'll do a few circles. If we still don't see anything let me know where you want me to set down."

Though she strained for any shred of hope, it wasn't to be found, and gestured for Lauren to take them down a couple miles from where the deputies were. After their feet were on the ground again, Nona watched Lauren yank a small feather with a hiss of pain and hold it out.

"In case you find him or need me."

"But I still have..." Nona pulled out the other feather from her pocket. Tried to. It wasn't there.

"One time use. You were probably too preoccupied to notice it turning to dust." The new feather danced in the light wind, its edges sparkling moonlight-silver.

Nona accepted the token and stowed it in a zippered pocket on her chest. She pulled her headlamp from her pack and turned the red light on, swung it over the area. "Trevor! Can you hear me?"

There wasn't a response. Ten minutes of calling didn't change that.

"I'll go back up and keep looking," came softly from Lauren.

"Hold on. I'll show you the map first," as she was digging it out. She laid it on the ground, put rocks on the edges. With her finger, she pointed. "We're here. This is the town. This is where Randal was found. These are cliffs. Trevor could have gone in these directions. He'd try to head for the town's lights if he can see them, but we've covered most of the area between town and Randal's body." Staying calm while she explained wasn't easy. Tension rose within her as she saw all the places Trevor could have fallen, gotten hurt, gotten trapped...

Lauren spread her hand over the map. "Want me to pass over that area again or should I search farther out?"

"There was a helicopter up all day, doing a grid."

"Does he have a phone or anything that might be glowing? A pilot could've easily missed that in the daylight."

"No phone. He might have gotten something from Randal's pack." Nona glanced down the mountainside. "If you don't mind, do a couple passes between town and here."

"Okay." A nod. "Not a problem. I'll circle a couple times, drop down to call his name in a few spots, come right to you if I find anything."

The easy confidence coming from Lauren was soothing. Nona managed a deep breath. "I have a glowstick too, so you don't have any trouble finding me." Green, she snapped it, watched it glow to life. An unbroken glowstick and a small flashlight, she passed over, caught Lauren's fingers. "He's shy and won't trust you. Tell him I made him eat an orange when he fought for Fruit Loops so he knows you've talked to me. We had a pretty big argument over it the day before he... His favorite stuffed toy is Mr. Grumbles."

Green and red light made Lauren's face a disturbing mix of shadows. Her wings caught the light prettily, however, and glittered. Lauren smiled at her. "You sound like you're a good mom."

Emotion choked her reply, "I do the best I can."

Gently, briefly, Lauren's hand gripped her shoulder. "I'm sure you do. I'll check in with you in an hour." She rose and disappeared into the sky.

Nona's hand went to her pocket and fingered the feather there. Small, but noticeable, a weight lifted. Even if they found Trevor in bad shape, Lauren's wings could get him to help faster than a rescue chopper. She checked the radio. It buzzed with fresh batteries, and she nodded. Toward the north, she pointed herself, cleared her raw throat and started calling for her son.

The darkness, mud, and the lack of trail forced her to move slowly. Carefully. It wasn't easy. She had to constantly remind herself that breaking her own neck or rolling an ankle wouldn't do Trevor any good. When she started to yawn, she looked skyward, nearly shrieked when the stars blacked out as a huge shadow passed overhead. It dropped some thirty feet away on a rocky outcrop.

She was fingering her axe when a voice came from the darkness. "It's me, Nona."

Hope flared. "Find anything?"

"Not yet."

"Shit." Nona kicked at a rock, listened to it skitter until it landed in pine needles somewhere.

Lauren was turning away. "I'll keep looking. See you in another hour."

Fatigue forced her to sit down before Lauren had returned. Nona considered setting up camp, but couldn't bring herself to do it. Compromise finally won out.

"After Lauren checks in again," had her resting in a level clearing that would make a good campsite and landing area. She yawned and wiped her face, huddled deeper into her jacket. "If Randal didn't put Trevor's coat on him before he got his sorry ass eaten, I will drag him back from Hell and wring his neck."

This time, when Lauren dropped out of the sky, Nona was ready for her. "Anything?" called out before Lauren's feet hit the ground.

"No," was the low, tired response.

She distracted herself by fussing over Lauren. Were those dark rings under her eyes or only shadows? "How are your wings?"

Rotating her shoulders, "I can go another pass." Her face tilted skyward. "Sun'll be coming up then."

Practicality made Nona call it a day. Her son needed her to be functioning. For that, she needed to close her eyes for a few hours. "I'm going to try and sleep." She unrolled her sleep pad. "I brought a two person tent just in case..." she swallowed. "But I didn't think to grab another pad. I'll leave out my extra shirt." Her eyes fell on the pine trees. Travelers had used pine boughs for millennia as impromptu cushioning. Well, mostly for insulation that Lauren wouldn't need, but also to keep off sharp rocks. "You could cut a few branches if you want a mattress."

"Branches? For a mattress?"

What a city girl. Nona chuckled. "The smaller branches of pine trees make a pretty decent cushion. Under the tent, they won't even poke you much. They'll be better than sleeping on rocks."

"If the wilderness expert says so." There was a tiny glow in her hand that suddenly snapped into a long line. Her spear flashed in the moonlight. A few short, deliberate movements later, and several new growth branches were stacked on the ground. "This good?"

The casual question and cute clothes made stark contrast to the glinting weapon and dark wings. It was both hilarious and disconcerting. Nona closed her mouth and made an agreeing noise.

"Need help or want me to get back up there?" without spark or light, the spear was abruptly gone.

Nona blinked. Her vision was blurry, and she yawned deeply. "Um."

"Let's get your tent up." Lauren made the decision for her. The two of them got the boughs arranged, tent up and staked, and bear bag full of food strung up within fifteen minutes. She hung the glowstick on a low tree branch while Nona tossed sleeping pad and bag in the tent. She quickly followed, unlacing her boots, setting them in the tiny vestibule by her pack. She held up a thick, long sleeve shirt. "I know you could use your wings if you actually get cold, but... well, it's here if you want."

"Thanks, Nona." Lauren smiled. "I'm sure it'll be nicer than rubbing on tent fabric."

———◆———

Nona was surprised to note she'd fallen asleep when she woke up to the tent zipper moving.

"It's me." Lauren's voice was rough, strained from yelling and exhaustion. She pretty much oozed into the tent.

"Anything?" was asked despite knowing the answer.

"Sorry."

Damn. She watched Lauren's shadow fumble with zipping the door up, then with putting on Nona's extra shirt. Nona remembered she had a tiny pillow. "Here. I'm too selfish to share the pad, but you can have the pillow."

"If by selfish, you mean you need it for insulation from the cold ground, then yea. Sure. But I'll totally take the pillow." Lauren cuddled it to her head and went horizontal with it. A pleased sound grunted out. "That's the stuff."

Nona's eyes stayed open until the sun had risen enough to give Lauren's face features again. Focusing on those, tracing the soft lines of her nose and cheeks was entrancing enough to lull Nona, and she allowed herself to close her eyes.

⬧

Despite only four hours of sleep, Lauren woke and followed Nona from the tent when she got up to pee. She yawned through a quiet breakfast of oatmeal and coffee. Camp was packed, and they returned to the search, alternating who yelled, both scanning the trees until their eyes hurt. Evening came. They ate, kept going. After sunset, Lauren took to the skies. The night wasn't much different than the previous.

Nor was the next day.

Nor the next night.

The following morning was as heartbreaking and dreary as the others.

It was late afternoon when Nona jerked to a stop and stared hard at the opposite side of the gorge they were walking along. Was that? She took a step backward. A strip of something bright yellow slid among a tangle of underbrush. She wanted to hit herself for forgetting her binoculars, for not changing to glasses or fresh contacts, for not having fucking eye drops! Her eyes burned. They were blurry and useless and... Nona remembered that she had Lauren. And Lauren had seen a hunting cougar across the damn valley without binoculars that winter.

"Lauren. That bit of yellow. His jacket is yellow and blue. Is it him?" Nona stabbed her finger in his direction.

"Stay here," was all the warning given before feathers slapped her in the face.

She sputtered and blinked. "Trevor!" shrieked out of her raw throat. "Trevor!"

The yellow didn't move. Maybe it wasn't his jacket, just a bit of trash. Her mind quickly brushed that aside, already convinced the yellow was Trevor's jacket, that she'd finally found her baby.

Lauren was halfway over the gaping trench. She flew right over Trevor, circled once over the thick carpet of trees, dropped down probably a hundred feet uphill from him where an old tree had fallen. While she picked her way down, Nona whimpered, stuffed a fist in her mouth. She was too far away, dammit! Was he breathing? Was he sleeping? Let him be sleeping and not... From foot to foot she danced until Lauren reached him.

The yellow moved, blue pants attached. He was backpedaling away from Lauren.

"Oh thank God," wheezed out. Alive! He was alive!

Lauren gestured away from them. Toward her. Nona jumped up and down, waving her arms.

He shot up and waved back.

Hot tears streamed down her face. They'd found her little boy. He was alive! And Lauren wasn't scooping him up and flying him over, so he must not be hurt. Her wings weren't out. Was she intending to wait for Nona to go to them? Walk all the way back to town? What?

Both Lauren and Trevor were gesturing widely. Were they arguing? Discussing? Lauren rose, looked toward Nona, made some arm movements. It took five minutes for her to figure out that Lauren was probably telling her to use the radio. Must be, because she stopped gesturing when the radio was in her hand.

"Deputy Jones, this is Nona Hummel. Come in."

The radio crackled back, and she repeated herself two more times before she got an answer.

"This is Jones. Go ahead."

"I found him." God, that felt amazing to say. "I repeat. I found my son!"

"Is he okay? Do you need a medical evac? Over."

"I don't know. He's on the other side of a gorge, and I can't get to him. Over."

"Alright, Nona. What's your location? Over."

Half an hour later, a helicopter roared overhead and circled a few times to signal that it'd seen them. She watched it land half a mile away. Lauren gestured at it. Trevor did too, then both of them were heading that way. As best she could, Nona paralleled them, trying to stay in sight, trying to keep them in sight. Every time the trees cut off her view, she panicked a little. "Keep your head, woman. He's got Lauren with him. There are rescuers moving to meet them. It'll be okay."

And it was. By the time she was level with the chopper, there was a natural bridge over the gorge, and she ran to throw herself around her son.

"Mommy!" cried into her arms.

※

Chapter Ten

Nona's House

"No. No, it's okay. I've got a camp to get back to. I just happened across him, saw his mom on the other side," finally cut into the stupor of having her baby in her arms again. Nona looked up to see Lauren waving the deputy off. "I'm good."

"If you're sure, ma'am." Deputy Jones murmured. He was eyeing Lauren's filthy street shoes and torn jeans.

"Totally. I'm just happy to help."

Nona took the opportunity to, "Thank you." She rose and enveloped Lauren in a tight hug, sobbing into her shoulder. "Thank you so much for helping me."

"Anytime," breathed into her hair.

"Mommy, can Lauren come to lunch?"

She blinked down at her son. "Sure, but I, um, think she's busy camping."

To her great surprise, he pouted. "But..."

From the half-hug they were still in, Lauren dropped away to kneel and be at Trevor's eye-level. "I need to get back to my camp. How about later, Snowman?"

His shoulders sagged. That tone was one he knew. A half-promise that usually never got fulfilled, usually by Duncan. "Okay," was muttered.

Lauren probably needed to get back to her life. It was a long flight home. A long flight... Nona's gaze went to the shirt on Lauren's back. The not-torn shirt. No sign that Lauren's wings had come out while wearing it. How? She remembered asking about it before, that Lauren had given some lame excuse about not knowing why the magic was that convenient. It still didn't stop logic from arguing that there should be huge tears down the back. Did the magic simply ignore clothing? Was it only Lauren who didn't destroy her clothes? What about others?

"Speaking of lunch, I bet you're hungry." Nona came back to the present and tried to distract her kid from disappointment. She grabbed a trail bar from her pack. "It has cranberries. Your favorite."

"Okay." He smiled, but didn't grab it from her hand and shove it in his face.

"Aren't you hungry?" her instincts worried.

"Not really. While that jerk was sleeping, I took the bear bag and ran away."

Now she noticed Trev's backpack on his shoulders, the half-full water bottle in its pouch on the side. "My smart little man. What'd you do when you got cold? We never saw a campfire."

"I didn't want him to find me, so I didn't make a fire. I found a little cave to sleep in one night. The next, I made a shelter under a pine tree. Last night, there was this big tree that'd fallen over and left a big hole." He suddenly craned to look at his pack. "Oops. I forgot my sleeping bag there. I'm sorry, Mommy."

Pride and love and a whole slew of emotions had her hugging him tight to her chest. She could care less about trading a sleeping bag for Trevor.

"That's quite a story," one of the deputies said. "It's probably best if we get him checked out at the hospital anyway." The deputy met Nona's eye. "Just in case."

Nona gave an agreeing nod. Off to the side, she saw Lauren fidgeting. "Deputy, could I borrow a pen and paper?"

The deputy pulled a notepad and pencil out, handed them over.

Home address and directions to it were written down. Directions that she hoped would be easy to follow from the air. "In case you change your mind about a meal," was given to Lauren. "You're welcome any time."

"Oh. Yea. It's no big deal."

Nona refrained from arguing that, especially with their audience. "Thank you again, anyway. Really."

"Yea." Lauren bobbed her head. Her eyes darted around, then she turned and headed away from them.

Heart in her throat, Nona watched until a deputy coughed and said they were ready to head back to town.

"Okay. Come on, Trev. Let's go home." Nona steered them toward the waiting helo. She cast another glance toward Lauren, but trees and rock had already obscured her from view.

◆

Light knocking on the door startled them both from the cartoons they were watching. Dozing through. Same thing. The point was that it was late. Duncan and the horde of well-wishers had gone home for the night hours ago. Lyleigh had gone to bed shortly after. She would still be up with them, would've called in to work the next day, except that Nona had spent almost an hour convincing her otherwise. She'd lost enough time at work worrying over Trevor. And sleep.

Lee needed a full night's rest. She needed the hours at work. So Nona had shuffled her off to bed, hugged her tight, thanked her again, and closed the door.

No one should be at the door this late. Who could it be? Nona hesitantly went to the door and peeked out. There was a tall woman out there wearing a familiar shirt.

"Lauren," puffed out of Nona.

"Lauren's here?" Trevor bounced up from the couch, suddenly full of energy.

In answer, she opened the door.

"Hi," came quietly from their scratched up, dirty guest.

"Lauren!" He ran toward them, stopped at Nona's hip. It freshly astounded her. He didn't warm up this quickly to strangers. An hour hiking surely wasn't enough, not if all they'd talked about was movies they liked and vegetables they hated.

"Hey, Snowman." Lauren grinned down at him.

"I'm not a snowman." He argued.

"You don't seem to mind the cold, neither do snowmen."

Trevor shifted. "You're weird."

Lauren chuckled and shrugged. "I've been told that."

"Come inside, Lauren." Nona gestured at the interior. "I know you two don't mind the cold, but I don't want it in my house."

"You're not wearing a coat." Trevor noted. "You're a snowm- um. Snowwoman."

83

"I might be," was Lauren's distracted reply. Her eyes were tracing the inside of the cabin. "Nice place."

"Shoes off at the door," ordered Trevor.

Snickering, "Aye, Cap'n Snowman."

While Nona watched the stained, torn-up shoes get toed off, she again wondered what Lauren had been doing before Nona had called her. Taking a walk? Shopping? Or maybe she'd been watching TV and thrown on whatever pair of shoes was easiest before flying? How had those shoes not come off while flying? Had she had to touch down for a layover on the way? Did she not expect to be gone long? Was that why she didn't have a purse or daypack, any supplies at all? And then it occurred to her that Lauren probably hadn't eaten since breakfast. "Are you hungry? There's leftover pizza."

Lauren's stomach answered with a rumble. She rubbed it while Trevor giggled. "Pizza sounds amazing."

"We've got a veggie pizza and a basic sausage and cheese."

"Veggies on pizza? Are you even American?" was the sneering rebuttal.

"Are you insulting the food I'm offering?" Nona returned.

"Only half of it." Lauren grinned.

Nona gave her a cool look, but went into the kitchen to retrieve a plate, open the box, and show Lauren where the microwave was. Half a cold slice of deep dish pizza disappeared into her mouth. She chewed eagerly, chomped more, finished the whole slice in three bites.

"That is fucking amazing," groaned out of her.

"That's a bad word!" Trevor scolded.

Lauren's hand paused on its way to another slice. "Um. Yea. Sorry?"

"It's okay," he allowed. "You didn't know the house rule. But if you say more, you have to do something good to make up for it. And Mommy says you shouldn't eat that fast."

What looked like a flush was rising up Lauren's neck. "She's probably right," groaned out as she dropped slices to the plate. It was shoved in the microwave, and she fumbled with the buttons.

Host duties had Nona offering, "Something to drink? We've got water, milk, and fruit juice."

"No hot coffee?"

"You want something hot?" Nona frowned at her, unable to tell if she was being serious or not. "Are you actually cold?"

The toothy grin that replied made her roll her eyes. Lauren finished with a laugh. "Not really. I just thought coffee with Kahlua sounded good. I'll take water."

A cup was dragged out and shoved at her. Nona waved at the faucet. "It's right there. Help yourself."

"Service around here is shi..." eyes darted to Trevor. "Sure terrific."

"You bet your butt it is." Nona said.

"Nice glasses, by the way. Bright red is very city girl of you."

Nona snorted, felt the glasses slide a little, pushed them back up. Her eyes loved them. If it wasn't a major hassle with how they fogged up, froze over, and broke too easily, she'd wear glasses on the trail. "Trevor picked the color."

"Red is my favorite!" He cheered.

Laughing, Lauren lifted a warmed pizza slice to her mouth.

"Are you going to stay the night?" Trevor asked.

"Um," Lauren froze.

"If she wants to. Speaking of, you want a shower? I'll grab you some clothes and a clean towel." Nona ushered her curious kid from the kitchen, deposited him on the couch, and went to her bedroom where she hunted down comfy, stretchy clothes. A clean towel and wash cloth were added to the pile. She considered her bed and whether she'd stay in it or out on the couch with Trevor.

She poked her head into the living room. "Pumpkin, you want to sleep on the couch or in bed with me tonight?"

Thoughtfully, Trevor looked at Lauren, who had joined him on the couch with her pizza. "Your bed, Mommy. Lauren can have the couch."

Pizza disappeared into Lauren's mouth. It was vanishing at a more normal pace than it had in the kitchen, thankfully. "What're we watching?" was asked halfway through her third slice.

"Adventure Time!" Trevor was aghast. "You don't know it?"Lauren shook her head.

"Have you been living under a rock?" he demanded.

"More like up in the clouds," puffed out softly, with an air of sad nostalgia.

Even tired and unfamiliar with her, Trev noticed. He pat Lauren's thigh. "Don't worry. I'll help you catch up. There's Finn and..."

Explaining the characters, their backstories, and the world took up the rest of the episode. Trevor was fully into the pop culture lesson, and cutely, Lauren was being a good student. Nona caught and shoved away what was probably an ooey-gooey expression on her face before anyone noticed. After the show finished, Lauren went for a shower, and by the time she got out, Trevor was yawning and helping put sheets on the couch. They left a much better smelling Lauren alone and headed into Nona's room.

Nona poked her kid as they snuggled in bed together. "You're really comfortable with Lauren."

Giggling, he squirmed from the touch. She chased those giggles with more pokes. "Mommy!"

"I'll stop tickling if you tell me what you like about Lauren so much." She wiggled her fingers along his tummy.

He wiggled and giggled. "The cougar ran away from her."

Ice wrapped around her heart. "What?" her breath should have fogged out of her, cold as she suddenly was.

Trevor stopped giggling, and his little boy face went serious. "I knew you'd freak out. It's why I didn't tell you before."

She couldn't breathe. Images of Randal's chewed body plastered across her vision, were replaced by Trevor's.

"It was really close and scary, but when it heard Lauren coming down the hill, it stopped moving. And when we could see her, it started hissing, Mommy. That big cat was scared of her!" His eyes were bright, excitement clear on him. "She threw her arms out." His own spread wide. "And hissed back at it!"

Terror banged at her skull.

"She kept hissing and walking at it until it ran away!" He giggled until he fell sideways.

Nona's chest felt like bursting, and a gasp popped out. Her lungs howled. Oh. Air. She made herself breathe.

"Mommy?"

She grabbed him and held him close.

Chapter Eleven

Scuffed Shoes and Jeans

A full body flinch woke Lauren up. She jerked upright, or tried to. She was tangled in a blanket and ended up rolling off her bed, crashing into the floor and jarring an elbow.

"Owww," whined out of her. Irritated, she pushed the blanket off and leaned back against the bed. She yawned and blinked, realized she wasn't at home and stiffened, eyes going wide, magic humming under her skin.

Bright light cut a line between curtains on the far wall. It highlighted boots lined up next to the door on a rubber mat, coat tree above it. Lauren's ruined shoes were on the mat. She'd taken them off and placed them there at Trevor's orders. Trevor. Nona's kid. The woman who she'd promised Amber that she'd never see again. For all their sakes.

Here she was though. Gierdes hadn't shown up in the middle of the night to silence them all, so Lauren must not have been seen. A huge yawn split her face, scrunched her eyes, made her whole body tense. She let it out. Another quickly followed.

"Damn." If she was still so tired why was she awake?

Her bladder answered. Oh. Okay. Lauren went to stand and groaned. Every muscle from her neck to her toes protested, whining that they were stiff, that they had been overly abused the past few days. She struggled to the bathroom. While using it, several more yawns erupted. She scrubbed her hands and eyed the mouthwash. Yea. Definitely needed that.

A cupful was poured, and she tossed it back. The moment she gargled, her throat burned like nitrous, and she gasped, choked, bent over the sink, coughing and spitting. After a long minute, she caught her breath and wheezed, but her throat still burned and her head was starting to pound. Great. She scooped water from the faucet into her hands and tossed that back.

Better. But she could use some Advil or something. She poked at the medicine cabinet and was rewarded with several bottles of over the counter painkillers. Two tablets were washed down with more water.

"Right," she croaked. A few days of yelling had torn her throat up. No mouthwash for a while.

What about coffee? Warm bliss. That should help. And food. Yea. Bacon on the brain, she opened the door and nearly walked into another person. Big eyes peered up at her.

"Morning?" Lauren offered.

"Morning, Lauren." Trevor blinked, grabbed her hand. "Mommy is still asleep. Can you cook?" as he was already dragging her to the kitchen.

"Sure." She let herself be guided to the fridge where eggs were put in her hands.

Trevor carefully pointed out the frying pan, utensils, spices, and how he liked his eggs. Then, he told her how to make eggs for his mom and Auntie Lee. He set up the toast by himself. Four types of jam were pulled out. He was standing on a chair, pulling plates down when Nona appeared, worry lining her face

"Morning, Mommy." Trevor set the plates on the counter. "Lauren's making breakfast."

"I got volunteered." Lauren chuckled.

"Mommy, are you okay?" Trevor frowned.

The last few days' horrors were written all over Nona. Her breath was shaky. Her bottom lip quivered.

"Nona?" Lauren prodded, taking the eggs off the heat.

After a glance at Lauren, Nona crossed to Trevor and threw herself around him. "I missed you so much." Three days of yelling in the backwoods and almost two weeks of panic made that whisper a raw croak. Damn. Must be painful to even breathe right now. Lauren's own abused throat throbbed in sympathy.

Trevor was hugging back just as tightly. "I missed you too."

Lauren turned away from the emotional moment. There were hot pricks at the corners of her eyes that she didn't want to encourage into tears. She focused on the eggs, scraping Trevor's sunny side up onto a plate. The rest would be simpler. Scrambled. She reached for the bowl of whisked eggs. Fingers on her wrist stalled her.

"Lauren?" Nona was beside her, the rim of her eyes red and flushed, deep bruises below them.

"Yea?"

"Thank you." Her arms wrapped around Lauren. "So much. I can't begin to thank you enough." She pressed herself close, burying her face in Lauren's neck. "I don't know what I would've done if..."

Caught off guard by and having a little trouble breathing under the forceful embrace, Lauren puffed out a weird noise that she hoped Nona registered as friendly.

"Trevor told me..." Breath stuttered into a sniffle. "He said you scared off a cougar." There had to be tears streaming down her face the way her body was shivering.

Oh boy. Had to stop this train of thought. "He's home now. He didn't get hurt."

Fingers dug into Lauren's shoulders.

"He's safe, Nona." Lauren stroked her back. "Trevor's fine. Right, Snowman?"

Trevor moved next to them and pat his mom's hip. "I'm okay, Mommy. You found me."

Instead of backing off, Nona whipped an arm out and drew him tight against them. She whimpered. Tears were definitely dripping. Lauren awkwardly resumed the slow strokes to Nona's back and endured the death grip until Nona was ready to let go. This had to be the first time she'd cried it out. There had been some tears on the trail, a few escapees as Nona pushed onward. Nothing like this. Maybe the moments when Nona first caught sight of Trevor and got to touch him. Lauren had been a little preoccupied with keeping a low profile and sticking to the simple story of being out on a walk from camp despite the looks her ripped jeans and sorry shoes were attracting.

Nona finally released her, sniffling, lifting her bright red glasses to wipe her eyes. "Cheese and rice. I didn't mean to blubber all over you like that."

Lauren chuckled at the reminder that Nona cursed with food. The dork. "It's fine. You needed it."

"I..."

Toast popped up. Slipping out from under Nona's arm, Trevor went for it, slathering mustard on it before putting his egg between slices and squeezing. Yolk oozed out. "You did it!" He cheered. "Auntie Lee always overcooks it. She thinks it's gross."

"She's not wrong." Lauren snorted. The sight of that runny mess made her lip curl. "Scrambled is way better, dude."

"No it's not," argued with her.

She cheerily bantered with him while she poured the egg mix into the pan and watched the edges cook. Nona eventually told Trevor to stop talking and eat while it was still warm. In the quiet, Nona started the coffee maker. The ambrosial scent of coffee filled Lauren's nose as she turned off the heat and divided the pan's contents into three. More toast popped up. Jam was offered. Peach accepted.

Mugs and plates steaming, they made their way to the living room. The house wasn't big enough for a dining room, and the kitchen only had a small breakfast bar. Lauren made herself comfortable in an armchair and tucked into her food. She was three bites in when noise from one of the bedrooms drew her attention.

"I'm late!" squealed a woman. A moment later, a younger version of Nona streaked through. Tall, blonde, pretty, though she lacked the scars and had blue eyes. She also wore mascara and a touch of blush.

"Breakfast is on the stove, Auntie Lee." Trevor announced.

"Thanks, Trev!" She gave him a smooch on his forehead and dashed into the kitchen. The sound of fork hitting plate sounded. Liquid splashed into a container. The fork made a few more clanks and scrapes. Maybe two minutes in all passed before Lee was back in the living room, travel mug in hand, shoving feet into boots, cheeks puffed as she chewed. She waved, started to open the door. "Who's this?" pointed at Lauren.

Nona went as stiff as Lauren felt.

"Lauren." Trevor answered. "She was camping in the mountains and found me. She came to visit."

"Oh." Lee's eyes went round. "Oh my God, thank you!" She made a jerking motion, like she wanted to jump Lauren with a hug, but ended up opening the door. "I'm sorry, I have to go!" The door slammed behind.

Lauren let out the breath she'd been holding. "Bye."

"Lyleigh. My little sister. She lives with us." Nona sighed. "She's never been great with her alarm clock. I sent her to bed about an hour before you showed up last night."

Lauren smiled. It felt like home, with Grace's usual morning dash because she was late again.

"Oh my cheese! Speaking of work. Do you need to use the phone or anything?"

Steve was going to kill her, at least fire her. Calling now might help mitigate that. But there was no way she was going to use Nona's phone. Amber had gotten word that Knight Tibbits had been assigned to watch Lauren and Nona after that blizzard. By now, there probably wasn't anyone physically watching, yet their phones were definitely still bugged. Lauren would survive if she lost her job. She wouldn't if Tibbits discovered that Lauren had flown up to Colorado.

"Nah. I'm good." She shoved toast in her mouth.

"Are you sure? Did you make some calls before you..." Nona glanced at Trevor, who was currently oblivious.

"Yea." Lauren lied. "It's fine."

Disbelief was clear on her furrowed brow.

"I'm heading back tonight anyway." The sight of her filthy shoes brought up, "Mind if I hang out and get my clothes washed before?"

"No, of course! Anything you need." Nona offered. "Anything at all."

After breakfast, Nona did laundry while Lauren and Trevor hung out on the couch watching some kids show on HULU. She fell asleep at some point, waking up to lunch and clean laundry. Chicken salad sandwiches and oranges. Lauren was pretty sure she'd never had chicken salad with raisins and walnuts and curry before, but she was definitely going to make it again. When Trevor went down for an afternoon nap, they talked about when and how Lauren was heading home.

That should be before Lee got home. She would be ridiculously curious and ask a thousand questions. Given that Lee would be home by late afternoon meant that Lauren would be stuck out in the woods for several hours before she could risk flying. Lauren refused the offer of a bus ticket. A paper trail wasn't an option. Nona made another meal that would travel well so Lauren wouldn't miss dinner. A water bottle and a thermos of coffee were given to her. And a compass and printed out map. And a snack for mid-flight. *And* a bag to carry it all in. Nona mom'd the shit out of Lauren all day. It was both annoying and adorable.

When it came time, Lauren was sent on her way with clean, though still horribly stained and scuffed shoes and jeans, a dark blue hoodie, and the bag full of goodies. Nona drove her to a trailhead for both the story that Trevor knew and because taking off from the woods was a better idea than in town, even if Nona's house was pretty much on the edge.

Lauren wandered in a way and found a fallen tree trunk to plop on. As boredom set in, she made a list of all the things she needed to do. Like make sure she kept her burner phone on her all the time. Or get another. Tibbits probably knew about the one she used for racing.

If she'd given it any thought, she could've saved her job, warned Amber, given her roommates a courteous "hey I'm leaving for a few days" -because they were both going to be worried- and it'd be a number she could contact Nona on. Lauren would have to send an unmarked letter to Nona suggesting a burner phone and Lauren's number.

She groaned up at the night sky. A phone would've helped her keep track of time too. She only knew that the sun had set a while ago. There was a highway somewhere close with traffic. She waited until that seemed to lessen before taking to the sky. Her entire body protested the effort, even her wings. Groaning, she forced herself into a steady pace and tried not to think about the long hours ahead.

⚊⚬⚊

Steve didn't fire Lauren. He should have. But he didn't. What he did do was chew her out for half an hour and tell her that if she was even late for work again, he had a cousin that was getting his ASE certificate soon and would happily take her place.

"If you didn't have so many damn certifications and weren't such a fucking Japanese import encyclopedia, Ren..." His rage trailed off. That she was obsessed with imports and could deal with the problems local kids brought to them was why she'd been hired in the first place. The certifications she chased had been why he'd kept her.

"I know," came quietly. Lauren picked at a thread on her pants. "I'm sorry."

He glared down at her. "What the hell were you thinking?" repeated from him for probably the hundredth time.

And like she had the other times, "I wasn't. Sorry."

"Hell, I should fire you for not even giving me the courtesy of a decent excuse." He fumed, though the rage was spent. "Had something to take care of. Jesus Christ, Ren. You know that's about the lamest line I've ever heard. You could say your grandmother died or something."

92

She met his eye. "Lying wouldn't be any better, Steve."

He suddenly sat down. "Are you okay? Are you in some kind of trouble?"

The concern was sweet. "I'm okay," was said with a smile.

Eyebrows furrowed at her. He and most of the shop knew she raced, that the other car she never sold wasn't street legal. They'd all suspected something was up with her since she'd come back from Colorado. Really, they had since that bad race a while back when that asshole had tried to kill her, not that she'd told them, but they sensed it. They'd been working together for too long. Since she never showed up drunk or high, never brought her problems into the shop, and always did quality work, they held their suspicions in check.

"Goddammit. Just tell me if it's your parents or if it's going to affect my shop."

"My parents are fine, Steve. It won't affect the shop. It won't happen again." She'd already bought that cheap burner phone and plenty of airtime minutes to go with it. Its weight hung heavy in her pocket.

He grumbled and scrubbed fingers over his buzzed skull. It was flushed with anger now, like in summer, when it would burn and stay burned until winter. Had to suck to be that white. "Goddammit."

She waited while he stared at her for another minute.

"There's an Acura with an engine problem the other guys can't figure out. Go take over on it."

She jumped. "Thank you."

A long sigh spewed out. "Goddammit, Ren. Don't fucking complain about the coffee here ever again."

It was shit and he knew it. She'd been harassing him to get something better so she didn't have to bring her own for months now. It was a bad day when she forgot. Like today. She'd run out the day before Nona had called. She stifled a yawn and nodded. "Sure, Steve."

"Go. Get out of my office." He waved at the door.

At her locker, she changed into her coveralls, let out a huge yawn and wished she hadn't decided to be responsible and come in right after that long ass flight. At the coffee pot, she sighed. The guys gaped at her when she strode into the garage.

"You've got to be shitting me."

"Where the fuck you've been?"

"He didn't fire your sorry ass?"

"It's about time. Come figure out what's wrong with this sewing machine." One of the older guys gestured at the Acura. He didn't think a car was worthy of a name unless it was domestic. Everything was sewing machine or donkey cart or cheese basket or crumpet carrier. Racist old bastard.

Lauren slurped her coffee, grimaced, and picked up the notes the customer had left. It was going to be a long Tuesday.

Chapter Twelve

Prepaid Phones

Looking at the selection of prepaid phones, Amber sighed. They should've thought of this sooner. Having spare phones that Tibbits didn't know about and couldn't monitor was a fantastic idea.

"Anything I can help with?" A salesperson smiled from behind the counter.

"Um. Yea. I need two phones. No monthly plan or contracts. Just something to keep on hand in case, um."

"To shove in the go-bag." Royce finished. "We're trying to do a little survival prepping, you know? Zombie apocalypse and shit."

The salesperson laughed. "Okay. You'll want something where the minutes don't expire. You thinking basic phone calls or maybe want to connect to local wifi? These smartphones aren't too pricey. They'd get you online and to email or news sites. Not fast, but they do the job."

An hour later, they had two low-end smartphones ready to make anonymous phone calls. They both called Lauren's burner and said hi. Then they went out for fruit smoothies.

Amber watched Royce take pictures of joggers and dogs, a skateboarder practicing some impressive tricks. She sipped her smoothie and leaned back on the park bench they'd claimed under a fat shade tree. Sweat rolled down her cheeks, soaked her back and armpits. She reveled in it. Unlike Lauren, she loved summer and its delicious heat. It could never come soon enough.

"Did I tell you I have a gig coming up?" Royce took her picture as she looked over.

"No. What is it?"

"Lollapalooza."

She nearly dropped her smoothie. Lollapalooza was a *massive* event. Four day music festival in Chicago that drew thousands. "What?"

"Yea. I've been assigned one of the stages. If I do this right, I might have a foot in the door for Afropunk Brooklyn."

She squealed. She loved Afropunk, all the music, the fashion, the black camaraderie. They had tickets already, but would happily give Royce's to a friend or sell it if he got a photography gig there. "How?"

He grinned. "That magazine editor I met at the last wedding I worked. She's got her hands in a lot of pots."

Weddings weren't his thing. They brought in good money and it was a cousin's friend, so she'd prodded him to do it. Extra cash in the go-bag was never a bad idea. Or, you know, extra cash for another cute outfit. "Told you it was a good idea."

He rolled his eyes. "Whatever. I'm not doing another wedding unless we are completely desperate."

"Mm hmm." Amber argued. "Or unless you see another camera or lens you want to buy."

Lips pressed tight together.

"Don't act like you don't have a huge wishlist of photography gear."

He laughed. "You got me." Grinning, he leaned in for a kiss that she rolled her eyes over, but accepted all the same. Damn she loved this man.

Chapter Thirteen

Fast and Furious

Late September found Nona happy and content in a way she hadn't been in years. She and Trevor were taking a roadtrip to Ohio that hadn't been possible since her divorce. Without Duncan's interference, summer business had been absolutely fantastic, plentiful enough she'd been able to take off a few weeks before winter tourist season. Bills were paid, some in advance, and a comfortable figure sat in her savings. She could finally take Trevor out of the state without worrying over what Duncan's lawyer would do. Since the kidnapping and the court awarding her full custody, he had no legal grounds to complain. She didn't even have to let Duncan see Trevor, though she did, when Trevor wanted to see him.

Trevor had never been farther from home than his gramma's, a few hours away. He'd been scared to go so far and almost decided to stay with his dad instead of joining her on this vacation. Almost. She bribed him with a little fast food and free reign to play on his phone during the trip. Worked like a charm. He was a happy little camper. When he got antsy about being cooped up, she pulled off to see a weird art installation in the middle of Nebraska called Carhenge. It was a parody of Stonehenge, made out of cars by some artist she'd never heard of. They got out, stared, laughed, and proceeded to run around being dorks for an hour.

Crossing the Nebraska-Iowa border, Nona noticed something off about her vehicle. For the next hour, she paid careful attention to what her battered vehicle was telling her, but couldn't figure it out. Not a huge surprise. Mechanical things weren't her forte. The shuddering could've been happening for months without her noticing. Too much time on lumpy back roads. Half an hour outside of Des Moines, the shudder became a jolting terror for a few seconds before returning to an unnerving shudder. Fear and adrenaline let loose a string of curses.

"Mom! Those are bad words!" piped up from the back. He'd been calling her mommy less and less since meeting Lauren. Or maybe it was the kidnapping, but she preferred not to bring that agonizing week up too often. Passing off the maturity as a token of meeting her favorite hero didn't make her heart ache.

She brushed hair out of her face. "I'm sorry, pumpkin."

"I'll forgive you if we can get burgers." He grinned at her via the rearview mirror.

She rolled her eyes and smiled back. "Deal." While he cheered, she used the voice command on her phone to GPS a mechanic. She groaned at the huge selection and considered calling a tow. What stopped her was the cost. The mechanic's bill alone could wipe out her savings. "I'm going to pull off for gas. When we get in town, we'll find a burger place, okay?"

"Yay!"

Luckily, the next exit had a large truck stop with an empty, grassy side lot where Trevor could run off the cabin fever while she thumbed through reviews on garages. The dozens of options had her thinking about a tow again. They'd have first-hand knowledge about what was best around here.

"That is one happy kid." A woman's voice caught her attention. Leaning against a ratty old pickup, a woman about Nona's age was lighting up a cigarette. She took a drag and smiled at Nona. "Hey."

Nona allowed herself a moment to both envy and ogle the woman's sumptuous cleavage before politely bringing her eyes up. "Hi."

"He's yours?"

Nona smiled. "He's mine."

"Looks like you." The pack of smokes was offered. "Want one?"

"No thanks."

Nona started to put distance between herself and the offensive smoke, but she caught herself. "Are you from around here? I need to find a mechanic."

"Kinda. I'm from the other side of Des Moines. Your car break down?" Open concern bloomed across the woman.

"Not yet." She glanced at her truck, checked on Trevor, went back to the stranger. "But it doesn't sound good."

"It is a car, right? Not a truck?" The woman gestured at the big rigs on the other side of the lot.

Nona had to pause before she replied. She'd always called her vehicle -and ones like it- trucks, but it was technically an, "SUV. Nothing special. I tried a Google search and found a few, but it'd be nice to get a local opinion."

"Yea? Let me see."

Nona proffered her phone and its daunting list of mechanics.

"Yea, no. Gordon's Auto is run by a pig fucker. I dated that asshole's brother for three months until he gave me the clap after cheating on me with a bunch of whores." She slid through the other options. A pull of smoke was blown away, but the wind brought it back to hit Nona, making her cough. "Sorry." The butt was dropped to the pavement and stamped out. She went back to the phone. "This place is probably decent, but it's in a shady part of town. Not a good place for a woman traveling alone with her kid."

Tension started to claw at her. Nona groaned and rubbed her thigh.

"Right. Being an attractive woman is a bitch sometimes." Her figure and cleavage were gestured at. "Get all the attention, whether we want it or not."

Nona sighed in agreement even if her weathered skin and scars turned more than a few off.

"Maybe this place. It's a little ways off the highway, but you've got GPS. A friend of mine took her Jeep there for her water pump. She said they were great and didn't try to gouge her with unnecessary shit."

That sounded promising.

Jarring metal music shrieked into the air, made Nona fumble her phone and the woman chuckle. The woman pulled a phone from her pocket and answered it. "Yea. Hold on a sec." She met Nona's eye. "Good luck, hon. I've gotta get going."

"Thank you."

The pickup truck's door creaked open, was slammed shut, and the engine growled to life. A black cloud billowed from the exhaust as it rolled away.

"That stinks," came from her hip. Trevor was holding his nose and frowning at the pickup.

She ruffled his hair. "It sure does. Let's get back on the road."

He galloped toward the car. "Burgers!"

"Hey!" ripped from her throat as a flashy car raced in. She managed to grab Trevor's shirt and yank him back before he was turned into mush.

"Watch your kid, bitch!" yelled from the open window.

Her blood boiling, she marched herself and her son to their truck. "What have I told you about holding my hand?" She snapped angrily, taking the belt from his hand to buckle him in herself.

"Always hold your hand if we're in a parking lot or crossing the street." He intoned. "I'm sorry," was honest and contrite. "Please don't yell at me."

Air stuck in her throat as her heart hammered at her chest.

"I won't do it again."

He would. Eight year olds didn't remember promises for more than two days. She closed her eyes, realized her lungs were burning for fresh air, and made herself breathe again. The rush of diesel stink made her wheeze.

"Can we still get burgers?" Big, watery eyes were pleading with her.

"We have to take the truck to a mechanic to get it checked on. If you remember to hold my hand next time we get out, we'll still get burgers."

Emphatically, he nodded. "I will!"

"Okay then." She kissed his forehead and closed his door. There was a slight nip in the air, and she pulled her longsleeve flannel from the passenger seat, buttoned it on. She glared at the bright red sports car that'd almost mowed down her child, clenched her jaw, and got behind the wheel again. She set the GPS to the mechanic's garage and prayed her truck would hold together a little longer. "Let's go find out how much of my savings is about to vanish."

"Ren!" Brody burst into the main garage, yanking her concentration from the manifold she was dismantling. "The best thing just happened."

Lauren slid wrenches into a pocket, stretched, and wiped sweat from her face. "What?"

"This babe walked in the office. Plaid button up over a tank, faded shorts. I noticed her tits first, perky and small and no bra, just how I like em. Then the blonde curls. Wow. Like Charlize Theron back in the 90's. You remember that giant gorilla movie she played in? Yea. But longer hair. It's pulled back, but I bet it gets past those sweet collarbones of hers when its down." He moaned expansively and grinned when she rolled her eyes.

"And then I saw a pair of legs that Tina Turner would be jealous of and looked at Steve. He was just noticing her in the back of the line. One idle glance, and he goes back to the old man who's paying for that shit-yellow Cadillac we replaced the alternator on. The old man leaves. Steve must've finally seen her legs, because he dropped the keys Betty was passing him."

Hard, rude laughter came out of him, and Lauren found herself smiling too.

"So, he's picking up the keys and staring at those legs and not hearing a word Betty's saying, and I'm over there by the coffee pot trying my damndest not to laugh. I bet Steve popped a woody looking at those legs. The woman's gotta spend half her life on a stairclimber to have calves like that." Brody leaned back to peek through the window between garage and office. "Oh, shit. The blonde's at the desk. Let's go watch."

She didn't hesitate, stuffing her gloves in the pocket with the wrenches, following Brody in. She went to pour herself a cup of coffee, and froze.

She knew those blonde curls. Green eyes. Dimple in the left cheek.

Nona.

Giddy excitement and horror flooded Lauren in equal measure. What the balls was Nona doing in Iowa? And at *Lauren's garage*?!

"We'll get your vehicle back on the road, but it might take a couple days if we can't get the parts in this afternoon." Steve was grinning his charming grin. He was a prince, rarely ever got turned down, could get any woman he smiled at, even when he fumbled. Women thought it was cute when he went stupid for a minute before sliding back into charmer-mode. "In the meantime, how 'bout I show you this little Chinese place I was going to hit for lunch?"

Brody was sniggering beside Lauren, while she felt like she could barely breathe.

Nona was smiling back at Steve. She'd be going on that date with him, would...

Lauren twisted herself to fully face the old coffee machine. She steadied herself on the cheap laminate counter, fingers going white as it cracked. This wasn't good. They'd agreed to never talk or see each other again, unless, you know, it was another emergency. So much could go wrong.

"Steve, you taking an early lunch?" Brody choked through a half-contained laugh.

"Don't you two have cars that need fixing?" Steve demanded.

"Yea, but we needed coffee," was Brody's easy retort.

"Didn't you just get a cup five minutes ago?"

"Mom! Lookit what I found!" Trevor's happy peal cut through the guys' bickering, yanked Lauren's sight to him. He was proudly holding up a scuffed plastic thing. Red and white. A ball of some sort. It'd been sitting in the lost and found box by the door for a week.

"A pokéball. Cool." Steve grinned and leaned across the front desk. "I love Pokémon. I begged my parents for all the games when I was a kid. Hell, I got roped into playing the darn game on my phone."

Trevor's hand snapped the toy protectively to his chest and he took a step back. His gaze went imploringly to his mother. Poor kid. Was he always this shy?

"Trev, this is Steve. He wants to take us to lunch." Nona smoothed Trevor's hair.

Steve nodded. "Yea. Golden Szechuan has great lo mein. And egg rolls."

Emphatically, Trevor shook his head in disagreement. "Mommy, you said we could have burgers."

"The Pit Stop makes a mean burger," came Steve's easy change.

Trevor sucked in his lips and looked around for an escape. His big, brown eyes found Lauren's, grew bigger. His face broke into a huge grin. "Lauren!"

Intense green eyes latched on her too. "Lauren?"

Lauren avoided meeting Nona's gaze as Trevor bounded over to hug her. Embracing him didn't stop her from feeling the eyes of everyone in the room though. She struggled to ignore them, focused on Trevor. "Hey, Snowman. What're you guys doing in Iowa?"

"On a roadtrip to see Mom's friends. She wouldn't let me stay with Auntie Lee." He pouted.

"You'll like Becky and her husband. And you'll love their dogs." Nona drew close to rub her son's shoulder and be within touching distance of Lauren. "Hi, Lauren. Fancy meeting you here."

Lauren's mouth opened, but nothing came out. Her eyes were latched onto the feather hanging from blonde curls and brushing a bare neck. A black feather, with scarlet edges. Nona's fingers reached up and touched it.

"I knew you were a grease monkey." Fingers moved from feather to Lauren's face. "But this is kind of overdoing it." Thumb rubbed across her cheek, came back covered in a good layer of black grease. "Don't you think?"

"Steve," was Brody's not-quiet whisper, "I think you're going to lunch alone."

Steve chuckled. "I dunno, man. Lauren's so scared of her own shadow right now, I might just have a chance."

"C'mon, Ren. Get your head outta your ass and take the woman batting her lashes at you to lunch." Brody prodded.

Batting her lashes? Nona wasn't flirting. Brody was fantasizing again.

"You'll go to lunch with us?" Trevor beamed up at her. "I can show you all the pokémon I caught on the way here!"

How could she say no to that face? But her eyes darted to the feather again. She was terrified of someone seeing her with Nona and putting two and two together. But if she didn't go, the guys would heckle her about it and why she was stupidly nervous, might start asking uncomfortable questions on top of the uncomfortable questions about the pretty woman. They didn't need to know that Nona had been the guide who Lauren had been trapped in a blizzard with. Their meeting would end up on social media and yea...

"Steve, you're sure I can take a lunch now?" She begged him to tell her no and give her an excuse to not be seen around Nona. "I was in the middle of that manifold."

"Whenever you want to take your lunch is up to you, Ren." Her boss shrugged, a silly grin on his face. "I'm sure the manifold can wait."

"Lauren, I'm really hungry. Can we go now?" Trevor grabbed and tugged on her overalls.

Shit. She swallowed the lump in her throat. "Let me wash up real quick, okay?"

Body and mind numb, she made her way back to the small locker room next to the toilets. She washed her face and hands and exchanged greasy overalls for jeans and tshirt. She frowned at her overly tight pants and the way her belly bulged out the top. Gross. Should've worn a different pair today. But she hadn't planned on being seen in public! She turned away from the mirror and shoved her feet into driving shoes. ID and cash stuffed in a pocket, she took a steadying breath and returned to the front.

Nona and Trevor were waiting outside in the brisk autumn air. The guys' eyeballs were pasted to the front window for the show. Lauren flipped them off as she passed.

"Oh good. Clean clothes. I can hug you this time." Nona announced right before pulling Lauren into said hug. "Don't worry," whispered into her ear, and the pleasant heat of it made her shiver. "Trev won't talk about how he really met you."

"But the feather," hissed out of her. "It's really visible."

"I usually wear it with others and people think I'm being fashionable. I think the other ones fell at a rest stop somewhere." Dangling threads and the colorful beads above them were noticed. It didn't do anything to calm the dread in her stomach. Nona retreated from the hug, reached up, tugged her hair free of the ponytail, and proceeded to redo her hair to hide the feather. It vanished under the mass of curls. "Better?"

Lauren nodded.

"Can we go now?" whined Trevor.

"I got his belt adjuster. I assume you have a car?" Nona held up a leather thing shaped like a 'Y'.

"Yea. It's a coupe, getting him settled might be a little work, but he'll fit." Moving helped steady her, and she took long strides to the back lot where the crew parked. Trevor jogged along.

"Isn't a coop for chickens?" He asked.

"Yea, but that coop is spelled different. When you say it in reference to cars, it means two-doored." Lauren explained. She clicked her fob to unlock the doors and gestured at her favorite car. "See? Two doors."

"This is yours?" Nona's tone was low and wondering.

"Sure is. Did most of the upgrading myself," pride answered. "She's won me a few..." She caught herself from talking about racing. Nona probably wouldn't appreciate her son learning about Lauren's illegal activities. "Car show prizes," was her lame finish.

Giggles came from Nona. "Looks like something right out of a 90's action movie."

"It is a 90's model. Funny that it'd look like something from a 90's movie." Lauren deadpanned. Nineteen-ninety-seven Acura Integra Type-R, she preened silently. Customized from engine to paint. Bronze, with black and red idealized feathers along the sides to mimic her own. A middle finger to Xuande's Law and all the bullshit about dark feathers.

"But not every 90's movie had an Integra this pretty. I begged for one as my first car, but my parents thought a used Subaru was a better choice." Nona stated as she bent into the car. "When they told me I had to earn the money to pay for half, I thought it was a better idea too."

The outdoor enthusiast could name the car model on sight? Lauren gaped.

Over her shoulder as she wedged herself into the tight back seat, Nona tossed, "I liked *The Fast and the Furious* too. And most of the sequels. All that eye candy."

"What's eye candy?" came from Trevor.

"Things you like to look at," was the mom's easy explanation from inside the car. Only her backside stuck out. Her excellently proportioned, easy to stare at backside. Glorious eye candy.

Lauren yanked her gaze away before her thoughts could degrade further.

"Like clouds?" innocence asked.

Nona chuckled. "Sure, pumpkin. Like clouds." She reappeared from inside the car. "Alright, get in."

The sight of Trevor crawling into Lauren's car twisted something inside her. It was a similar reaction to watching Nona smile and giggle with him. Warm and inviting, putting images of an impossible future in Lauren's head. She bit her lip and looked up at the clouds. They were fat and wispy, lazily drifting to the east, occasionally dulling the glare of the spring sun. Heat pricked her eyes.

"He's buckled in," was announced.

Sun-dazzled gaze shifted down. Lauren blinked rapidly to regain her focus and chase away the moisture that'd built up. Trevor was in back, the leather contraption attached to his belt, forcing the thing into a shape that fit the kid. Oh. Nice. It was one of those things she'd seen on TV, but thought was stupid. Did they make them for adults too? Maybe it could keep the belt from cutting into her boobs.

"Cool. To the Pit Stop we go."

She adjusted her seat, buckled in, and turned the engine over. It purred to life, familiar and soothing. Lauren started to relax, and she put the car into motion like usual. Nose halfway out the exit, she remembered she had passengers.

Lauren found Trevor's eye in the rearview. "I'm not used to little passengers. I'll try to drive carefully, but let me know if the acceleration gets too much, okay?"

"What's axel-ray-shun?"

Nona was laughing and responding before Lauren had translated his question. "Just let Lauren know if you feel uncomfortable. Her car is a lot different than our truck."

"It doesn't have rust," was Trevor's agreement. "And it's really shiny."

There was a huff from Nona. "Yea. It is." Was she blushing?

Lauren put her focus back to the road and nosed onto the street. She took the stop and go traffic between lights carefully, getting to the restaurant about five minutes slower than normal.

"Hey, Lauren. Whoa. Not only are you here earlier than normal, but you brought friends today," cheerfully greeted them. Monty, her favorite server. He was the same age as her own dad and looked a little like him too, with the same gorgeous black hair and big, lovable smile. That he was gay and treated her like one of his own kids made his attention even more comforting. He was half the reason she ate at the Pit Stop at least once a week.

"Yea. Friends from out of town. Nona and Trevor."

"Welcome to Des Moines, Nona and Trevor." Monty's winning smile even had Trevor grinning. "You want a booth or table today?"

"Booth," whispered up from Trevor.

After a glance up at the adults for agreement, Monty nodded. "Super. Booth it is! Right this way."

Barely finished giving Monty their drink orders, and Trevor was showing Lauren a hefty smartphone, talking about how he'd caught ten really cool pokémon at rest stops and gas stations on the road.

"Wow. You're really good at this." Lauren praised. "And your phone is even better than mine." She didn't mean to toss a judging look at his mom, but it happened.

"I know," groaned out of Nona. "He's eight and doesn't need one, but his aunt got it for him, and he gets out a lot playing that game, and it has really good signal."

Really good signal. Memory took her back to a terrified, exhausted mother screaming in the woods for her stolen kid.

"I suppose those are good excuses."

A strained smile appeared. "And Lee helped me figure out the parental controls. What he can do on that thing is really limited." Nona tossed her gaze up for a moment. "Thank God."

"I'm not allowed on the internet." Trevor informed her. "And I can't get new apps unless Mom puts the password in."

Their drinks arrived, along with Monty wanting to take their orders. Lauren made a quick decision from among her usual choices. Grilled chicken sandwich sounded good right now. With the sweet potato fries. Unlike a lot of places that mashed theirs into tots before adulterating them with extra sugar, these were crispy, hand-cut slices with a dash of salt.

"Turkey burger. Can I sub a side salad for the fries?" Nona asked.

Salad. Should've gotten that. Lauren felt her stomach practically gain an inch. She really needed to eat better. She wasn't a teenager training with the Gierdes five days a week anymore, hadn't been for years. Even if she had slimmed down a little bit since winter, she was far from where she'd once been.

"Of course." Monty was smiling. "And for you?" He asked Trevor, who looked to his mom.

"We've talked about this, Trev. You know what you want." Nona didn't order for him. "Speak up for yourself."

Trevor spoke down at the table, too quiet to be caught.

"You have to say it loud enough for him to hear, pumpkin."

His eyes darted up, down again. "Junior burger with pickles. No tomatoes." Another flashed look. "Please."

"Sure thing, bud. You want regular or sweet potato fries with that?"

Trevor looked devastated at the choice.

"Ever had sweet potato fries?" Lauren stepped in.

He shook his head.

"They're a lot sweeter than normal ones. Hence the name. And they're orange."

There was a definite struggle on his face.

"Tell you what, order the regular ones and try mine when they get here. If you like them. We'll trade." She offered.

"What if I want both?" he whispered.

"Then we can share."

His little face screwed up in thought again. "Okay," came the serious response. "We can share."

She chuckled and looked up to find Nona smiling at her in a way that made her breath hitch.

"So," Lauren reached for anything to say to distract herself from that smile. "What's wrong with your car?" And instantly regretted it. Nona's smile died.

"I don't know, but it can't be a simple fix, not the way it was shuddering." Frustration tugged at curls. "I got the tires replaced before I came out and asked them to give the rest of the truck a lookover. They sure as cheese charged me for the inspection, but they said everything looked fine except the front brakes are a little thin."

"Steve will put Brody on it. He knows his stuff. He'll get it fixed for you and do it right," Lauren tried to assuage. "And I'll tell him it needs a proper inspection." Another inspection would cost $70, she realized. "Actually, I'll do it myself so the shop won't have to charge you. But it'll have to wait until I'm either done with my current project or after hours."

"No, Lauren. I wasn't complaining to try and get you to give me a discount," attempted to wave her off.

An idea that appealed to her on several levels made her blurt out, "How's your cooking?"

"My cooking?"

"Can you cook on a real stove with stuff that isn't dehydrated or prepackaged?"

Properly insulted, Nona glared at her. "Yes. I make a mean stir fry."

"My usual game night got canceled, my roommates are out of town, and they left me a fridge full of stuff to use up. How about I drop you two off at my place, you cook dinner, and I get your car inspected? If the car needs repairs that take more than today, I'll find Grace's spare sheets. She won't mind. I get a home-cooked meal and company on Friday night. Sounds like a fair trade to me."

Dimple and a chuckle bubbled up. "It is Friday, isn't it?" She stiffened. "Oh, it's Friday. Is the shop open tomorrow?"

"For a couple hours."

"We get to stay with Lauren tonight?" Trevor perked up. "Cool!"

Lauren laughed. "Yea, sure. We can watch movies or play a game or something. Pretty sure Jeff has a bunch of board games stuffed in a closet somewhere."

"Jeff is one of the roommates? How many of them are there?" Nona was teasing.

"Just me, Jeff, and Grace. We could all manage it on our own, but none of us actually want to," she shrugged.

Food arrived and changed the topic to the best burgers they'd ever had. Monty came by again and got Nona to admit this restaurant was now in her top five burger places. They tipped exceedingly well, giggling as they headed toward Lauren's car. The drive was pleasant and full of stories about restaurants and people who worked in them. When the city and houses started to thin out, Nona questioned where they were going.

Jeff's house was out on the edge of town. Good thing Steve had texted her saying take all the time she needed. Of course, he was teasing her, but she was going to use it. Her lunch hour was turning into two with the 20 minute drive home. "I figured you guys wouldn't want to sit in the shop all day. We're going to my place."

"Oh." Nona seemed startled.

Bad idea? "I should've asked first. Sorry. Should I turn around?"

"What? No." A hand pat her knee. She tensed until it vanished. "We appreciate it. Right, Trev?" She turned around. "You'd rather hang out at Lauren's place than be stuck sitting in those hard chairs at the shop all day, right?"

He nodded enthusiastically. "Yea! I'm tired of sitting."

"Okay. Good." Relieved, she took the next turn down that led into an upscale neighborhood. It'd take a good arm to throw a football from one house to the next and their prices marched steadily from half a million up. She spied Nona narrowing her eyes at her and bit her tongue. There were days she couldn't believe her luck with her living arrangements. Pulling over to help out the stranded truck on the side of the highway had been one of her best decisions ever.

Jeff had been on the phone with AAA when she'd said she was a mechanic and might be able to help. A few questions and inspection of an otherwise clean, new engine narrowed it down for Lauren. Bad alternator. They hadn't been far from a parts store and the alternator had been easy enough to get to. She'd replaced the thing right there on the highway. Truck had started right up and the electrical issues he'd mentioned earlier were nowhere to be seen. In thanks, Jeff offered to buy her dinner and since they'd already established that she was gay and he was a decent guy, she accepted. He asked where she worked and brought all of his business there. Several of his employees followed.

Lauren had still been new at the shop, working part-time, going to classes for her first certification, and living out of a rusty Honda Civic. She'd been evicted a week before. The shitty little apartment had been in her former roommate's name, and she hadn't paid rent for three months. Blown it all on partying. Jeff found out a couple weeks later. She was pretty sure that Steve mentioned it to him. Jeff invited Lauren to lunch one day, brought his roommate Grace, introduced them. They hit it off, and Lauren was offered a room in Jeff's enormous, nearly empty house. Smiling at the memory, she pulled into the long driveway.

"You live *here?*" squawked from the back.

She chuckled at their awe. The place was damn impressive. Jeff's design was like a modern castle, and the interior, well, the living room was big enough she could turn it into a car showroom. Kitchen could make a five-star chef drool, and the gym downstairs? To die for.

Then there was the massive four car garage, enormous driveway with extra parking for Jeff's truck collection, and titanic backyard. All for three people. And two dogs.

Lauren tapped the remote to open the garage and backed the car in. Two bays were taken up by Grace's Volkswagen Bug and Jeff's only car, a classic Shelby Mustang. Grace had taken an Uber to the airport. One of Jeff's siblings had picked him and the dogs up for his family fishing trip. The last bay was a workshop. One wall was lined with toolboxes, half of them Lauren's, the other half Jeff's. The other wall held most of Jeff's fishing and camping gear. A single, dusty snow shovel was stashed in a corner. Jeff paid a local kid to do all the yard work, including picking up dog poo and removing snow.

She was spoiled beyond belief living here.

"Are all those cars your roommates'?" Nona was gaping through the still open door.

"This adorable pink Bug here is Grace's. The Mustang and trucks are Jeff's." One was a monster Dodge Ram she'd helped modify so he could go mudding and other redneck shit. "He owns a construction business. Most of his equipment is at the office."

Nona finished helping Trevor climb past the folded front seat. "What about the other three?" She waved at the cars parked beside the trucks.

"They're mine."

Blankness stared at her. "Oh."

"You've got three cars?" demanded Trevor. His fingers went up as he counted. "Four cars! Wow. Are you rich?"

Laughter barked out of her. "No. Not even close. I buy cheap cars, fix them up, and sell them for extra cash. There's normally one over by the tools, but Jeff needed to get his fishing gear. And that one is my daily driver." She pointed at the black Mazda. Unlike her Acura, it was street legal and wasn't worth half as much. Stereo was better in it. Kept good all-season tires on it too. Racing tires were amazing on dry asphalt. On snow, not so much.

"I just felt like taking this one to work today. It'll be cold and icy soon and I won't be able to drive it then." She almost hated winter, when she couldn't race. On the up-side, it got dark a lot sooner, and she was sometimes able to sneak flights in on cloudy nights. People tended not to go outside in the dark when it was cold.

"I think you're a lot bigger fan of *Fast and Furious* than I am," dryly pointed out.

"All that eye candy," laughed back.

Chapter Fourteen

Lauren's Disaster

One look at the disaster that Lauren called a bedroom had Nona thinking about running for the metaphorical hills. This kind of mess and disorder would drive her bonkers! The lone bookshelf held dusty keepsakes, tools, framed photos, what looked like packages of batteries -Lauren hadn't turned her light on and indirect sunlight through her window was casting shadows everywhere- and a jar of coins, everything except books. Those were all over the floor in haphazard stacks.

Also on the floor was a laundry hamper full of gym pants and tshirts. An involuntary sniff brought the scent of vanilla candle and engine grease. It wasn't entirely unpleasant or strong. Was the car smell from Lauren herself? It didn't look like there were greasy clothes in the hamper. Did she just do a load of work clothes or what?

Nona shifted her attention to the slew of books. Mostly automotive stuff, but a few comic books and science fiction novels peeked out. The literature almost overshadowed the paperwork lumped on the dresser, the envelopes strewn around the floor, the magazines and receipts and various other poking up from between the bills and important-looking papers. Nona's fingers twitched. She thought longingly of her file cabinet and paper shredder, the neatly organized shelves and bins of paperwork in her office. The only thing neat in here was the shut closet doors.

"So, yea. My room." Lauren waved at them to keep going down the hall.

"I thought adults had big beds." Trevor remarked.

A twin bed. Cheese, she hadn't had a bed that size since high school! Couldn't Lauren at least have gotten one of those long twins like in college dorms? Having her feet hang off the end couldn't be comfortable.

"Big beds are for big rooms." Lauren muttered. "Do you see space here for a bigger bed?"

Trevor studied the room. "I guess not."

There was plenty of space. If Lauren ever picked up the books and paperwork, a queen-sized bed would fit fine. Even another bookcase or two. She could afford to invest in cars, not like she couldn't afford some furniture. She was out, cute, well-adjusted. Did she not bring women home? Maybe she only did one-night stands in hotels. Or maybe she simply liked a lot of walking space between bed and walls? Nona continued to wonder about Lauren's dating life as the tour of the giant house went on.

Lauren gestured through an open door into an extremely clean, stark bedroom with a grey palette. "Jeff's. Master suite, has its own bathroom. The man has no appreciation for color." Compared to Lauren's tye-dyed rainbow bedspread, no.

Another bedroom had soft greens and yellows with metallic grey accents. It exuded a lovely, feminine appeal, aside from a sharp, spicy scent that wrinkled her nose. From the candles everywhere or a perfume? Either way, Nona decided that she'd much rather stay in the room that smelled of engine grease and vanilla.

"This room smells weird." Trevor said.

"Trevor," she admonished.

Petulance frowned up at her.

Chuckles burbled out of Lauren. "He's not wrong. Grace burned one of her incense sticks in my room once, and we had a huge fight over it. I agreed to pile my smelly work clothes in the laundry room and do a load at least once a week. If I buy her dinner, she'll do it for me."

Nona laughed. "What's her part of the bargain?"

Lauren grinned. "She's not allowed to burn incense with her door open or when I'm home."

"What does Jeff think of her incense?"

"He's got no sense of smell, probably why he can handle having two dogs sleep in his bed."

Dogs? Nona sniffed and realized that she'd been smelling a faint scent of dog, but hadn't seen or heard evidence of them yet. "Two dogs?"

"Yea. Bubba and Moxie went with him since Grace's vacation was longer than his." Lauren waved at the next door. "Grace's bathroom. Mine was across the hall from my room." She pointed at the last two doors, both closed. "Grace uses this one for an office, the other is the dogs' room. Their kennels and stuff."

No spare beds for guests? Did no one ever invite anyone over? What about family?

"So that's the upstairs." Lauren ushered them back to the stairs and down to the finished basement. There were a few closed doors, but was otherwise one huge gym with huge mirrors, giant TV, enormous speakers, and enough equipment to service a small army. Treadmills, benches, racks of weights, mats, balls, and ropes. An interesting PVC structure that looked good for things like chin ups and tricep dips. And a taped up punching bag that was bolted to the ceiling. Everything looked heavily used. Did Lauren train down here? The martial arts she'd once spoken about? What would it be like to watch Lauren go through exercises, flushed and sweaty, clothes clinging to...

"Storage. Bathroom. Laundry room."

Nona blinked, hoped her blush wasn't too noticeable.

Lauren opened a door that let out the strong scents of laundry and soaps. "You're welcome to use any of the gym stuff, the washer and dryer, whatever."

"Sounds nice."

Trevor was poking at the punching bag. "You have your own gym too? Wow."

"It is nice. I like being able to work out without people staring."

Nona's hot cheeks hit a boiling point. She pointedly did not look at Lauren's chest. She refused to acknowledge the lovely cleavage that the straining shirt exposed.

"Why do they stare?" Trevor asked.

"Um." Both women glanced at each other, mutual understanding passing between. "Not only are some people rude, but I'm a lot stronger than normal people."

Trevor gaped. "Are you stronger than Mommy?"

A light smirk formed. "Yep."

"Really?" He couldn't believe it. He'd seen other women at the gym when Nona sometimes took him, had him exercise on the kids' rock wall or help with survival courses or just play with other kids when he wasn't in school.

"She might be." Nona allowed.

"I'd prove it, but I have to get back to work soon." Lauren shrugged, somehow both confident and shy at the same time.

"What about tonight?" Trevor prodded.

Nona chuckled. "Lauren doesn't need to prove she's a beast. We already know that. Come on, pumpkin. Back upstairs."

"Okay."

"So, all three of you rent here?" Nona asked when they were back in the kitchen.

"No." Lauren shook her head, wavy hair wagging from the motion. Was her hair longer? Wow. Yea. A few inches at least. And the blue streak was purple now too. "The place is Jeff's. He built it."

She'd assumed that someone had a mortgage that was bigger than their wallet. "I suppose his construction business is a lot more successful than I expected, what with all the roommates."

Lauren was nodding and shoving her feet in the shoes she'd left by the garage door. "Yea. Like I said, none of us really want to live alone. Grace has abusive ex problems. Jeff doesn't bring anyone home. And ever since Wh–" she suddenly stopped, like she'd just realized she had an audience. "It's nice here. Look, sorry, I'm pushing my lunch hour as it is. I've got to get back. Make yourself at home. If you need anything, you've got the number for the shop, right?"

The business card was in her pocket. She pulled it out to double check. "Right here."

"Good. Oh, wait." She opened what looked like a junk drawer, the kind everyone had in their kitchen with the odds and ends. A key on a bright yellow string was held out. "Spare house key if you want to take a walk or something. Shop closes at five. I'm usually home before six." Garage door was opened. "Like I said, make yourself at home. Anything in the fridge or cupboards is fair game. Watch whatever movies are on the shelves. You can use my Netflix ID on the TV." She looked a little lost. "See you."

"Bye, Lauren!" Trevor waved.

"Thank you." Nona added. "We'll see you later."

"No problem." An odd roll of her shoulders. "Bye."

The door closed. Mother and son looked at each other. The Acura's engine roared to life, was mildly muffled by the distance, then suddenly peaked. They saw the car zip by through the front windows.

"Want to explore the neighborhood?" Nona suggested.

"Yea!"

She had them both drink some water and use the toilet before spending an hour wandering around, taking in the expensive homes, a nearby golf course, and a cute little trail that cut through a wooded area before spilling into cornfields. They encountered a handful of joggers, a cyclist, and an old man taking a stroll. Crows squawked at them, but otherwise it was a quiet walk. Trevor was yawning for his nap when they got back shortly before two. He didn't even try to watch TV with her, just went right up to Lauren's room and crawled in her bed.

Sweet cheese and crackers.

Why couldn't Lauren be a normal woman? One who didn't have all this dangerous baggage, who Nona could muster up the courage to ask on a date, who might be willing to relocate to Colorado.

Nona sighed. If Lauren was normal, Nona would have died of hypothermia. Then again, if Lauren was normal, she'd probably never have hired Nona, and they'd never have met at all. Ugh.

She headed back downstairs, texted her friends and Lyleigh about her roadtrip getting a delay, and found a TV series to watch. A lighthearted comedy. It managed to distract her from wondering if Lauren might let Nona start a friendship with her. A real one. Where they communicated for mundane things like talking about TV instead of life-threatening problems.

In the middle of the third episode, her phone rang with an unfamiliar number. Figuring it was the garage, she paused the show and picked up. "Hello?"

"Hey. Nona?"

"Speaking."

"It's Lauren. I'm calling from my cell."

Lauren? Her voice sounded higher on the phone. "Hi."

"Hey, um. So, I've got good news and bad news." Her heart sank. Either her car would take a week to fix or it would totally wipe her savings, or both. "Which do you want first?"

Nona sighed. "Good? I guess."

"My car is in fantastic condition."

Her car? Her car?! What kind of rude joke did she think she was spinning?! Damn, she'd really misjudged Lauren. Hot, livid anger snapped out on her tongue, "Look here, I don't k-"

"You can borrow it," cut in.

"I... what?"

"Borrow my car, finish your vacation, and pick yours up on the way home."

There should be steam billowing with how fast her anger cooled. "You'd loan out your car like that?"

"Yea. The biggest problem with yours is that the parts will take a few days to get here. The repairs won't take that long." Lauren hummed. "So, borrow mine. You'd planned a week visiting your friends anyway. This'll be fine. I'll have time to do that inspection and let you know if there's anything else. And if there is, I'll have time to take care of that too."

This generosity was too much. She couldn't accept it. Yet... she'd have to find a place to stay the entire time her car was out of action, and that would be an expensive hotel; even a cheap one would become pricey. Lauren's roommates were due back in two days. Nona's pride didn't want to keep accepting the hospitality, even if the roommates stayed away longer.

She sucked in a tight breath.

"You have full coverage on your insurance?" Lauren asked.

"Yes."

"See, no problem with borrowing my car." She went on to explain that the truck's problem was worn CV joints and driveshaft. The spark plug wires needed replacing too. Cost of parts and estimated labor was detailed. It wasn't cheap, but it was a lot less than Nona expected. "I have to officially ask if you want me to order the parts and do the repairs when they come in."

"Do it. Let me know if anything else comes up while you've got it ripped apart."

"Will do. Oh, um, I suppose I should ask if you can drive a clutch."

Nona snorted out a laugh. "Yes. It's been a while, but as long as it's not super touchy, I should be fine."

Lauren was chuckling too, soft and warm. It made Nona's heart skip a beat. "No. The Mazda's not like the Integra. It's all about comfort in that one. Remote ignition, power everything, satellite radio."

"I'm going to get spoiled driving it."

"Yep. Enjoy. Hey, I've got to run. You've got my cell number now if you need anything. See you in a couple hours."

"Bye."

Thick silence grew around Nona. She stared at the stilled frame on the TV long enough that the DVD player went into sleep mode. Eventually, her fingers drifted up to touch the feather in her hair. She needed to feel the reality. Lauren was too good to be true. Like magic was supposed to be. But it was real. The feather proved it. Lauren really was this good of a person.

Fun to be around, smart, generous, enjoyed the outdoors, was great with Trevor. All of that on top of being Nona's kind of attractive. Fantastic curves over what had to be a lot of muscle. Weak women couldn't hike easily in the mountains let alone carry an adult and all their gear. It was probably a good thing that the winter clothes had mostly hidden Lauren's figure from Nona's eye. She'd have been caught ogling for sure.

Cuddling for warmth would have been even more difficult. Not to say that she hadn't been affected by Lauren's closeness, but she'd been more overwhelmed with the wings and magic and remembered stories of false angels. She'd seen the curves this spring, but again she'd been overwhelmed with other things. Thinking about Trevor's kidnapping got her up and going to check on him.

He was snoring with a little bubble wobbling from his nose. Gross, yet oh-so-cute. She brushed his hair back, kissed his cheek, tucked the blanket in. He grunted, and the bubble popped.

"If you weren't ridiculously cute..." she playfully threatened. Another impulsive kiss, and she left him to his nap.

Too wired now to sit back down in front of the TV, she wanted to take another walk, but with Trev sleeping that wasn't an option. Chores weren't really an option either. This wasn't her house, she didn't have laundry to do, and Lauren's bathroom was impressively clean. The gym! She killed an hour on a treadmill, watching a documentary on the Weather Channel, checked on Trevor again, decided to let him sleep himself out, and went into the kitchen. Might as well start chopping veggies for dinner. Were there enough bowls with lids or plastic wrap to keep them fresh for a few hours?

Cabinets and drawers were rummaged through. Bowls and matching lids were found. Sharp, elegant knives were discovered. There were high quality pots and pans and other cooking utensils. It was a relief really. She'd half expected the kitchen to be stocked like a college dorm when she'd seen the roommates' mismatched furniture.

The chicken breasts and veggies she'd seen earlier were pulled out. Bok choy and peppers and carrots. How appropriate that she'd mentioned stir fry. "Do you people have a rice cooker too?"

Other cupboards were poked in. A low one finally gave up a family sized cooker. She started to stereotype the roommates since she'd seen the pictures in the living room. Jeff had what looked like Chinese features. Don't be an ass, Nona. They're adults. Any of them could've bought a rice cooker. She didn't remember talking much about food on the hike, and she wondered about Lauren's palate. Huh. Well, if Lauren didn't like what Nona was prepping, she could order a pizza. She went to work washing vegetables.

Hands covered in veggie juices, eyes watering from onion fumes, Lauren's comment about car shows hit her. Those words were a cover up. Though she'd driven gently, the power in that Integra was impossible to miss, the rumbling purr of its engine, the extra gauges on the dash, the specialty body work and paint. That thing didn't win car shows. It won races. Street races, not legal rallies, or Lauren would've just said so.

"Oh crackers. She's a criminal."

She laughed. Lauren had broken lokref law by saving her life. What kind of hypocrite would she be judging Lauren for breaking normal human laws to make a living for herself when Nona was encouraging lokref law breaking by staying alive? It wasn't like she could imagine Lauren putting lives at risk when she raced. But what would she know? She barely knew Lauren.

Above rings of onion, the knife paused. That wasn't quite right. You couldn't spend days alone with a person, hiking in the deep backcountry, sharing campfires and meals with them without learning a lot about them, even when they were the quiet type, which Lauren was not. Not until the blizzard hit them had Lauren's tongue grown reticent to share.

Then her actions had spoken much louder.

She could have saved herself a lot of trouble by letting Nona die. Leaving a feather had only added to Lauren's troubles. Flying across the country, exhausting herself to help find Trevor, then flying home, none of that had been easy on her. How often had Nona thought about this over the past few months?

Her knife began moving again, and she blushed at the thought of how she didn't mind cooking for Lauren, at the image of future dinners with her at the dinner table. Lauren was the kind of person she wouldn't mind as a role model for her son. Minus the law-breaking part of her. That she wasn't keen on, but the rest of Lauren... She was courageous and generous and had a great laugh, beautiful smile, nice body. Wonderful cleavage. What would it look like in a bathing suit? Or...

"Get your mind off her tits, woman." But the reminder of Lauren's shirt stretched tight across her chest remained in the corner of thought, no matter how ardently Nona tried to think of other things. "Ugh," she groaned. "Nona Hummel. You are a shallow creature!"

Chapter Fifteen

Discovered

"Commandant, there's been a development." Tibbits reported.

Commandant Meisenger sat forward, peering intently at the knight on video chat. That Tibbits had requested a video conference in lieu of the usual email already had him on edge. The knight's opening statement set his nerves on fire. "What?"

"The hiking guide that Trent hired last winter," a glance at notes, "Nona Hummel. She went to the garage Trent works at. She stayed overnight at Trent's home and borrowed her vehicle to continue a road-trip to Ohio."

They were friendlier than Tibbits' reports had led him to believe. "Why did she borrow Trent's vehicle?"

"Apparently, sir, her own was in dangerously bad condition. I don't think she knew that the garage she chose for repairs was where Trent worked, but it was obvious that she was pleased to see Trent." Tibbits frowned. "Very pleased, sir. Her attraction to Trent is rather obvious."

"Attraction?" He demanded, his mind furiously trying to draw up details from the reports he'd read almost a year ago. "Doesn't Hummel have a child with an ex-husband?" "Yes, sir."

His lips pressed together in confusion.

"Hummel's sexuality doesn't appear to discriminate between the sexes, sir."

Dammit! This wasn't good.

"And, sir. There's something," Tibbits swallowed. "Else."

"What?"

The knight took a stuttering breath. Meisenger stared. Tibbits was never nervous, one of many traits that made her a successful spy. What could possibly make her nervous? "Hummel wears a black feather in her hair, sir."

Ice streaked through his veins. "You're certain?" He needed to be perfectly clear what Tibbits' nervousness was implying.

"Absolutely, sir. It's unmistakably Trent's."

The black-wing had broken the law. He would have to approach this carefully. Stealthily. Garrett couldn't... Garrett. "There's a possibility that Knight Garrett-Mansour is aware of Trent's criminal behavior. We'll have to arrest both. Separately. Quietly. Put teams together and in place within 48 hours, Knight Tibbits, but do not act until I give the order. And keep it silent. No one is to know who the targets are until it's time to act."

"Yes, sir." Tibbits returned briskly. "And of Hummel and her child?"

"You'll send a team to capture them as well. Keep them alive and have them confined until Trent and Garrett are in custody."

"Sir."

Meisenger ended the call and leaned back in his chair. Slowly, a satisfied grin sharpened his features, revealed his teeth. Having an ironclad reason to put Trent under lock and key was perfect. If the teams approached her correctly, she wouldn't have a chance to put up a fight, though she might if she realized her slug was in danger. He may have to offer the black-wing a carrot. Seeing as there hadn't been any rumors of angels or magic coming out of the mountains that Hummel called home, it appeared as though she was keeping Trent's secret.

Hummel might be able to continue to keep that secret. Threaten the life of her child, and she certainly would. This could work. Promise Trent to allow the slug to live as long as she never breathed a word of lokref or looked for Trent, and Trent would do anything asked of her. It left a foul taste in his mouth to allow a slug outside of the law to continue living. He hated it, but he had done worse, tasted worse, in his position as a commandant of the Gierdes. It would be necessary to keep the black-wing docile.

At least until he was able to brand or kill Trent without her fighting back. Then he could dispose of the slugs. And Garrett would stay in prison, possibly die there too, without ever knowing differently. A shame. Garrett was an exceptional knight. He pushed the guilt aside and moved forward, as he always had, as he always would. It was for the good of all.

"Royce! Husband, you are a beautiful creature, and I love you, but if you don't stop taking pictures and start helping me cook, I will take myself out for dinner and leave you with this mess." Amber halfheartedly scolded him.

He set the phone on the counter and bent down to kiss her neck. "If you insist, wife."

She couldn't resist dipping her head to allow his affections. They'd been married for going on five years, but he could still get her hot and bothered with barely any effort. "You keep this up, and neither of us are getting dinner tonight."

Pleasantly warm chuckles drifted along her nape. "I don't see how that's not a win."

"Royce, I am hungry and w–"

Rapid knocking on the sliding glass door made them both jump. On the other side of the transparent barrier was a good friend. Blake Freeman. The hell was he doing at the back door? Amber had a good idea, but she refused to let the thought fully form. It couldn't have happened. No. She couldn't even push herself to open the door. Royce had to do it.

"We have ten minutes." Blake announced as he darted in. He met and held each of their gazes, spoke calmly, firmly, but with an undeniable air of urgency. "Get dressed, grab your go-bags, and don't bring your phones."

"Why?" was her last effort at denial.

"Knights are on their way to arrest you."

Shit. Shit! Shit! It had happened. She turned off the stove burners. "Ren?"

Blake made a frustrated noise. "Knight Tibbits was sent to collect her. I barely found out in time to warn you. Nothing I can do for Ren."

Tibbits. Meisenger's most trusted spy, a dangerous lokref, fast and strong with dozens of arrests and kills under her belt. Few knew her face, but everyone knew her reputation.

"Shit." Amber grabbed up her phone as she jogged to the bedroom, dialed Ren's number, set it to speaker, and went for the little safe under the bed.

"This is Lauren. Leave a message."

"Dammit, you aren't working, pick up your phone!" Amber hit redial.

Behind her, Royce had already changed out of his ratty gym pants into jeans and a sweater, was grabbing their bug-out bags that had been packed and waiting for months. Ren's voicemail answered again.

Clouds darkened the afternoon sky, and the air had gotten noticeably cooler when Lauren paused her post-work run at a busy intersection. She kept up a stationary jog as she waited. Her breath fogged on the air. Under the noise of the city and her own breathing, she heard her phone's ringtone, but didn't get to it before it stopped. Amber. Three missed calls. What was she calling for? Lauren hit the call back, but it went to voicemail. She sent a quick text asking what was up. There wasn't an immediate response, so she shoved her phone away, let her eyes drift up to the grey mess above her.

"Good afternoon, Lauren Trent." A hard voice interrupted her momentary daydream of flying.

Startled, she blinked at the cluster of people around her. Two of them met her eye. She flinched at the violence in their gazes, felt her magic buzz in response.

"You'll want to come quietly, Trent." The voice belonged to a slim person with smooth, caucasian features and black hair styled in a crew cut. The dark blue leather jacket looked expensive. "Or the hiking guide and her son will regret it."

Lauren went rigid. Gierdes. They'd found out. That they were here and threatening Nona meant there was no way Lauren could bluff her way out of trouble. Hot anger -at herself, at the law, at the commandant's ruthless action- pooled in her gut, and she burned to fight. "If you're here, that means you're going to kill them."

"The commandant has seen fit to offer you a choice," calmly responded. Neither voice nor face exposed any emotion. "If the pedestrian can continue to keep her silence, she may keep her life." Sharp hazel eyes held her immobile. "As long as you cooperate and accept the full judgment of the law."

To her left, the crosswalk light was blinking, and one person from the cluster around her took the opportunity. Four others and the crew cut remained. All Gierdes. Even if she fought, she didn't have a chance, would never get to Nona before a phone call could be made. Lauren doubted the commandant would allow Nona to live after he'd secured Lauren, but she didn't have any other choice at the moment.

Her next thoughts were for Amber and Royce. Amber would immediately be suspected of knowing Lauren's activities. Then, almost guiltily, she thought of her parents. They might be punished as well. Shit!

"What is your choice, Trent?"

Trembling, she forced her hands to uncoil from the fists they'd curled into. She held them palm up and away from her body. "I'll come quietly."

Sturdy handcuffs were clamped around one wrist before her arms were twisted behind her back and the other clamped as well. Irritation prickled around the metal. How mundane it felt to be restrained by mere handcuffs. She knew better though. These cuffs weren't simply thicker and stronger than normal ones, they were imbued with nullen. Summoning a weapon now would be impossible. Wings would come, with excruciating pain from the nullen interference, and flying with her arms restrained like this would be difficult at best, but they would come.

Rubberneckers ogled as the plain-clothed Gierdes cuffed her, took her phone, and tugged her toward a dull brown SUV with rust along its edges. She was being pushed inside when a familiar call stabbed through her chest. Her frame twisted in her captor's arms, toward the east, where Nona had screamed her name.

"What are you doing, Trent?" Crew cut asked quietly. "Did I not make the..." trailed off.

"Let me go!" She was yelling, struggling, bucking against the three bodies holding her down, preventing her from answering the call. She howled and bit one, dug her teeth in until the man screamed and pushed her away. Only two sets of hands on her weren't enough. A twist and kick set her free.

Pain, white hot and sudden, smashed into her back. Another sent her to the ground. Crew cut was over her as she fought to breathe normally. "I will not offer the choice again, Trent. Get in the car."

She narrowed her eyes and tried to regain her feet, was kicked in the chest almost casually for it. Her head cracked against the pavement. The world became a flash of light, and she was left dizzy and weak, but she had to try to rise, to obey Nona's call. Blearily, she lifted her body only to have a heel crash down on her face. White hot pain exploded in her skull. She sucked air through her teeth until the pain faded to a manageable throb and her senses returned.

"This is Tibbits," focused her fuzzy vision on Tibbits. A phone was at their ear. Maybe? "What?" was shouted into it. Yep. A phone.

Despite the blurry vision and watery thoughts, Nona's call remained crystal clear, continuing its forceful pull to the east. Pain and anger and fear became desperation. Lauren had to get up, but she knew the moment she tried, Tibbits -shit, *the Tibbits?* shit!- would kick her back down. Another pair of arms would be nice.

Another pair. Her wings. The thought of more pain made her hesitate. Was it worth it? The call sang a desperate ballad in her chest. Yes. Absolutely yes. Gierdes wouldn't expect her to flaunt magic now, and she didn't give a damn if she made the nightly news.

"I see." Tibbits lowered the phone. "Knights, ma-"

Black feathers shot out, slapped Tibbits sideways, forced Lauren upright, launched another knight at a car. She went to run, but a body jumped her, sent them rolling along the ground. Her knee found a soft spot. One of the Gierdes grunted, let her go, giving her enough room to find her footing. Slippery footing. Her vision blurred, and when it cleared, she'd been surrounded. Wings weren't enough! She needed her weapons and her hands free. Dammit! The call yanked at her chest, made the repressed magic burn in her veins, made her scream in rage.

"Trent. Stop this. You endanger us all." Tibbits hissed at her.

Rage spat back, "Fuck you."

"Calm yourself, and we'll take you to her."

The call latched onto the words, but she shook her head at the attempt to trap her. They'd ferry her until they could stick a needle in her neck and put her to sleep. She would wake in a prison cell, chained down, inked with nullen-tattoos and trapped for life. She'd *never* be able to answer Nona's call. That certainty kept her from hearing Tibbits' continued lure. Magic roared in her blood, howled in her ears, turned her vision red. It would not be denied!

⸻

A picture of what looked like a drunken artist's attempt at immortalizing flames was on Meisenger's phone screen. What had once been a pair of thick, steel handcuffs were twisted, shredded things turned a strange, disconcerting orange. He shuddered. It was easy to imagine the black-wing's magic as a proverbial dog, rabidly digging into the metal and using its powerful jaws to rip the nullen filaments out. That couldn't be what happened. Enough magic must have been thrown at the cuffs until they were overwhelmed and exploded. Either way, lokref magic wasn't supposed to be able to do that.

Power needed boundaries, but this black-wing refused to obey them. Fear licked at his spine. Could even a solid nullen cage hold Trent now?

The sound of cracking plastic shook him from his reverie. He tilted the phone to glance at the frame and found it caving under his knuckles. His entire hand was clenched and shaking. He switched hands to relieve the pressure. A fine line appeared across the screen, and he silently cursed.

"This happened after she received a call?" he clarified.

"Yes, sir. Trent began struggling right before I got the message about Hummel's feather turning to dust, and we could no longer restrain Trent or convince her we'd take her east." An audible swallow. "I have never seen a lokref break null-cuffs."

There were reports of lokref bending them, slipping free, especially when they received a call while restrained, but nothing like this. He would flay whoever had screwed up and allowed that slug to call the black-wing. Flay them, demote them, burn them at the stake, whatever struck his... He yelped at a burning bite to his palm.

Shattered glass and plastic clattered to his desk, erratic flickering coming from what had been his phone screen. He looked at his hand and watched blood well up from his cut palm. It dripped upon his desk and the freshly signed paperwork there. Scarlet pooled and spread, obscuring the broad strokes of his signature, spreading to his printed name and titles, glistening darkly in the afternoon light.

Chapter Sixteen

Twisted Halloween Decoration

Nona glared at the cracked door of her cage. She'd put those cracks there kicking it for twenty minutes before it'd opened, a ham-sized fist had knocked her silly, and a stout woman had glared down at her. "Every time you kick the door or one of my men or even scream, I'll make your kid scream. If you break the window or try to escape, I'll make him bleed."

Her heart pounded at the cold, unflinching tone the woman had used. That'd been three hours ago. Three hours trapped in a sparse bedroom with newspaper-covered windows through which the streetlights barely pierced, without knowing where her son was or what was happening to him. She went back to pacing. The carpet and mattress were stained with things she didn't want to think about and held no appeal for sitting even if she could've stayed still.

With a jolting creak, the door opened, revealing the stout woman. "Come on, slug. Piss break."

"Where's my son?" jumped out of her.

"Locked up like you. Get your ass out here."

Needing to relieve herself and hoping to hear or see Trevor or an escape route, she made her way to the door, got shoved forward and into a huge bathroom that should have been nice. There was a broken mirror; its glass filled the sink and littered the floor, speckled and filthy. Urine stains trailed down the side of the toilet, and filth coated the bowl's interior. Mildew pinked the shower stall. Revulsion made her lip curl, stomach knot, head shake. Her unpleasant guard stood at the door, staring at her.

"A little privacy?" Nona demanded.

"Piss here or piss in the room and deal with the stink. I don't care."

Nona cursed, unbuttoned her pants, and made herself sit to empty her bowels under the unflinching gaze of the guard. It was a good thing her body didn't care if she had an audience. She stared back as she let her body do its thing, wondering at how the bitchy guard wasn't as filthy as everything here. Did she bathe here? In this filth? Not that Nona could have smelled her over the house's stench.

She finished and had her pants halfway up when a heavy thud sounded overhead.

"Check the roof," was already being yelled by her guard. "Check the fucking roof!"

Commotion roiled up from the others in the house as a second thud came, this one closer, sounding more like falling wood.

"Roof breach!" roared from the guard as a huge, double-bladed axe and blue medieval armor appeared.

Three sharp flashes preceded a chunk of the ceiling falling down in the middle of the bathroom, followed quickly by a dark shape that the guard attacked. Metal clanged, walls exploded, someone screamed.

The guard was down, armor and weapon gone, eyes closed. Above her was another armored figure. It turned toward Nona. Half-terrified, half-excited, she flinched and backed away, remembered her near-nakedness and tugged uselessly at her pants.

"Nona." Her spoken name made her pause. Her breath caught when the helmet retreated to reveal a battered face. It was angrily swollen, dried blood and scabs all down the right side. Dark hair with a purple streak was matted above. Lauren. "Where's Trevor?"

Thoughts of her son returned control to her hands. "Somewhere in the house. Downstairs I think." She finished yanking her pants up.

Lauren's expression went dark, and her helmet returned. "Stay right behind me. We'll find him," barely preceded another fight. Tight quarters didn't seem to bother Lauren. She bashed her opponents into walls with her shield, her spear appearing and disappearing as she fought, until the last lokref was impaled on it, the spear wedged between plates of armor.

Blood replaced armor, spreading, crawling across clothing, skin, carpet. Nona tore her sight from it to call for, "Trevor! Trevor, can you hear me?"

Faint and trembling, his answer funneled up the stairwell. Lauren's gauntleted palm on her chest stalled her from dashing right down there. "Be careful." She warned and launched herself down first, colliding with another armored lokref.

They were rolling and struggling when Nona jumped over them to chase Trevor's voice. He was behind a locked door in the living room. A closet! Her child was being kept in a closet! There was a solid deadbolt keeping it secured, and the door itself barely flinched when she kicked it. Shit! "Trevor!"

"Mommy!"

"I'm here, Trev. I'm here. I just have to get the door open, okay? Hold on." She whirled, looking for a key, a hammer, a crowbar, a miracle.

Lauren's spear would work, but she was still fighting, didn't look like she was doing well, actually. Adrenaline and need had Nona grabbing up a heavy brass lamp and swinging it at the false angel's head. It connected with a metallic ring that paused the universe for two seconds, gave enough time for Lauren to untangle from her opponent with a twist and slam her shield into their chest. Repeatedly. Until the wall cracked and buckled behind them, puffing dust into the air. Their arms dropped. Panting, shoulders rising and falling with the intensity of it, Lauren stood over her fallen, unarmored enemy. A middle-aged man in jeans and a Metallica tshirt.

Nona shook herself before she could wonder about his mundane life and tried to find Lauren's eye behind the matte black of her helmet. "Trev's locked in a closet."

Drooping shoulders barely spoke of extreme exhaustion, but the helmet nodded, and Lauren followed the mad dash to the closet. The spear lifted and delicately sliced through the lock.

Nona jerked the door open to throw herself around her baby boy, who gasped, "Mommy, there's a statue!"

In her peripheral, she saw Lauren's helmet move, a wide turn that took in the whole of the house.

Trevor gasped. "It moved!"

"That's because I'm not a statue, Snowman." Lauren's battered face smiled down at him, but her eyes were hard and caught Nona's. "We need to go."

"Lauren?" He squeaked.

"Are you going to fly us out?" Nona asked.

"Driving would be less conspicuous." She glanced over her shoulder, to the hallway that her body was blocking Trevor's view of. "Know if any had car keys on them?"

"Um," her overloaded mind tried to think back over the past day.

"Don't you have a spare key to your car?" Trevor demanded of Lauren. Confusion stared down at him.

"They brought us here in it." Nona explained.

Relief warmed Lauren's face. "There's a spare hidden on the bumper. Is it in the garage?"

She barely nodded before Lauren was moving. "Keep him close. Stay behind me on my left."

With Trevor's hand in her own, she followed as ordered, her head swiveling, eyes darting to every shadow. They went out a back door. Tree branches creaking in the light wind nearly made her scream. Lauren's hand coming up to stop her had the same effect. She squeaked, and Lauren peered back, put a finger to her lips.

"Wait here."

The corner of the house kept them in shadow while Lauren darted from it to the garage's rolling door. She went to the small side door and peered in through dirty glass before testing the handle. It moved smoothly, and the door opened quietly. She went in and came back out.

"Come," was gestured at them.

They darted in, and Nona immediately got Trevor buckled up while Lauren dug her key out from under the front of the car. Nona straightened to get in the front. Movement at the doorway caught her eye. A man, no armor or weapon, but he was one of the people who'd kidnapped them, another false angel. Shocked, terrified, she made a short, weird screech that drew the man's attention, and she froze. What to do? If he was a bear or a cougar or even a rutting elk, she'd know what to do. But this was a person, a false angel, and...

Thud.

His body jerked backward, thrown against the open door, and he had the dumbest look on his face when he looked down at the spear pinning him to it. The spear vanished. Hesitantly, he touched the new hole in his chest, gurgled, and puddled to the floor. Blood, bright and quick, was staining across his white shirt. Terror that matched Nona's own appeared on him before he collapsed face first to the ground.

"Nona." Lauren's voice. "Get in the car."

Yea. Good idea. The garage's main door was curling upward. They needed to flee. Her body remained frozen, her eyes on the second pool of blood she'd watched spread that night. How many people had Lauren killed? For them?

"Mommy?"

"Nona, get in the car!" was accentuated by the engine's rumble.

Shaking started in her hands.

Abruptly, she was yanked down and into the car by a fist in her shirt. Lauren. Her face was twisted into a terrible grimace.

"Close the door," snapped at her.

She did manage to do that before Lauren shoved her back into the seat and dragged the belt across her, punched it into place. The engine roared as the car launched backward. Lauren snapped a 90 degree turn, and the engine roared again as the car heaved forward, tires squealing, physics tossing Nona around like a ragdoll. It took her a minute to realize that Trevor was crying.

It took her several more to realize that she was too.

———◆———

Maybe ten minutes later, maybe twenty, Lauren finally pointed the car into the parking lot of a busy Walmart, and found a spot in the middle. People walked past the car. She flinched, but knew the horde would hide them. She peeled trembling hands from the wheel, set the brake, closed her eyes. Dead bodies hid behind her eyelids. They snapped back open.

Dead lokref. The first, well, she might not be dead, but probably would be soon. Matt was definitely dead. Lauren's spear had gone right through his chest. She'd trained with Matt. He wasn't a bad guy. He hadn't even been armed or armored or made an aggressive move toward them. Yet she'd killed him. If her spear wasn't made of magic, he'd still be hanging on that garage door like some twisted Halloween decoration. Luck had been on her side. Matt had always been stronger and faster than her, not a surprise, but he was one of the best of their cadet class, which was why he'd been invited to special ops. Add on that he would have kept up training over the years where she'd gotten fat and slow, and it was a miracle that she was alive. If Nona hadn't screamed...

Lauren peered sideways at her silent passenger.

"What are we doing here?" came Nona's low question. Her eyes were bright, the skin around them puffy and red.

"Hiding in the crowd."

"Can we go home now?" whispered from the back. Trevor's face was as tear-stained as his mother's.

Lauren looked out the windows. There was a gas station across the street with a bright ATM sign. Her debit card was in her pocket. They needed cash. And a different car. This one could be bugged. Gierdes could be tracking them right now. She looked up through the windows, didn't see any dark shadows in the sky above the parking lot's blinding lights. Were there even stars up there?

At least winged assassins wouldn't fall down on them now. The Gierdes wouldn't attack in such a public place. That she was certain of.

"Lauren?"

"We need cash before they shut our bank accounts down. If they haven't already."

A weird laugh came from Nona. "Well, they left my purse in here." She was digging through it, pulled out a wallet, a scratched bank card. "If they can shut them down, they'll be watching them. Is it safe to use it?"

"They already know we're in this city. That doesn't matter. Gierdes won't attack in a public place and besides, if they have someone watching the accounts, the transaction will take a few seconds to show, minutes if we're lucky. It'll take a minute to get a phone call through. Several more minutes to get knights here, some seconds to figure out where the place is, to look for us…"

"I wanna go home," demanded Trevor.

Lauren glanced at him, then at the cooler on the seat beside him. "You've got some groceries in here?"

"Some lunch meat and oranges and stuff."

Cash. Map. Those were the two priorities right now. "Got any cash on you right now? We need a map and it'd be better to buy it before hitting the ATM."

Several twenties were held up.

Run over to the ATM or drive the car over and keep her passengers close? Quick decision later, the car was put in reverse, and she slowly backed out, nearly screamed at the teenagers walking slow as fuck down the middle of the lane. They glanced at her and kept walking slow as fuck right in her way. "You little fuckbags," she seethed.

"Bad language," came a meek whisper from the backseat.

She bit her tongue to keep from screaming.

It took nearly five minutes to get through the crowds, down the lane, and across the street. Emotions on the edge of snapping, Lauren backed the car into a spot, and gave a quick, "Wait here." She darted into the convenience mart.

"Hi, welcome to Fast Stop," greeted the bored attendant. When the young man's eyes fully latched on Lauren, the way he scanned her figure had her glancing down at herself. Lightweight running clothes stained with blood. How had blood gotten on her? She'd been in armor the whole time.

It took her a long moment to realize that frowning hurt, and she touched her face. Too hard. Pain burned trails of fire across the right side of her face. Oh. Her own blood. The fight in Des Moines. Her face must look like hell. She looked up and met the attendant's eye, intending to spin a story about a bicycle and a squirrel.

"That asshole won't hit me again," came out.

His jaw dropped.

"You have maps of the area?"

A hand gestured to Lauren's right. "Under the, uh, postcards, ma'am."

There were maps of a dozen different states on display. Which one was she in now? All she knew was having flown east for hours. Some northeast too. Nona had been heading to Ohio, right? Had she made it that far? Shit.

Rising panic almost had her asking the attendant. Bad idea, dumbass, she scolded herself. Just grab a handful. Ohio, Indiana, and the states that led to St. Louis.

Was Amber waiting? Was this why she'd tried calling yesterday? It had to be. Lauren mentally slapped herself. Not only had she missed Amber's calls, but she'd left the burner phone at home that she'd specifically gotten for these situations. She could buy another now, but she didn't know any phone numbers by heart. Damn she was useless.

A round display of hoodies caught her eye, and she grabbed a dark red one. It was cheap and plain. Perfect. She tore the tags off as she walked back to the car, unpleasantly conscious of her swollen cheek and scabbed features.

"You go first." She told Nona.

"Be right back, pumpkin." Nona reached to touch Trevor. "I'll be right there. Okay?"

Some low noise came from him. Lauren pulled the hoodie on and scoured the area, hunting for shadows and watching eyes.

"Your turn," alerted her to Nona's approach. She looked as terrified and lost as Lauren felt. Shame at having brought Nona into this danger heated her cheeks, and she looked away from those bright green eyes. She fumbled putting her card into the machine, entered the wrong PIN twice, and nearly summoned her weapon to break into the thing.

That wasn't a horrible idea. Stealing from an ATM wouldn't be hard, and she sure as hell wouldn't feel guilty about doing it, but she tabled the idea for later.

"Pick a direction," was what she entered the car with. She could figure out where exactly they were later and redirect them, but right now they just needed to be moving.

"Can we go home?" Trevor tried.

"No, Trev. Not yet." Nona answered. "Unless you have a destination in mind, we can head south. I've spent time in Kentucky. There's a lot of places we could hide. F-"

"No." Gruff and clipped, Lauren shot the idea down. "We're going to Missouri. St. Louis."

"St. Louis," was repeated, an edge to her voice. "Sure."

You're such a bitch, Lauren mentally slapped herself. "Sorry. Your idea is good, but St. Louis is where Amber is waiting. She knew we might end up in this situation and made up an emergency plan after the, uh, blizzard."

Nona's expression and tone were soothed. "Okay. I like emergency plans. Don't I, Trev?"

"Always have a plan." He was clearly quoting words he'd heard many times. "Stay calm and follow your plan, and you'll make it through."

That sounded familiar. Lauren glanced at him.

He nodded sagely. "I made a plan when the bad man took me from the playground. I made it through til you found me."

"Yes, you did." Nona agreed. "And I'm so proud of you."

A big, rust-eaten panel van was inching up on Lauren's rear. Her heart thudded.

"We're going to be okay, because we got a plan." Trevor smiled confidently.

The van set its blinker and curved around their left, slowly passed, and returned to the slow lane. Lauren heaved out a breath and felt Nona's eyes on her. "Yea. We'll be okay."

"So. St. Louis. Are we meeting somewhere specific in the city? The outskirts?"

"Yea. It's a..."

Now a police car was inching up on their tail. Reflexively, she checked her speed, which was two miles under the limit, then mentally checked her registration. Good for a few more months. Why would... Oh. Shit. Tibbits could've called Lauren in as a kidnapper or something. Or the cop could simply be a douche and make their lives more difficult than they already were. Shit. Shit. Shit!

"Lauren?"

She flicked a glance at Nona, but didn't know how to respond, not without scaring her or Trevor, because what if it was another false alarm?

Lights, glaringly bright red and blue, spun into panicky existence. Her hands squeaked on the steering wheel. Her immediate reflex wanted her to hit the gas, to run because she'd been caught racing. But she wasn't racing. Not doing anything illegal at all, not by pedestrian standards, she tried to soothe her nerves. Just pull over.

She was peeling her hand off the wheel to hit the turn signal when the cop car went around, accelerating quickly down the highway. Not after them. An exit appeared on their right, and Lauren swerved down it, hitting the brakes hard and pulling off the road. Breath shuddered in her chest, and she dropped her head to the wheel.

"Damn."

Fingers draped over hers. "Want me to drive for a while?"

Her pride said no. She swallowed. "Y-yea."

There weren't any places to properly park. It was a simple junction for a county highway. She set the hand brake, got out, breathed, smiled in gratitude as Nona walked over. "Thanks."

"That's what I should be telling you."

Lauren shrugged. "This is all my fault. You don't need to thank me for trying to put things right."

Nona shook her head. "None of this is your fault, Lauren. You haven't done anything wrong."

Broke the law. Xuande's Law of Quiet. The only one that really mattered.

"And don't look at me like that. That law is ridiculous. How can it be wrong to use whatever is at your disposal to save another life? No one else got hurt, and I was perfectly capable of keeping your secret."

She couldn't find it in her to argue.

"Laws change every day. That one definitely needs to."

"Yea." It really fucking did.

Nona touched her elbow, then moved around to settle in the driver's seat. The interior light was flicked on, and she fingered through the maps, picked one, popped it open. Her gaze shifted up from the map, examined their surroundings, and nodded. Fingers traced lines along the map. "We're heading east right now. We can either turn around or head to Interstate 77. That'll take us south where we can cut back on a state highway or get to I-64, which goes all the way to St. Louis."

Thoroughly impressed and mentally exhausted, Lauren shrugged. "Whichever makes you more comfortable."

"East is fine." Nona folded up the map so the section she'd been studying was facing out and stuffed it down the side of the seat. "Anyone thirsty?"

Trevor eagerly opened the cooler beside him and dug out a big bottle of apple juice. Nona pulled cups from somewhere behind her. Crackers also appeared. Both were shoved in Lauren's hands. She stared for a moment. Liquid? Food? Her brain woke up and howled about how her stomach was *completely* empty, her throat was *absolutely* parched, and her hands *definitely* needed to be doing something about these problems. The apple juice went down in one gulp and multiple crackers were shoved in right after.

The untouched cup halfway to Nona's lips paused. She dumped the contents into Lauren's cup and refilled her own.

Lauren blinked at her, felt heat in her cheeks. She glanced at Trevor, the puffy red around his eyes, and shame cranked the heat in her cheeks to volcanic. She shoved the rest of the crackers in her face, then the juice, and sat feeling distinctly out of place in the silence of the passenger seat.

"More juice?"

She flinched.

Nona noticed. She set her juice aside and got out of the car, went to the trunk and rummaged for a moment. A water bottle, full of sloshy goodness, was put in Lauren's hands. A banana and a bag of beef jerky quickly followed. "I'll get us back on the road."

The interior light was switched off. Seat belts were buckled. Tires crunched on asphalt. Headlamps and taillights glared in the darkness. Lauren tried to distract herself from the painful quiet by eating, but the moment she opened her mouth, she blurted, "We were taught how to use maps in training. But I was never really good at it, especially the ones with all the squiggly lines."

Nona glanced at her. "Training?"

She started to bite her tongue, but her mouth didn't want to stop. And why keep anything from Nona and Trevor now? "The Gierdes. They're kind of like police for lokref. I joined when I was sixteen, pretty much right after I learned I was lokref. They're the ones hunting us now."

"What's low-kef?" Trevor asked quietly.

His face had lost most of the terror from earlier, but his eyes were still bright from tears. Fucking Meisenger. How dare he do this to him! He didn't deserve to be caught up in this stupid shit. Balls! What she wouldn't give to punch Meisenger and Tibbits right in their throats.

"I'm sorry," squeaked out of him.

Confused, she blinked. "Uh?"

"Your face, Lauren." Nona's voice was low. "You're scowling."

Oh. Shame barked at her heart. "Sorry. I'm not angry at you, Trevor. I'm just angry at what those people did to you and your mom. It's okay to ask me questions."

Trevor's eyes were looking toward his mom. His question was clear though he didn't speak. "Does she mean what she says?"

"I mean it." Lauren spoke firmly, yet softly. "I won't get angry at you for asking questions."

Hesitance remained.

"Unless it's about poop." She fully turned to offer what little smile she had. "Poop questions are for your mom."

Reflex had her glancing at the road when another car drove by, yet when she turned back, he was smiling. Tiny and wavering, but it was a smile.

"Okay," he said.

"Cool. So, you want to know what lokref are?"

He nodded, all eager curiosity.

"Lokref are people with magic. Remember when you thought I was a statue?" Talking was helping ease her tension, and she was able to make her smile kinder, fuller, even if it hurt to stretch the scabs.

"Yea."

"That's my armor. Lokref have weapons and wings too."

Trevor shot his mom a look.

"She's not making it up," was Nona's reinforcement. "I've seen them."

Shadows raced across his face. "That stick that came out of that man's chest. He was in the garage."

Lauren's smile died. "Yea." She answered the question he didn't ask. "That was my spear."

"He was going to hurt us, wasn't he?" Trevor's voice was small.

Her peripheral caught Nona's hand lifting to cover her mouth.

"Yea," breathy, almost a whispered bark. He would have. Maybe. She'd never know.

"Why?"

She swallowed, blinked, felt hot liquid seep from her eyes, felt her throat tighten.

Nona twisted in her seat to reach back and touch his leg. "Remember last winter, when I was stuck in that blizzard?"

He frowned and nodded.

"Lauren used her magic to protect me. She saved my life, but she also broke a lokref law. Regular people like us aren't supposed to know about them."

"But if she was the one who broke the law, why are they being mean to us?" He demanded.

"Because they're afraid I'd tell other people." Nona replied.

"Did you?" He asked.

"No." Nona shook her head. Curls, flat and messy, shifted. How long had they been shut up in that house? Since they'd left Saturday morning? Three days? "But maybe," trailed off. Nona shot an intense look at Lauren.

"What?"

Nona bit a lip, rubbed at her thigh, glanced at the rearview. "Maybe we should tell everyone."

Dumbfounded, Lauren squeaked, "What?"

"You did say the best place to hide was in the crowd." Nona waved a hand. "If everyone knows, what would be the point in chasing us anymore?"

"Retribution. Simple hatred. Sending a message."

Irritation scowled at her. "Oh yes, Lauren, let's focus on the good things."

"You asked."

"You don't need to be a sourpuss."

Sourpuss? *Sourpuss?* Perplexed laughter startled out of her. "All of this is happening, and you call me a *sourpuss?*"

There was a light upturn of Nona's lips. "I call 'em as I see 'em."

She started to reply, but the car dinged. The fuel gauge's warning light was on. Lauren sighed at herself. "We need gas."

Nona's eyes narrowed at the gauge, rolled, and she poked at Lauren. "Weren't we just at a gas station?"

"Hush."

"Not just a sourpuss, but a half-wit as well."

"Half-wit?" Lauren's brain boggled. "What century are you even from?"

"Asks the woman whose armor looks like something from *Tron*."

"*Tron?*" Lauren balked. "I do *not* have neon lights advertising my every move. Besides, how is that a good example of a different century? That's an 80's movie world based in computers. If you're talking about the sequel, it doesn't count either."

Nona lifted her chin. "Fine, some crazy cyberpunk duds that'd look at home in *Minority Report* or *Ghost in the Shell* or *The Matrix*."

Stunned, pleased, feeling silly, "I don't know if I can handle all the geek culture that's pouring out of your mouth right now."

"I have to be able to talk to the unwashed masses. It's part of my job." Nona gave a sly side-look as she took the next lucky exit. Several gas stations beamed their prices in bright neon at them.

"Unwashed masses, says the woman whose job keeps her away from real showers for *weeks* at a time."

"What's a half-wit?" broke into their silliness.

"Someone who doesn't notice the car needs gas until *after* we leave the gas station." Nona tossed a smirk at Lauren. "Frankly, I'm surprised she even knows what it means."

The easy, relaxing banter lasted until Nona spied a QT.

"Lauren?" Nona's tone lost the joking bounce.

Worry, almost panic made Lauren tense. "What?"

"If they can watch our bank accounts and track our phones, couldn't they have a way to look for your plates? Or have police searching for us under a false premise?"

She started wishing that they'd stolen one of the lokref's cars, but they'd be just as easy to track. "Yea. I was thinking about that earlier." She eyed the handful of cars in the parking lot. "Don't suppose you know how to steal a car?"

"I don't think the stealing part is hard." Nona gestured loftily. "I think it's the unloading and loading of our gear without being seen and not having the stolen car get immediately reported that's the hard part."

"And what did you do in your teenage years?" Stressed and scared, Lauren defaulted to making a joke.

Nona glanced at her curious son. "Not much."

Curiosity peaked. Had Nona boosted cars? Or something else equally delinquent and juicy? "Now I need to know."

She shrugged, her attention shifting from them to a vehicle pulling into the lot from the other direction. "Maybe we don't have to steal anything. How do you feel about an 80's Buick?"

"Not great, but I'll look at it." She found the car that Nona was looking at, read the "For Sale" sign in the window. Twelve hundred bucks. Too much, but maybe they could talk the owner down a few hundred. She rolled the window down to listen to its puttering engine before it cut off with a rattle. A lean, white man with scruffy grey hair poking out from under a grimy baseball cap exited, dropped a glowing cigarette to the ground, stomped on it with a cowboy boot. Ew. A smoker's car.

Nona got out and smiled at the man. "Hello."

He turned, gave her a once-over. "Hullo."

"Your car still for sale?"

He fully turned to face her, lifted his cap to scratch a balding, sun-burned scalp. "Yes, ma'am. You interested?"

Nona shrugged. "We were thinking about getting a second car."

His dark eyes traveled Lauren's car, the stuff packed in it, Lauren and Trevor. She tried to hide her injuries with a hand over her face. "Well, she's an old girl, but she runs well enough. Rebuilt the transmission last summer. Tires are good. Radiator leaks. Engine burns oil."

Nice. Not the heavily-used condition of the car, but that the guy was being straightforward about its shortcomings. No big surprises to screw them over.

"Why you selling?" Nona asked.

"Oh, it mostly sits in the garage. Wife wants it out. She said I could get that Mustang I've been lookin' at if I sell this one. Been drivin' it mostly to let people see it's for sale."

Nona was nodding. "How much?"

His lips pursed, tacked from side to side, and he glanced at his car. "Price says twelve, but..." He sighed. "What you ladies looking for a car for?" His eyes were back on Lauren. Balls. He'd seen the battlefield of her face. "You ladies in trouble?"

More than he'd ever believe.

"Someone hurt you, miss?"

Nona's hand went to where she'd once worn Lauren's feather. Her fingers groped at the dangling string before sliding back down to hide in a pocket.

The man's eyes followed the awkward movement. "It's pretty late. You ladies have a place to stay tonight? We've got a couple spare rooms for when family comes up. Could stay the night and see about business after breakfast. You can put your car in the garage tonight."

"That is awfully generous of you, sir." Tone tight, uncertain, Nona hesitated.

"Wife would kick the tar outta me if I left coupla young ladies and a kid out in the cold. You two look like you could use some sleep." Pointedly, he looked at Lauren. "Hot showers."

Nona was biting her lip and seeking Lauren's opinion. What to say?

"Shit." The man kicked the pavement. "Name's Keith. Wife is Jeannie. Got three big, stupid dogs that might try an' lick you to death."

Seemed like a decent guy to her. They could always check the place out, meet the wife, the dogs. If anything felt off, well, Lauren was never unarmed or defenseless. "I could use a shower."

Nodding, Nona added her own agreement, and that settled it. They exchanged first names and a brief explanation of where his house was. Both cars got full tanks. They trailed the man to his home, an old farmhouse on a modest acreage some five miles away, with a gravel drive and a crazy amount of pink flamingos in an overgrown yard. What felt like a hundred little black eyes stared at Lauren as she stepped out of the car. Creepy.

"Granddaughter is obsessed with those stupid things." Keith waved at the flock of evil birds. "Can't wait til she outgrows it, and we can trash em."

The front door creaked open, a short, weather-worn woman stepping out, giving them a welcome in a voice as raspy and smoke-roughened as her husband's. The promised giant dogs dashed out. Keith gave gruff orders for the excited creatures to behave before they bowled their guests over. Nearly bowled Nona and Trevor over. Like most animals, they gave Lauren a more subdued greeting.

"Lokref, huh?" The woman snorted.

Lauren's neck popped at how fast her gaze shot to her.

"Keith called on his way over. The way them dogs acting, and the way your head just snapped, well," she shrugged. Lazily, she opened her right hand, and a curved, forearm-length blade appeared. It gleamed wickedly in the yellow porchlight. "You must be the black-wing, Lauren Trent."

Adrenaline hot and magic thrumming, Lauren murmured, "Yea." She shifted into a more battle-ready stance.

"You running from police or Gierdes?"

Was Keith lokref too? She eyed him, wondered how capable either were in a fight, if there were more lokref in the house. Jeannie and Keith waited. The dogs sensed the dramatic air and withdrew from licking Trevor to crowd around Keith.

"Gierdes." Lauren said.

"They just decide they hate you that much or you break the law?"

Both. But how to respond? Could they trust these people? Every shadow on their property was making her itch. Her muscles were starting to complain about the tense posture. Too much time flying and fighting today. She hurt. Exhaustion was starting to rear its head, *and* her skull was starting to throb again. Her head swam with indecision.

"Uh huh." Jeannie grunted. "I see. You ain't bonded to the blonde or they wouldn't be chasing you. Why'd you tell her?"

"She was going to die. I broke the law to save her." Lauren barked.

Jeannie made a gesture as though tossing her knife aside. It vanished. "Good enough for me. You ladies are safe here with us. My brothers and all my kids are lokref. Ain't none of us have reason to be friendly with those Gierdes pricks. Bunch of elitist bastards, Meisenger worst of them all. Might do the world some good to know there's magic in it. Come on in."

She backed her door open, stood waiting. The dogs trotted inside. Keith offered a smile and nod of his head. "Hungry? Jeannie's not much of a cook, but I can whip somethin' up."

"You're lucky I love you, you asshole." Jeannie grouched at him.

He planted a kiss on her cheek as he passed. "Chain your bitch up a little, hon. They look like they've had a rough day."

"Yea, yea. Come on in, kids. Let Keith play mother hen while I go spruce up the guest rooms."

"She's scary," whispered Trevor from around his mom's back.

Nona shrugged. "Yea. But I think she's just the grouchy grandma kind of scary."

A description that Lauren agreed with. "I could use dinner."

"Okay."

The interior of the house was decorated in a typical country way, blue and white checkered curtains, designs of hearts and chickens and cows everywhere, pictures of family on every available surface. Dust made a fine topping on all the little figurines and bookshelves. Lauren's nose was delighted to realize that the place smelled of vanilla and cinnamon and dog instead old cigarettes. Nice. The couple must smoke outside.

Closer up, she noticed Jeannie's broad shoulders and square jaw and a few missing teeth. She had dark features and a big, flat nose. Wrinkles cragged her face. She looked a lot older than she probably was, even if she had grandkids.

"God damn. I thought you were tall from far away." Jeannie glared up at Nona. "Got yourself some Amazon blood in you?"

"German, I'm afraid." Nona smiled.

"You want pancakes? Mac and cheese? Got some leftover pot roast, could make sandwiches." Keith brought their attention to the rather pink kitchen. Its counters and stove nearly sparkled. Must be the only dust-free place in the house. "Lots of fruit." A hanging, three-level basket full of apples, oranges, bananas, pears, and lemons was gestured at. He opened the fridge. "Some bean salad. Pickles." He chuckled. "If you can pickle it, I'll eat it."

Cold beef sandwiches, salad, and fruit made its way to their stomachs. Trevor picked at his, but Lauren ate heartily and Nona deliberately. Lauren's sandwich was nearly gone when she felt her head bobbing and her eyesight blurring. Exhaustion had one eye half-closed, the other watery.

"Rooms are ready." Jeannie announced, jerking Lauren upright. "I put some fresh towels in the bathroom. You need anything? Soap? Band-aids?"

"We should be good." Nona answered. "Lauren?"

"Um." Bed. All she could think of was crawling into a bed.

"You don't have a spare toothbrush, do you?" Nona asked. "Lauren only has what she's wearing. She kind of dropped everything to fly from Iowa."

Eyebrows rose. Jeannie and Keith exchanged looks. "Is that how you broke the cuffs? She called you?"

"Um?" Cuffs? Oh. When she'd been arrested and... Lauren stood so fast the chair crashed to the floor. Shield and armor flashed into existence. "How do you know about that?"

"Cool your jets." Keith said softly. "Hon, get your laptop and show the kid she's famous."

Famous? Her brain tried to connect dots while Jeannie left the room, made small sounds down the hallway. She came back holding a laptop. On its screen was a news page.

"Here. Watch." Jeannie tapped the play button, and a news story about a possible angel hoax in Des Moines, Iowa began. The news anchor laughed at the possibility of angels. He especially didn't think they'd come with black wings or be handcuffed or...

She'd stopped listening. Beside the news anchor's face was a jumpy, handheld video of Lauren being arrested by Tibbits. Her initial calm acceptance, the abrupt change of heart, her struggle, Tibbits' casual superiority. The black feathers that exploded from her. How she looked like a cornered animal.

"You endanger us all," and her answering scream echoed memory.

A dangerous, frightening glow outlined the cuffs before Lauren's arms whipped apart, sending the cuffs and blood flying. Sleek bronze armor appeared. Spear and shield lashed out. The lokref around her stood no chance without exposing their own magic and went down quickly. She watched herself launch skyward and become a dark shape, then a dot, as she followed Nona's call.

Lauren's magic retreated, and she slumped, staring down at her wrists. Scabs ringed both. Gingerly, she prodded them, hissed in pain. Some of the cuts felt like they were all the way to bone. Shit.

"In case you're wondering," Jeannie's voice cut through the fog of Lauren's shock. "Those are special cuffs designed to keep us lokref from using our magic. Never heard of anyone escaping them like that."

Nona and Trevor's eyes looked ready to jump out of their skulls.

"Famous." Keith said.

"Yep." Jeannie nodded. "And asleep on her feet. Come on, we'll help you get whatever you need from the car for the night. Up."

Herded by the older woman, they stumbled to the car, got backpacks and such. Keith moved a truck out of the garage for Nona to replace it with Lauren's car. He was their guide up to the second floor where the guest rooms were. Both had queen size beds. When was the last time she'd slept in a bed that was long enough her feet wouldn't poke off the mattress?

"There's a fan you can stick in the window if it gets too warm. Or extra blankets in that closet if you feel otherwise." Jeannie gestured. "Make yourselves at home. Get hungry, help yourself to anything in the kitchen."

The couple left them in the room that Nona and Trevor claimed. Right across the hall was a bathroom. Lauren's room was next to it. Lauren looked down at the packaged toothbrush, brain numb, eyes foggy.

"Come on, Trev, let's get you ready for bed." Nona had a bundle of clothes in one hand and prodded her kid toward the bathroom with the other. A minute later, the sound of running water reminded Lauren of her own unwashed state.

How bad did she smell? She hadn't showered since yesterday, or was it the day before? She'd worked on a car all morning until deciding to go for a run, then that fight, hours of flying to reach Nona, another fight. Her face throbbed. She glanced at a body-length mirror on the closet door and hoped there wasn't too much dirt or worse in those scabs, but closer inspection revealed that there was. They'd have to be soaked and scrubbed off for the wounds to get cleaned.

It was going to hurt. A lot. Infection would hurt more, she told herself. She might deserve it, a dark voice in the back of her head whispered as it showed her a picture of Matt touching his bloody chest. Lauren poked a scab for the simple reason that pain distracted her.

Steam rolled out of the bathroom. "Hope you don't mind us jumping in first." Wet-darkened curls framed Nona's flushed face, somehow made her eyes greener, brighter, prettier. "Water was still hot when we finished."

Lauren blearily nodded and made her way into the bathroom. She vaguely noted the strong perfume of Nona's shampoo, frowned at the memories the feminine scent tried to drag up, but she stuck her face under the spray of water and blurred everything away with the pain of scrubbing her face. Scabs and tiny hard things moved under her fingers. A shard of white plastic came out of her cheek. Was that a piece of someone's phone?

When the pain reached a boiling point, she grabbed a bottle from the edge, the thick layers of dust becoming gooey in the spray. Strawberry shampoo. Something left behind by a grandkid, no doubt. Overly sweet and gross, but worked. Clean and rinsed, she got out, toweled off, threw on the borrowed shirt and sweatpants, and asked Nona to play doctor.

"Sure thing. Bed. Sit."

Lauren fell more than sat. A fierce inspection informed her that the wounds looked nice and clean. Goo was slathered on them. Little bandages followed. Lauren did her best not to let her head bob. Her eyes closed of their own accord.

"Lauren."

"Nuh," was her grumble.

"We're all done."

Nice. Oblivion welcomed her back to its embrace.

"Lauren," prodded her again. "Sweetie, you need to get up and go to bed."

One of her eyelids peeled open. A blurry Nona was bending down toward her. "Muh?"

"Up. Come on. I promise, you'll be more comfortable when you actually lay down."

She wasn't already? Her other eyelids peeled apart, and she found that she was still sitting on Nona's bed. Oh. Hands were tugging on her. She allowed them to get her up, guide her, tuck her into bed. Hair was brushed from her face. The hand stalled over her ear, and Lauren used the last of her willpower to look up at Nona.

"Thank you," was whispered. "Thank you for saving us."

"Always," she managed before her eyelids dropped.

⁙

Holding a baggie of ice to her jaw, Tibbits sat at her computer. Not only had Trent escaped her custody, but she'd managed to get to Hummel and the child, take out the guards, *and* escape before the backup team arrived.

Plastic popped. Frigid water trickled down her hand and arm. "Dammit," she groaned. She got back up and went for another baggie. Two more. Who knew how many she could tear through in her frustration.

There hadn't been enough Gierdes in the area. No. That wasn't true. If they'd been allowed to fly, they would have gotten there before Trent. But

Xuande's Law was absolute. No lokref could be seen. Even in times of emergency. It was frustrating at the best of times, crippling at the worst.

Tibbits watched the video of Trent using her magic and read a few dozen comments. Lokref came up once. She traced the user to an anonymous profile. Another glance at the comments showed a few more mentions of lokref and Gierdes, even weavers. Not all anonymous profiles. Some were only repeating rumors they'd heard, things they'd recently read on the internet. She booted up a program designed to find mentions of lokref and Gierdes, set it to hunt.

Hundreds of forums and blogs were popping up about lokref. Talking openly, shaming Trent, applauding Trent, complaining about Xuande's Law, condemning the Gierdes for inhumane practices. Some suggested a mass walk-out. Thousands of lokref exposing themselves would change the world. They also talked about the shadows. There were rumors of sightings in Brazil. Rumors! Tibbits had investigated rumors before. Nothing. They were always nothing. And they weren't in her jurisdiction anyway. Irritated, she refocused on finding the black-wing.

Where had Trent gone? Trent's face and license plate were being looked for. Nothing since the transactions at the ATM. And Knight Garrett-Mansour had vanished with her husband as well. Excusable for the vacation hours she was on, but more likely, Trent and Garrett-Mansour would be trying to meet up. The only question was where. Convincing pedestrian law enforcement that Trent had abducted Hummel and her child had been easy enough. Maybe they would be helpful, maybe not.

Tibbits spent the rest of her night perusing every place the friends had ever traveled to together. Discussions they'd had on social media or over text were scanned. Popular places to escape to were considered. She didn't stop until she heard her neighbors get up for work. Knowing that exhaustion would make her sloppy, she made herself call a break. A quick email update was sent to the commandant with her conjectures and status before she went to bed. She *would* find Trent. She closed her eyes to that promise.

Chapter Seventeen

To St. Louis

Morning found Lauren's face turning a brilliant collection of purples and blacks. An equally brilliant coloring was across her chest where Tibbits had kicked her. Breathing was a chore today. Yesterday there'd been a ton of things to keep her mind off a little pain. Her shoulders and back, wrists, hips, *everything* was sore and tight and completely unhappy with life. She hadn't been this sore since the last time Nona had called her with a feather.

Lauren sighed and left the bathroom. Nona slipped in for her turn and when she was done, she pushed into Lauren's room to inspect her injuries.

"Swelling hasn't gone down much." Nona kept her voice low. Trevor must still be asleep. "We should've put ice on it last night."

Lauren waved the concern away. "We had bigger things on our minds than my face, Nona. It's fine."

Lips pressed together.

"You don't have to mom me." Lauren snapped, suddenly angry.

The lips parted, and anger snapped back. "I'm concerned about my friend, not mothering you, you ridiculous woman."

She took in a huff of air, ready to fight, flinched at the throb of pain, and deflated. "I'm sorry. I didn't get much sleep." She'd woken from a nightmare a few hours ago and had tossed and turned since. "I hurt and..." She focused on the wallpaper behind Nona, the little blue and yellow flowers dancing in a vintage pattern. "I'm scared."

Warm hands abruptly linked with hers. "Lauren." The hands squeezed. "Look at me, Lauren."

It took a few breaths to find the energy, the courage. Early, golden sunlight was shining across Nona's face, making her skin glow and illuminating a thousand shades of gorgeous in her eyes. Lauren's breath hitched. Those priceless emeralds smiled at her, and her heart stuttered.

"It's okay to be scared, Lauren. You're doing a great job of holding it together, but you have to remember that you aren't alone here. Okay? I'm here with you. You can vent and share the stress with me, like I know I can with you."

Nona was too close. The enticing perfume that she'd noticed last night was clogging her mouth and nose, filling the space where precious air should be. Or was it Nona's declaration of togetherness? Both. Oh, definitely both.

"Lauren?"

"I..." Her body twitched. Her lungs screamed for air. She wanted to drop Nona's hands so she could hug her. She wanted to drop them so she could run away. Nona's hands squeezed. It gave her a reason to break eye contact and look down. "Thanks," wheezed out. "I think I, um, just need coffee. We need to get going."

And yet, she still couldn't pull her hands away from Nona.

"Lauren, we c-"

"Mom?"

They both looked to find Trevor in the doorway.

"Did we wake you, pumpkin?" Nona asked.

He shook his head. "I need to pee."

"Bathroom is right there." Nona tipped her head in its direction.

Yawning, he stumbled to it.

"How the hell are you keeping it together," cracked from Lauren.

Nona looked at her. The golden rays of morning were gone, left Nona looking tired and stressed. "I did the shock and crying yesterday."

"Oh."

Awkward quiet hung heavy until Trevor returned, asking about breakfast. Lauren escaped Nona's hands and spearheaded the way downstairs where Keith and Jeannie were sitting. Must've gotten as little sleep as Lauren had. They both looked awful. Keith held out the giant mitt he called a hand. Car keys were in it. "Figured you kids would be up early. Take the Buick. You can leave yours in the garage for a while."

The idea of leaving her car in the hands of a total stranger made her cringe.

"That's very generous of you." Nona said.

It actually was. Handing the keys of the car you'd been trying to sell to a total stranger without payment was insanely generous, even if Lauren's own car was kind of collateral.

"What'd Meisenger do to piss you off?" Lauren needed to know.

Jeannie and Keith looked at each other.

"Other than being a typical elitist bastard?" Jeannie grunted. "Had a friend back when I was a kid. Tracy's magic showed up when some asshole tried to take her in a back alley. Nice big sword that she skewered him with. Gierdes took her in like all new lokref and started showing her how to control her magic. Everything was fine and dandy until her wings appeared. Big, dark things, like yours."

Lauren suddenly didn't want to hear the rest of the story.

"There was a suicide note, written in her hand, but..." Old pain and anger were clear on Jeannie's face. Keith pat her knee. "I know Tracy wouldn't have done that. There aren't any dark feathers in the high ranks. Black-wings have been disappearing and dying under unusual circumstances for decades, probably longer."

A shiver went down her spine.

"Meisenger refuses to look into it, just like his predecessor."

Her fists curled. Things she hadn't wanted to think too hard about screamed for attention. Too many close calls, too many offers for her to go places where she could easily vanish. Whitney showing interest shortly after Lauren summoned her black wings for the first time. Could... could Whitney have been one of Meisenger's flunkies? But why? Why not just get rid of Lauren? Her parents didn't have enough influence in the pedestrian world to cause him trouble. Didn't have any lokref friends aside from Amber.

Amber. She'd already been a knight when Lauren had first shown up for training. Several years older, she'd quickly become a big sister. Amber had gorgeous golden wings, incredible strength, and a solid position in the Gierdes. She would have raised a fuss. She could be real trouble for Meisenger. But she couldn't do much about Lauren choosing to quit the Gierdes because her ex-girlfriend had ripped her heart out and turned every other friend against her. Seeing Whitney's sneering face every day meant getting her heart ripped out every day. Knights spit on her black wings. Everyone hated her. Life was hell in the Gierdes.

"Lauren?" Nona was touching her arm.

Her palms were damp. She uncurled them and was surprised that her nails hadn't broken skin. It was just sweat.

"I think Meisenger's been trying to get rid of me for a long time." She announced. That time she'd been racing, had realized she'd been drugged, that the asshole had tried to shoot her when she'd climbed out of her burning car. A news report that Lauren had happened to come across said his body had shown up a few days later. At the time, she'd written it off. How many other close calls were Meisenger's doing?

Nona's light touch was now a hard grasp.

"You could hide out here for a while." Keith suddenly offered.

"Keith!"

"What? The kids are terrified. We got the spare rooms. Ain't no reason Gierdes would come lookin' round here for 'em."

"No." Lauren put in before the couple could argue. "It's okay. We have somewhere to be."

Jeannie sighed. "Look here. You don't have to put on a show. Keith's right. We've got the room."

Her heart warmed at their generosity, at their willingness to give Meisenger the middle finger. "Seriously. It's okay. I figured I'd screw up one day and have to hole up somewhere for a while. That's where we're headed. A safe place." Where Amber should be. Hopefully. Unless… No. She cut off her own terrible thought. Amber got out. That's why there were a bunch of missed calls from her the other day.

And Amber was probably smart enough to have taken her prepaid phone with her. She'd probably memorized Lauren's number too. If only Lauren could remember more than two digits of Amber's, she'd find a payphone or buy another phone and call her, save herself some damn anxiety!

"What about help?" Jeannie pressed. "You got help waiting?"

"Yea." Lauren nodded. "But thank you."

Arms crossed, Jeannie sat back. "Alright."

"If you need more help." Keith was pulling a pen from his shirt pocket. He looked around until he found what looked like a bill, ripped a blank chunk off the envelope. He scribbled on it. "Here's our number."

It felt like a weight in Lauren's hand. "Thanks."

"Or, you know, when you're ready to trade cars." He grinned. Lauren doubted he really believed he'd ever see his car again.

She was sure she'd never see hers. "Yea. Okay," was her uneasy response.

"Hey, little man, I bet you're hungry." Keith changed the topic by smiling at Trevor. "How 'bout some breakfast? Bacon?"

Lauren's stomach rumbled at the suggestion. Food was quickly set to cooking, coffee poured into cups, more set to brew. The table got all five sitting down to bacon, eggs, toast, and sliced fruit. Actually, Keith never really sat down. He had a plate that he occasionally took bites from as he continued to putter in the kitchen. When everyone was done eating, he presented them with several plastic containers of, "Food for the road."

"Got you a bag with clothes too. Stuff one of the kids left behind. Keep what you've got on." Jeannie added.

Lauren gratefully accepted the secondhand clothes and the cleaned ones she was handed.

"Did a load while you were sleeping." Jeannie shrugged. "Wasn't going to get any sleep last night anyway. Got most of the blood out."

Why was a handful of clothes making her teary eyed? She bit her lip and went outside, started shifting stuff from the Mazda to the Buick. She considered moving and hiding her car somewhere else to protect Keith and Jeannie, until she concluded that if there was tracking equipment on it, Gierdes would have attacked during the night. The cooler sloshed in her grip. Must need more ice. Another mental note was made to get more at the next stop.

She was almost done when Nona and Trevor came outside, their overnight bags on Nona's shoulder. Instructions back to the highway were given, thank yous and goodbyes said, and they loaded into the car. It stank like an ashtray. When she sat down, a fresh puff of acrid stench burst up. Nasty. Why did people smoke? Lauren held back her disgust, rolled all the windows down, and backed out of the drive.

They made it back to the gas station from last night, then the highway without trouble. Mostly because Nona was navigating. Lauren had forgotten the instructions after the second turn. Nine in the morning saw them heading south.

"Hey, so, um." Lauren picked at her shirt. "Where are we?"

Nona side-eyed her. "What?"

"All I know is that I flew for a long time before I found you. Are we in Ohio or what?"

"Northern Indiana."

"Oh. Okay."

"Is there a plan beyond meeting up with Amber?" Nona asked.

"Other than staying alive?" Lauren shrugged. "No."

Nona sighed, a hand lifting up to sink into her hair. "Okay. Let's talk about the options. Running and hiding. Confronting the Gierdes. T-"

"Confronting them is a death sentence, Nona!"

"I know. I'm listing the options, not if they're good or not." Nona replied calmly.

She coughed, "Oh."

Nona kept going. "Telling the world about lokref. Surrendering. Bonding together."

Bonding. The hair on her arms stood upright.

"Did I miss anything?"

"Huh uh," not that she could think of. She was still stuck on the thought of bonding with Nona. Well, with anyone really. But mostly Nona.

"Alright. Obviously we aren't fans of the ones that get us hurt. If we choose to hide, do you know how to get fake IDs?"

Fake IDs? Not personally. She could probably ask around the racing scene. That'd require going back to Des Moines though. "No."

"What about..."

"What's bonding together mean?" chirped from the backseat.

Lauren looked at the rearview. Trevor was staring curiously. "Um."

"It's kind of like getting married," came softly from Nona.

Trevor made a face. "Do you love Lauren, Mom?"

Lauren choked, heard Nona do the same.

"Mommy?"

"Bonding isn't..." Nona shook her head. "Lauren, can you explain it?"

Explain the super complicated problem to the eight year old? She wasn't the mom here!

"Please."

Ah, balls. Why was Nona's soft tone impossible to argue with? "The law doesn't want pedestrians, normal humans, to know about lokref." She found the words easier than she'd expected. "We can bond to one person, and then they don't need a feather to call us anymore. The bond basically makes them family, and family are allowed to know about lokref."

A minute of quiet passed.

"We'd be family?" Trevor pursued.

"Yea." Lauren sighed. "Yea, we'd be family."

He stared hard at her, then his mom, until he switched to the landscape outside.

Nona's hand appeared on Lauren's over the gear shifter. "Thank you." She retreated too, leaving Lauren to her swirling thoughts about family and how much she wanted what Meisenger clearly didn't want her to have.

The rest of the drive was quiet. A frustrating, nerve-twisting quiet. Trevor and Nona seemed done with words. Every stop for gas or restroom breaks was hurried and anxious. Every time a cop passed or glanced in their direction was a white-knuckle-event. Lauren put on the radio, but couldn't find anything besides country or moldy oldies that wasn't fuzzy with static. She missed her satellite radio. She missed her car. She wanted nothing more than to go home, maybe visit her parents in Nebraska for a day or two, crash on their couch, help around the house, eat mom's cooking, laugh and joke and tell stories about the guys at the garage.

Steve was definitely going to fire her this time. He'd been ridiculously understanding the last time that Lauren had disappeared. He wouldn't be this time. Couldn't be. He had a business to run. Not that it really mattered. Lauren couldn't go back to her life. Nona had been right to start thinking past St. Louis. Unless the world changed tomorrow, she needed to start thinking of how to live on the run.

Fingers tapping on the steering wheel, she let her mind wander. What would happen if Lauren stepped in front of a news camera and exposed her magic? If enough people knew who and what she was, wouldn't the Gierdes back off? Other lokref would stand up with her. She'd met enough disgruntled lokref in her brief stint as a knight. Hell, she'd met one yesterday! Jeannie seemed like the type to jump at the chance to live freely.

To fly freely.

Wow. Would the government try to regulate that? Would she have to file a flight plan first? Designated lokref flying areas? She'd be fine with abiding by some zoning restrictions and such. No reason to expect commercial traffic and leisure fliers to share the same airspace. The military would probably scramble to recruit as many lokref as possible. Law enforcement too.

She could join the police academy or FBI or even NASA if she was feeling really frisky. On paper, no one knew about her illegal racing. She'd get rid of her Integra and keep away from the street scene just to be safe. Meisenger knew, had to. But if the world was changing, then that asshole could be tossed from his seat of power and someone new put on it, someone who didn't murder black-winged lokref and worked *with* pedestrians to make the world livable.

"What'd you find to smile about?" asked from her passenger.

Lauren blinked out of her daydream to glance at Nona. Her brow was raised, a grin lurking on her lips. Lauren looked back to the road for a quick sweep before peeking at Nona again. "Daydreaming about flying in the daylight."

"Are you thinking about breaking the law again?" Her playful tone asked.

Silliness started to reply, yet she fell into serious thought. "Yea. I think I am."

Chapter Eighteen

Slop

Finally. *Finally.* The opposing traffic let up enough for Lauren to get out from behind the slow as balls farm combine. She hit the gas, making the old girl roar, and shot around it. An intersection with a single red light appeared. It blinked, slow as a bored cow, and she expected to hear mooing at any moment. They'd played a game of counting cows earlier. They'd gotten bored of it after a few hundred. Cows were everywhere, munching on the stalks of harvested fields, depositing manure, lazing about.

"Are we still going the right way?" She asked.

Nona came up from the outdoor magazine she was reading to consult the map. "Yes."

"Okay." Lauren sighed and crossed the empty intersection. The light blinked a bored goodbye in the rearview.

Nona went back to her magazine, Trevor snored lightly from his chair, and Lauren tried to find something other than their dilemma to think about. There was a curve in the road ahead. She couldn't help thinking that anything could be on the other side. Freedom. Gierdes. A portal that could toss her back a few months and stop this entire mess from happening. If only. She spent too much of her life watching sci-fi movies.

The car hit a patch of ice.

Ice?! What the hell? It was too fucking warm for ice! Lauren continued to swear as she wrestled for control of the car. Another patch of not-ice sent the car spinning right off the road. She couldn't stop it. Luckily, a farmer's fence caught them. They came to a jarring halt, left side of the car lodged against wooden posts, facing the wrong direction. Her heart hammered at her throat hard enough to hurt.

As she sat there panting, she stared back at the road, saw what looked like puddles. Grey, lumpy puddles. "What the fuck?"

"What happened?!" screeched Nona as she half-turned, already checking on a stunned Trevor.

"Don't know. You okay?"

Nona checked herself. "Bumped my head, but we're fine."

Cheers burst out of Trevor. "That was awesome, Lauren!"

Okay, the kid was an adrenaline junkie. That, she could relate to. A chuckle wheezed out at his happy noise. The chuckle drifted away as she caught sight of what was ahead of them on the road. There was a truck in the middle of it, an overturned eighteen-wheeler, blocking the way through. If she hadn't lost control, she probably would've driven right into it.

And trailing from the open-top freight container was a wide smear of something grey and lumpy. What the? As the thought coalesced, the sludge's stench slammed into her.

Her gag reflex triggered, and acid jumped up her throat. She swallowed and coughed at the burn.

"Oh sweet cheese and crackers," hissed out of Nona.

"Ew!" squealed Trevor, his hands covering his nose and muffling his voice. "That's gross!"

Lauren coughed again. There was what looked like bits of animals in the sludge on the road. Skulls, bones, hooves. Holy balls. Spoiled meat. Rancid, fermenting for who knew how long, meat. Tons of it. Literal fucking tons of it. She tried to breathe shallowly, tried not to taste it, failed miserably. She'd thought an empty meat package left in the garbage for a couple of days smelled bad. That was nothing compared to this!

She swallowed again as the vomit tried to creep up. No time for blowing chunks. There were still Gierdes on their asses, and the blaring of sirens said they were about to be surrounded by cops. She moved to put the car back in drive. Her gaze flicked to the Buick's crumpled side mirror. No, check the Buick first, make sure there wasn't any significant damage. It'd be hell if a cracked axle gave out on the highway.

Is that what happened to the truck? Some mechanical failure? Or was the driver in trouble? Asleep at the wheel?

No sign of them on the road. Couldn't see inside the truck's cabin from this angle. No other cars nearby. Driver must have called 911 or there probably wouldn't be those sirens in the distance. But where was the driver? On the other side of the truck? Trapped in the cabin? Unconscious?

"Lauren?"

"I don't see the truck driver."

It only took a moment for the implications to hit Nona. "Trevor, stay in the car. We're going to make sure the driver of that truck is okay."

Nona got out, Lauren scooting out after since her door was wedged between car and fence. She eyed the blind curve they'd spun out on. "Get your emergency kit, but stay here. Anything could come flying down that road and lose control. I've got armor to protect me. You don't."

Nona nodded. "Be careful."

"Sure." She aimed a beeline for the truck, yet the sludge was everywhere. All over the road, the shoulder, through the fence to the field beyond. She couldn't jump the fifty feet to dry road. Backtrack. As she jogged back, she discovered there were several puddles along the curve that she could dance around. Driver must have lost control further back where the first puddles were, sloshed the load over the edges.

The other shoulder was dry. She followed it up to the truck and around. No sign of anyone.

"Hello?" she called.

Nothing. Even the engine was quiet.

"Hello?" She yelled louder and scanned around, hoping the driver was peeing behind a bush or something. Nope. "Are you in there?"

Around the front, she peered in. The driver was slumped, eyes closed, blood matted in her greying hair. Lauren went to knock.

"You find him?" startled the shit out of her.

"Nona!" She growled. "What the fuck?"

"I can cross a road by myself." Nona ignored her outrage and looked inside the truck. "Oh cheese. She doesn't look good. Get in there and kick this window out."

Kick the window out? "Like in the movies? Have you ever tried doing that?"

"No."

"Don't. It's not worth the effort." Lauren went to the underside of the truck and jumped. She got a grip on the siderail and hauled herself up. The driver's side door was locked, the window down an inch. Lauren peered inside. An older woman, with a pixie cut and denim vest. Her eyes were closed, and she was still strapped into her seat. Man, dangling like that couldn't be comfortable.

The noxious sting of a cigarette attacked her nose even over the sickening stench of rotting meat. She scrubbed at her nose and wished for an easier life before rapping on the door. "Hey, can you hear me?"

Eyelashes fluttered. No other response.

The sirens that she'd heard were finally taking the curve, slowly maneuvering around the puddles. Two cars. Probably local sheriff and deputy. They should be trained for this kind of problem, but it'd be a hot minute before they got to the truck.

"Help me up, Lauren." Nona demanded.

She twisted and braced herself, held out a hand. Nona didn't really need it, not with how cleanly she mounted the truck. It was more to keep her from sliding off once she was on the slippery edge.

"You smell that?" Nona asked.

"The cigarette smoke? Yea."

"That's not…" she trailed off and stared inside. "Oh fudge. Something's burning in there."

Fire in a truck? Not good. "I'll get the windshield."

"Hurry, Lauren. It looks like something is wrong with the seatbelt. A fall like this will hurt."

She jumped off at the same time another police car appeared down the clean side of the road. She hesitated a moment. "Fuck it." Her spear made a new entryway through the windshield. Flames burst into existence at the bottom of the cabin. Fast food bags? Did she drop a cigarette in them?

"Lauren!"

Armor covering her legs, she stepped in. There was the sound of snapping metal, and the driver fell into Lauren's arms, her shoulders popping at the sudden, considerable weight. She wheezed and stumbled backward.

"Nice catch. Let's get her away from here." Nona was on the ground, waving toward the road's edge. Lauren hoisted the driver over and gently lowered her as Nona crouched down. "Are you awake? Can you hear me?"

A groan that sounded like a question returned.

"I'm Nona. Can you tell me your name?"

"Ca…" heaved out. "Casey."

The police car came to a jerking stop and spit out a state trooper.

"Is anyone hurt?" The trooper puffed.

"Casey is. She's showing signs of concussion." Nona said.

He gave her a look. His nametag flashed Johnson at them.

"I work in search and rescue." She supplied. "Her seatbelt broke, but Lauren and I got her out before the situation got worse."

Johnson nodded and pulled out a little pen light, flashed it in Casey's blinking eyes. "You said her name was Casey?"

"That's what I got out of her. There's also a fire in the cabin of the truck."

At that, Johnson grabbed his radio and passed the danger on. It garbled about how firefighters were ten minutes out. "Okay. Let's get you ladies farther away. You don't want to be near if it explodes."

"Trevor." Nona rose, made to run for their car, except the trooper caught her arm first. "My son. He's all alone in our car."

"Ma'am, there's a sheriff over there. He'll be fine."

Nona tugged for freedom, but the man didn't budge. "But he doesn't handle strangers well!"

"Ma'am, he'll be fine." Johnson repeated stiffly. "We have to get you away."

Desperate maternal instinct burned in Nona's face.

"I'll make sure he's okay." Lauren ran before Johnson could try to stop her. She skidded around the truck and its putrid sludge.

"Lauren!" screeched out from the car. A beefy cop straightened from looking inside.

"Trevor!" Lauren called back.

"Lauren?" Trevor squeaked. "Lauren!"

Her foot slipped on a rock. Maybe a bone. She couldn't tell what with the dive she was taking right into the pit of hell. She landed with a massive splash, putrid gunk squirting and squishing everywhere. For a second, she lay stunned. Then horror set in. She shrieked and scrambled to her feet, slipping twice, falling and soaking what wasn't already coated in slop.

Oh balls. Oh horrible, hairy, fucking balls!

"No!" screeched out of her.

"Lauren, what happened?"

Tears already streaming down her face, Lauren squeaked. She coughed and cleared her throat, realized that her face wasn't dripping gross, and she found the presence of mind to reassure the kid. "It's okay, Snowman!

I just fell. I..." needed a bath so bad. Her throat clenched. Bile rose. She couldn't stop it. More gross splashed into the sludge.

"Ma'am, are you okay?" The sheriff was a broad-shouldered man with silver hair at his temples. His nose wrinkled.

"No," pouted from her. "But I'll live." She shook goop from her hands and arms and trudged toward the car.

Trevor leaned back from the window as he took in Lauren's dilemma. "Ew!"

"I know."

He shifted. "Where's my mom?"

"There's a fire in the truck. The trooper didn't want her running by it to get back to you, in case it exploded. I ran anyway." She answered.

His returning smile was worth it.

"Ma'am, we should all get further back from the truck." The sheriff tipped his head toward the curve. "Firefighters are on their way."

"You heard the sheriff, Trev. Let's go."

He turned away for long enough that she started to call his name. He jumped out of the car before her mouth opened. His backpack was on. He reached for her hand, frowned, and curled his away.

She coughed out a laugh. "I agree. I need a shower." Something dripped off her elbow, splat to the ground. "Or twelve," she gagged.

"Hey there, sport." The sheriff smiled and held out a hand. "Let's get you back to my patrol car."

Trevor shrugged away. His hand splashed into Lauren's.

Cops shrank from them as they passed between the cars. Gloop drooled down her arms and back, made her shudder and swallow bile. She was directed to the safety of a hundred feet from the semi. As she was considering sitting on the pavement, more emergency vehicles came around the bend.

Another fire engine and an ambulance carefully nosed their way around the slop. The ambulance drove right up to Lauren, and paramedics rushed at her and Trevor. They came to a startled stop a few feet away. What were they staring at? The awful goop? The cuts and bruises on her face? Both?

"No injuries here, guys." The sheriff lifted a hand. "But these two sure need a shower."

A firefighter in full gear jogged up, took in the mess.

"These two are all yours, Joe." One of the paramedics waved.

"Hey, Smith. Hey, Bones." Joe raised a hand in greeting.

The paramedic who hadn't waved shook her head and sighed. "My name is Kearney. What's it going to take for you to stop calling me Bones?"

"Let me buy you dinner." Joe grinned.

She closed her eyes and muttered under her breath.

"What was that?" Joe pushed.

"Oh look, there's a nice woman waiting for you to start decontamination, Mr. Penton." Kearney said loudly. She pointed at Lauren. "Maybe you should do your job instead of harassing me?"

Lauren grinned at Kearney's reprimand. At Joe's glance, she smoothed her face. Maybe not a good idea to antagonize him. At least, not until she got washed off.

"Follow me, ma'am." Joe beckoned toward the fire engine. "We'll get that gunk hosed off you."

Trevor in tow, she followed, watching other firefighters mill around.

"What a mess." The sheriff muttered. "Going to take forever to clean this shit up."

"Yep." Smith answered. "Who do you call for this? CDC? EPA?"

"The paperwork will…"

The voices faded as she got farther away. In front of her, firefighters were being ordered about by Joe. A fat hose was connected to the giant truck. Voices argued, Joe yelled over them, and Lauren was waved over.

"Okay, ma'am." Joe waved at the firefighter holding the hose. "We've got the pressure on this hose very low. It'll get you nice and clean without hurting you."

"I'd let you spray me if it flayed the skin off my bones!" Lauren gushed. She cringed at the rank goop, flinched at the slime on Trevor's hand. "Clean up Trevor first though, okay?"

Thankfully, it didn't take any prodding for Trevor to stick his hand out as far as it would go to get hosed off, then wait beside Joe when it was Lauren's turn. Beyond eager, she nearly skipped into position. The firefighter smiled knowingly before adjusting the hose and telling her to close her eyes. She pressed eyelids and lips tight together and focused on the sunlight warming her face.

It was a slow, thorough process. Without anyone to stare at, her mind started to wander. How was Nona doing? Was Amber at the meetup spot? Who else would Meisenger send after them? How long could they hide? Would she have to kill anyone else?

A body pinned to a door filled the darkness.

Her eyes flew open. She nearly summoned her wings and took to the air, but a glance at Trevor stopped her. He frowned at her expression.

"Okay, ma'am. The next part is a little embarrassing, but it's for your health." Joe announced. "She's got a set of clothes and a blanket for after." He gestured at Kearney, who was keeping a good distance between herself and the man, a pile of cloth in her hands.

Clothes. Right. Lauren was wet in weather that had people in jackets. Anyone normal would be shivering or close to it. She tried to look uncomfortable. "Okay."

"Ma'am, I'll need you to strip down. Totally. Then you'll get another hose off, okay?" Kearney explained. "The guys will hold up some tarps for your privacy. If you want, I can be the one with the hose."

Lauren looked from one set of serious eyes to another. "Oh, balls." She threw up her hands. "Yea, okay. I don't care. Let's just do this quickly."

"Lauren?" Trevor frowned.

"It's fine, Snowman. They just want me squeaky clean." She looked down at her dripping outfit. How long would it take to scrub the stench from her skin?

His little face considered it. "Okay."

Tarps went up, soggy clothes came off, and another spray went over Lauren. She didn't have to fake being uncomfortable. The spray was cool, she was naked with a paramedic probably cataloguing all of her bruises, and she really wanted a hot bath, bottles of bleach, and a scrub brush. And a bottle of whiskey.

A disposable towel was presented, then navy blue scrubs and a blanket.

"Great." Kearney smiled. "We'll get you two to the hospital for a real sanitizing wash, a shot of antibiotics, just in case, and you'll be good to go."

"What about Mommy?" Trevor squeaked. He already had a handful of Lauren's blanket crumpled in a fist.

The paramedic raised a questioning brow at Lauren.

"We were helping the truck driver, and the firefighters kept her on that side of the truck." Lauren supplied.

Joe raised a radio to his face, talked to someone on the other end. An answer sputtered back: the fire was contained and the woman would be walked over. The sheriff appeared.

"Could you answer a few questions before they take you to the hospital?" He flipped open a notepad.

Trapped, she nodded.

"What's your full name?"

Her name? Oh shit. Should she lie in case Meisenger had decided to involve pedestrian authorities? What name would sound good? Uh...

The sheriff eyed her. "Ma'am?"

"Lauren Trent," rushed out. So much for lying.

"Lauren Trent." He scribbled. "Where were you coming from when you encountered the truck?" And other much easier to answer questions, ones she had no fear about answering with the truth. When a firefighter and Nona came into view, Lauren nearly dropped the blanket and rushed over.

"Mommy!" Trevor had no such reservations. He would have run right through the slop to reach Nona had Lauren's reflexives not shot her arm out and reined him in.

"Whoa!" Lauren held tight on his sweater. "We can wait right here, Snowman."

Confusion wrinkled his brow. He looked at what lay between him and his mother, nodded, the wrinkle shifting down to his nose with disgust. "Okay."

Past the goop, Nona dipped to accept the child leaping into her arms, stayed in a crouch to kiss his forehead and whisper something in his ear. She rose and frowned at Lauren's new outfit.

"Lauren slipped." Trevor supplied. "The firemen gave her a bath."

Nona's face wrinkled. "Oh no."

The sheriff chose that moment to pull Nona aside to interrogate her as he had Lauren.

"How's the driver?" Lauren asked when the sheriff finished with her.

Nona smiled. "Casey will be okay. She's on her way to the hospital now."

"They want to take me and the Snowman there too, pump me full of antibiotics and scrub us both down. He grabbed my gross hand," she said when Nona's face widened with panic.

"Is..." Panic slid away, and she glanced at the milling emergency workers, lowered her voice. "Do you need that?"

Somehow, it made Lauren grin. "I'm still human, Nona."

"Alright!" Kearney strode up with a professional smile. "We'll get you and your kid to the hospital for your Sunday bath." She looked at Nona. "The boys can get your car hosed down and an escort to the hospital to meet them."

Though her eyes tightened, Nona nodded agreeably. "Sure." She reached for Lauren's hand, stopped before they made contact, made a strange little frown. Another kiss for Trevor, and she allowed the paramedics to hustle them into an ambulance.

As they settled into the uncomfortable ride, Kearney smiled. "How long have you two been together?"

Together? Lauren blinked at Trevor. "Um?"

"Sorry. I didn't mean to pry. You and his mom act just like my cousin and his boyfriend. In public, they're all quiet looks and quick touches." A shrug as she watched Lauren's face. "Anyway, I'm Amanda. It's about twenty minutes to the hospital."

Wait. She was talking about her and Nona. They looked like a couple? Lauren's stomach twisted.

"Your cousin is a boy and has a boyfriend?" Trevor asked softly.

The paramedic's smile was gentle. "Yes. Some boys like boys how other boys like girls."

Trevor's little face screwed up in thought. "Is that true, Lauren?"

Dammit. She wanted to plant her face in her hand, but she took a breath and answered calmly. "Yes."

"Does that mean some girls like girls?"

Another breath. "Yes."

Kearney – no – Amanda's eyes went wide and they flicked between Lauren and Trevor. Her mouth made a silent apology.

His head tilted. "Can some people like both?"

Why was she the one having this conversation with the kid? "Yea, Snowman. Some people like both."

"Oh." He looked at his shoes. "What do you like, Lauren?"

Her face must be about to burst into flames with how hot her cheeks were. It hurt like hell. "I like girls."

His shoes needed to be tied. The loose strings dangled, and he looked at them for a little while longer before fixing Lauren with a serious stare. "Do you like my mom?"

Someone shoot her now! Something dry and strangled wheezed from her throat.

"Dad says mean things about people like you. I don't get it. You're nice. You're really brave and strong. You talk to me like I matter. I'd rather be around you than Dad."

That curve ball had her head spinning. Trevor wasn't asking about gays because he'd just learned about them. He was asking other peoples' opinions because his dad was a homophobe. And the kid just made his own mind up about the matter! "Are you really only eight years old?" She gaped at him.

Amanda looked ready to wrap them both in an ooey gooey hug.

The seriousness on Trevor's face didn't waver. "I'm okay if you like my mom." He pat her hand.

"Th-thanks." She managed. "I, uh, um. I appreciate that?"

Waiting for the firefighters to not only hose down the car, but allow her to coax the battered thing back onto the road made Nona want to pull her hair out. She was pretty sure that she'd rubbed a hole in her pants with all her anxious rubbing. Finally on the road, behind a police escort, she was definitely wearing the steering wheel thin. Thinner. It had seem some better days.

The hospital was twenty minutes away. She'd been driving for ten. But she'd been apart from Trevor for almost an hour. Her only consolation was that he was with Lauren. In fact, it calmed her a great deal knowing that.

She wiped sweaty palms on her thighs. She could also admit that half her anxiety and fear was that *she* was separated from Lauren. What if Gierdes found her now? The last feather she'd used was gone, and Lauren hadn't given her another. The poor woman had gone through hell for her. Lauren's face was a warzone. And under her clothes, she was covered in bruises, even if she hadn't said anything. Her stiff movements spoke pretty loudly.

The exhaustion that Nona felt must be nothing compared to Lauren's. All that fighting and flying. How much energy did it take to use magic? Did it take any at all? What did the magic feel like?

What was it like to call armor and weapons into existence? To grow enormous wings? To feel someone else's heartbeat from across the country?

Was it a visceral sense? Like wind in her hair or water sliding down her throat? Her thoughts continued in a tangled mess about Lauren, magic, and fear. She barely noticed arriving at the hospital. Once she did, she leapt out, eager to see her child and Lauren.

The hospital was a decent size for its rural location, but small enough and old enough for its awful sixties' color scheme and facade to not be out of place. Its automatic doors were so agonizingly slow she had to quell a scream of frustration before they registered her presence, then took an eternity to actually open. How could an ER operate like this? There should be laws to prevent doors this awful!

"Kidnapper? That one?" someone laughed. Nona froze around the corner from it. "You've got to be kidding."

"I swear, she matches the picture!" A young man's voice countered.

"If someone actually reported her as a kidnapper, they're probably an abusive ex trying to get her or the blonde back." The first speaker. A woman, with a good head on her shoulders, it sounded like.

There was a noise like a boot scuffing the ground. "Either way, we should bring them in for questioning. If they're running, we can help."

"Look, O'Keefe." The voice got forceful. "You can ask them if they need help, but you are *not* taking them to the station!"

"But what if they're acting?" O'Keefe pursued.

"The women, I could see that. But the kid? That kid adores both of them." She argued.

Trevor liked and admired Lauren immensely. Almost as much as Nona did. Heat crept up her neck. Was her own attachment to Lauren as obvious as Trevor's? Cheese and rice, woman! Forget about your crush! The police thought Lauren had kidnapped them. Someone would try to arrest Lauren eventually, might even succeed if she was tired enough.

What she needed to do was come up with a plan to get everyone out safely. O'Keefe may very well ignore his friend and attempt that arrest. She looked back at the parking lot. If they could get to the car, great. They should leave it somewhere soon though. She had their personal bags on them, mostly for Lauren's change of clothes, but their money and most important gear was in them too. She'd made sure of that.

Okay. Get to Lauren and Trevor. Try to get them to the car quickly. If that didn't work, they had Lauren's wings. Nona bit her lip. How far should they go? Would it matter once people saw a proverbial angel flying away?

No. That was a bridge to cross when they came to it. First, escape. Then, figure out the rest. It shouldn't be that hard. She and Lauren were partners in this. They would get through it together.

Plan made, confidence restored, Nona strode around the corner with her chin up and shoulders back. She smiled at the deputy and paramedic. "Hey, do you know where my partner and son are?"

The paramedic smiled back. She was the same from earlier, who had gotten into the ambulance with Lauren. "Yea. They're in room two." She half turned to gesture down the hall.

"Thank you." Nona nearly swallowed her tongue. She'd called Lauren her partner out loud! That wasn't at all what she'd meant to do.

Behind her, she heard them return to whispering. "See?"

"What?"

"She wasn't kidnapped. She's with her family."

"She could still be acting." O'Keefe grunted. "The other woman has her kid."

"You are such a pessimist." The paramedic sighed. "They..."

Nona was too far to hear more, not that her pounding heart took notice. She swallowed and focused on the receptionist. "Hi," came out a little strangled.

The receptionist looked up. "Oh, you must be the boy's mother." A friendly smile. "Go on back."

Nona headed for the door into the ER.

"You know where you're going?" called after her.

She glanced back. "Room two?"

"Yep."

She went through, eyed the handful of nurses and techs, found room two, and knocked. An unfamiliar face opened it, but smiled and admitted her. "You are definitely this little one's mom, aren't you?"

"Mommy?" preceded Trevor's usual running jump.

She caught him easily, sighing in relief at the renewed contact. Her eyes found Lauren sitting on the bed the nurse walked back to. She was in a hospital gown. "You two all scrubbed up?"

Trevor nodded furiously against her hip. "My hand doesn't stink anymore."

"Lucky," was muttered across the room.

"I was just about to give Lauren her shot of antibiotics." The nurse informed her. "After that, the doctor can sign her release papers and you all can go home."

Home. Wouldn't that be nice? "Thank you." Nona said.

Trevor peeled himself away to go watch Lauren being stabbed. As the nurse retreated, Nona went in for a hug, put her lips close to Lauren's ear.

She whispered, "Police might be coming soon." She retreated and spoke louder. "You do still stink."

Lauren blinked at her, glanced at the nurse who was tossing the needle in a sharps disposal. "Yea."

"Okay. The doctor should get those papers signed in a minute." The door closed behind.

"They've been eyeing my wrists." Lauren touched the fresh bandages on them. "And my other injuries."

The gesture made Nona flinch yet again. Poor Lauren. She'd taken so much abuse for Nona.

"Is the car drivable?" Lauren asked.

"Driver side won't open. Mirror is gone. It rides rougher than before and stinks even worse." Nona shrugged. "But it got me here."

"I don't suppose you found another pair of shoes for me?" Lauren grimaced.

"No. But we can do that later."

Lauren sighed at the rubberized hospital socks currently gracing her feet. "Oh well." She looked at the door. "So, you know that those papers could be here in five minutes or an hour, right?"

"I know. ER doctors are always being distracted. There's a lot of deputies out there too." Nona put Trevor's backpack on, handed over Lauren's. "Lauren?"

Shadowed eyes met hers. "Yea?"

"If we can't get to the car, can you fly us out?"

Her lips twitched. "Yea."

Good. "Trev, hold my hand." Nona peeked out the door. No one was looking at them. "Let's go."

Quietly, they darted from the room, down the hall, and right into O'Keefe. His eyes went huge. One hand went to his service pistol, the other up in a stopping gesture. "Hey, whoa. Where you off to in such a hurry?"

"We have somewhere to be." Nona said.

He glanced at her with a frown. "Ma'am, I need you to step away from Ms. Trent."

Lauren scowled. "Please move."

He ignored her to keep eye contact with Nona. "Ma'am, I know you're in danger. I can help if you step away from Trent."

"You have it all wrong, deputy." Nona shook her head. "She's the one protecting us."

His mouth moved.

Lauren looked at her, kept her own mouth shut.

"Deputy, please let us pass." Nona tried.

O'Keefe gaped another moment before gathering himself. "Then let me help. Let me take you down to the station. There's no safer place."

Lauren laughed. It was a harsh, unpleasant sound. "Balls, man. You have no idea what you're dealing with. Just get out of the way."

"Lauren!" She chided.

In response, huge black wings appeared. Armor followed. The deputy made a noise like a screaming frog. "The ones hunting us are just like me." She pushed into the deputy's personal space as he stared and quivered. "And bullets aren't shit against this armor."

He stumbled back as she loomed, both hands coming up in a defensive motion, eyes ready to launch from their sockets.

Armor and wings vanished. "Thanks for trying though." She brushed past, Nona a step behind.

O'Keefe wheezed and stared after them.

"Why was Lauren so mean to that police man?" Trevor whispered.

"We need to move fast." Nona replied. "And the deputy didn't listen when we asked nicely."

They jogged across the small lot, and Nona hustled Trevor into his seat. Lauren made to open the busted driver side and swore at her forgetfulness.

"Ms. Trent?" A nurse was calling across the lot.

Trevor's seatbelt clicked, and Nona dove in, sliding across to the driver's seat, Lauren only half a breath behind.

The nurse was almost at their car, another deputy following, when Nona slammed her foot on the gas. Tires squealed, and the car lurched forward with an angry grinding sound. Putting aside the thought that it sounded horrible, she continued flooring the gas, sending them shrieking out the exit and down the road.

"We have to dump this car." Lauren said.

"I agree. Somewhere it won't be found for a while. Those nice people don't deserve the attention it would bring."

Lauren growled. "Yea."

She kept looking in the rearview mirror, expecting to see flashing lights at any moment. She took a turn at the next intersection. And another at the following. If her mental map was right, they were heading north and away from the highway they'd crashed on.

"Got any idea where we're heading?" Lauren asked after a while.

"I do." She nodded. "North."

Her expression crinkled, then she shrugged. "Okay." She leaned back and yawned. Her eyelids dropped, abruptly shot back up. "What do we do with the car? Literally dump it in a river? And then what? We need another car. I can't fly us all the way to St. Louis."

"Is it a matter of stamina?" Or was she still afraid of being seen even after scaring poor O'Keefe?

"Of course it's a matter of stamina. I'm not an amazon like you." Lauren griped.

The almost-insult curved her lips. "It's okay, shrimp. We'll find another car."

A glare and a growl were thrown at her.

"What if we found another Walmart and just left it there for a while? Do you know how to steal a car? Can we hotwire another one we find in the parking lot?"

Lauren's jaw worked. "I might be able to hotwire one, but it'd be a lot easier to just open up the ignition switch or drill it out and use a screwdriver as a key."

"Really?"

"Sure, if it's an older car." Lauren shrugged. "Something ancient like this beast." Her nose wrinkled. "Something that doesn't stink as bad though."

The addition of the rancid slop hadn't improve its rankness. It would be stuck to the tires for weeks. "That'd be nice." She checked on Trevor. He was watching everything with big eyes. Her free hand reached to pat his leg. "I suppose we should find ourselves a slim jim first."

A cute little cafe that Ren had fangirled over when she'd tasted the coffee was where Amber and Royce sat waiting for her arrival. Every day at eleven, they came and waited anxiously for an hour. For three days they'd waited. They waited and looked over their shoulders and suffered in their ignorance of what was happening.

"This is bullshit." Amber muttered.

Royce looked up from his coffee. Ew. Coffee. He and Lauren sucked that sewer slop down like water. What was wrong with water? Or juice? She slurped at her orange juice. Damn delicious.

"What's bullshit?" Royce asked.

"I'm not a spy." She peered at a suspicious looking guy walking in. Torn jeans and leather jacket. Was he Gierdes? No. Didn't walk like one. Maybe? "I'm sick of looking over my shoulder."

"And you're worried about Ren." He said.

She glowered into her juice. "And worried about Ren. Where the hell is she? It's been days!"

He fiddled with the phone that they'd bought so long ago, that'd remained mostly silent since Blake's arrival at their back door. No amount of calling had gotten any response from Lauren. Only Blake had called, to let them know Lauren and her hiking guide were being chased. Meisenger was rabid at Tibbits' failure. He'd actually given Lauren's face and name to police with the story that she'd kidnapped the guide and her kid.

Lauren a kidnapper. She was more likely to eat a big, steaming pile of dog crap. Amber snorted, finished her juice, and rose. Royce followed suit. They dropped off their dishes and trash in the bins and headed out. Ren wasn't magically waiting outside the cafe, so they got into their car and went back to the hotel.

Amber brought up and watched the video of Lauren smacking Tibbits' teeth in and flying off. For the dozenth time. If Lauren had stayed a Gierdes or at least kept training, she'd be one hell of a badass.

Chapter Nineteen

The Guiding Stone

The only weaver contact that Meisenger had, and he was as loathe to help as Meisenger was to reach out. They glared at each other over the video connection. Even on the tiny screen of his phone, the weaver's dislike and distrust was vivid.

"This is to repay the favor you owe me." Meisenger repeated.

"Hunting down your own kind." He spat. "Because you're afraid of her feathers."

"The black-wing has broken our laws!"

The weaver leaned in. "'The black-wing.' Yes. You're especially afraid of those. How many have been born in the last few hundred years?" He sneered. "How many have lived to a fine old age?"

"Will you honor your favor or not?"

Lips curled back even further, wrinkling nose and brow. "I will give you what you want, Commandant Meisenger. But none of mine will ever help you again."

Whatever must be done to catch the black-wing. "Fine."

Disappointment and disgust colored the weaver's sigh. "A guiding stone will be delivered to your agent tomorrow."

Black replaced the weaver's face. A little message blurped that the call had disconnected and would he like to give feedback on the call's quality?

The screen of his brand new phone shattered.

"Dammit!"

179

Ahead of them, the cafe sign gleamed in the midday sun. Anticipation picked up their pace. Almost immediately, a man stepped in front of them. He was average height, mahogany skinned, and deeply freckled. Blocking their path, he looked from Nona to Lauren to Trevor. He smiled as Trevor hid behind them.

"Meisenger used up the last of his goodwill with my friends. The leader of the team hunting you received a guiding stone an hour ago."

A what? Nona wanted to ask, yet the terror edging along Lauren's face said it was exactly what it sounded. A stone to guide the Gierdes right to them. Melting popsicles! How could this situation keep getting worse?

"Why are you telling us?" Lauren growled.

He smiled wider. "We're tired of the way things are." He shrugged. "We're doing something about it."

"Who's we?" Nona had to know.

Piercing brown eyes met hers. "Weavers."

"Weavers?" she questioned. The term tickled her brain, but she couldn't recall anything about it.

Laughter, loud and uninhibited burst out. When he finished, he smiled at Lauren. "You haven't told her everything yet."

Lauren's jaw flexed.

"Not that I imagine you know all that much. The scarecrows are rather short-sighted like that. I would invite you to lunch, enjoy spending it and the rest of the day talking about our magic, but that can't happen today. You have scarecrows hunting you." He rooted in a jeans pocket, came out with a business card. "When you've figured out this problem, give me a call."

The card was placed in Lauren's hand. Its beige surface was mostly blank. Only a phone number was neatly written in purple ink across it.

He moved as though to walk away, paused. "For a pair that isn't bonded..." he trailed off. His gaze flit between herself and Lauren. "I wonder if this is what he's so afraid of," was softly muttered. Louder, "Good luck."

He vanished into the crowd.

Lauren whirled, searching the dense crowd - doing a couple little jumps to peer over it - and frowning. She'd clearly lost sight of him as quickly as Nona had. Lauren brought up the card to frown at it. "What the balls just happened?"

Nona opened her mouth. Before she could say anything about her own confusion, Lauren was rushing at the cafe and yelling, "Amber?"

"Ren?" yelled back.

"Amber!" Lauren collided with a shorter, darker woman with close cropped hair and bright jewelry.

"Ren!" The intimidatingly pretty woman gasped before thrusting Lauren back to look her over. "Damn, Ren! You look like shit."The back of her mind buzzed over the shortened name. Was she saying Ren, just a shortened version of her name? Or wren, like the bird? Or was it an unintentional play on words and nobody had ever noticed except a nerd like her before?

"Yea. Thanks." Lauren groaned. "You look gorgeous, as always. Did you keep this shit in your go-bag or have you been shopping?"

Amber laughed. "Shopping. A girl can look good even when she's on the run and working on a tiny budget."

She did. And so did the brown-skinned man who Lauren tackled next with a cry of, "Royce!" All lean edges and sleek cheekbones. He wore a tailored blazer and stylish jeans in muted colors that made her wonder what Hollywood fantasy he'd spilled out of.

Amber was in an equally stunning outfit of tailored lines and bold colors. Was she from a New York magazine? Her makeup was perfect and complimented her outfit. Had she put mascara on him too or were his eyelashes naturally that perfect? How were these runway models friends with the rebel greasemonkey?

Long dreadlocks swung as he corralled Lauren in a tight hug. "Dang, girl. I hope the other guy looks worse." Suddenly he frowned. "What is that smell?"

Lauren groaned. "Long, awful story." Her expression hardened. "We need to talk." She glanced meaningfully at the crowd bumping them.

Amber nodded, directed them across the street and through hedges that opened into a nice green space. A fountain bubbled in the center of the cozy park. There were joggers, moms with strollers, and business people with phones and unbuttoned suits.

"They have a guiding stone." Lauren revealed as soon as they were more than twenty feet from the crowd.

Harsh and pitched as a strangled cat, Amber gasped. "No."

Lauren nodded vigorously, her short hair bouncing. She was abruptly on her toes, looking ready to run, eyes darting. "Yes. We can't sit still." She froze a moment. "You know what? It's just me it'll be tuned to. You guys can hide. I'll keep moving."

Nona hugged Trevor close, her heart twisting at the thought of Lauren being alone, of Lauren not being there to protect them.

"Yea, no." Amber grabbed a fistful of Lauren's cheap hoodie. "First of all, how the hell do you know they have a guiding stone? Meisenger didn't have one before today. There's no way he'd have one and not use it."

Lauren looked at Nona, uncertainty written across her. "A weaver just told us."

"What?!" shrieked at her.

A passing jogger eyed them.

Amber swallowed, watched the jogger for a few breaths.

"Literally right before you came out of the cafe. He told us he was sick of Meisenger and wanted to help, so he told us about the stone."

Amber stared at her. "A weaver?"

Another nod.

"They won't attack in public or during the day." The pale sky was glanced at. "We've got some time to set up an ambush.""Ambush?" Lauren squawked. "Have you lost your mind?"

"We have to get the stone from them." Amber growled. "Or would you rather be the one ambushed?" She flicked eyes to Nona. "While you're sleeping."

Anguish and terror boiled in Lauren's expression. "But it's just us. A full team is five knights. Five of the best hunters and fighters on this continent. I know you're the equivalent of three, but compared to them, I'm just a garden songbird. And we have them to protect!" She waved at Nona, Trevor, and Royce.

Amber's fist tightened, dragging Lauren closer. "You're damn right we have them to protect," hissed into her face. "That's why we have to get the stone."

Lauren's lip quivered. Her voice dropped so low that Nona barely heard, "But I don't want to kill anyone else."

Shock stared up at her for an eternity.

A line sparkled down Lauren's cheek. Reflex or instinct or just a need to move had Nona's hand lifting to swipe it away. Big, doe eyes fixed on her.

"You didn't do anything wrong." Nona found her voice. "Now. We have a plan. We can move forward."

"What's an ambush?" a voice asked at her hip.

Reflexively, her hand went to smooth Trevor's hair, though his curls refused to be tame. "It's where you lure someone into a trap."

Confusion crinkled his face, but was quickly replaced by understanding and fear. She'd taught him about snares and traps to catch animals out in the wild. He'd seen what happened to those rabbits. He'd refused to eat them too. Was it a good thing that he hadn't yet connected cows and pigs to the beef and pork he regularly enjoyed?

"Hey, you going to introduce us or what?" Amber let go of Lauren's hoodie to gently - not so gently - slap Lauren's arm.

"Oh." Lauren made a sheepish gesture. "Amber, Royce, this is Nona and Trevor." A deep breath. "Nona, Trevor, these are my best friends."

Royce smiled a big, friendly smile and dropped to a crouch. He offered a well-manicured hand. "Hi, Trevor. It's nice to meet you."

Trevor flinched at the immediate attention, yet he didn't shuffle away. He glanced up at her, then Lauren. "Your best friends, Lauren?"

She nodded. "Yep. Royce is the nicer one though."

Lauren's little grin, Amber's huff, and Royce's soft chuckle got Trevor smiling and taking Royce's hand. "Hi."

Pride glowed in her chest at her little boy's courage.

Amber followed suit and greeted Trevor, got a quicker handshake, then moved up to grasp Nona's hand. "You like the cold too, huh?"

Nona shrugged. "There's no bad weather. Only bad clothes," was her neutral response. Personally, she'd rather face frostbite than heat stroke.

Amber rolled her eyes, nudged Royce in the ribs. He glanced at Lauren with a chuckle.

Lauren grumbled under her breath.

Soft, yet firm, his hand closed around Nona's. "I bet she complains how you're taller than she is too."

Memory flashed of Lauren making jokes about Nona's long bones. "It was practically the first thing out of her mouth when we met."

A smirk spread Amber's perfect lips. The couple stared at an increasingly uncomfortable Lauren, their amusement underscored by deep affection.

"Hey, Ren, remember that abandoned factory we went to a couple years ago?" Royce asked when Lauren seemed ready to explode.

"You mean the one Amber couldn't go explore with you because she couldn't get vacation time and wouldn't let you go alone, so you dragged me?" Lauren replied. "And I still couldn't keep you from slipping on broken glass, falling, and needing fifteen stitches anyway?"

He nodded. "That's the one."

What did…

"You are fucking brilliant, husband!" Amber grabbed his face, planted a thrilled kiss on his mouth. "It's a perfect ambush site."

"But wouldn't staying in a public place be better?" Lauren questioned. "They won't use their armor in public."

"No. We'll exhaust ourselves looking over our shoulders all the time." Amber countered. "They'll be picking when they attack, Ren. That's why we're talking about an ambush, so we can control the where."

Lauren fidgeted, scuffed her feet. She lifted her gaze to Nona, her expression asking something. Permission? Guidance? "Okay." She said quietly. "But do you have a safe place for them?"

An uncertain frown pinched Amber's features.

Nona felt herself shifting closer to Lauren.

"With you." Royce broke the quiet. "We'll be right beside you." He smiled. "But maybe in the shadows, behind a nice, sturdy wall."

Chapter Twenty

The Old Marshmallow Factory

Temperate fall weather came to a sudden, inevitable demise at the hands of an angry storm. It slapped the group with icy wind as they dashed from Amber's car to abandoned factory. The twilight sky howled and dropped buckets of frigid rain, punctuating its rage with flashes of lightning. Old metal rattled. Broken windows crackled. And the entire place threatened to collapse on their heads.

Lauren expected Trevor to quiver and cling to his mom's side. Big eyes swung about the dusty, open area of the rusted factory. "Wow! Where are we?" Awe instead of fear poured off him. She shook her head as the kid bounced with excitement.

"Place used to be a marshmallow factory." Royce supplied. He grinned down at Trevor. "Doesn't look it, huh?"

"No way!" Trevor's eyes couldn't be bigger as he ogled the abandoned shadows.

"Yes way." Royce chuckled. One of his hands settled on Trevor's shoulder, the other gestured dramatically. "Where all this dust and broken glass is now, there used to be giant cauldrons and machines whipping up marshmallows all day long."

Trevor peered up at him. "What're cauldrons?"

"Iron cooking pots. They were so big, all five of us could've hung out in them."

"Whoa."

He pointed further away and punctuated his words with wide gestures. "There were huge conveyor belts leading from machine to machine. Funnels spit out gooey blocks onto the belts and they cooled on their way to the people that boxed and bagged them up to send to the stores."

"Neat!" Trevor got distracted by the tagging on the walls. "Why are there weird words? What's a..." he frowned. "Cu-"

"Oh man." Royce cut in. "Some people come to explore like me, some come here to hang out and paint, and not everyone puts nice stuff up. That word you see, that's a mean word. Only jerks use it."

"Oh." He studied the wall for a long moment. "Okay." The rest of the place got his attention again. "Do you think there are any old marshmallows left in here?"

"Maybe." Royce chuckled. "You want to go look?"

Trevor barely glanced at Nona before scampering after Royce.

"They have the stone by now." Lauren said quietly.

"Yea. You've been here before, know the layout a bit. Where's a good place to wait?" Amber asked.

"There's an office up there," Lauren gestured. Nona and Amber swung their flashlights up. Broken, dust-covered glass looked like teeth in the jaws of the managers' office. "You can hide up there while I play bait down here, drop down when they show."

Amber nodded. "Are there st..." she trailed off, looked at her, then Nona and shrugged. Her golden wings came out and dust billowed as she launched herself at the office.

"Oh cheese." Nona gasped.

"Yea. Amber's not just pretty. The bitch is a fucking queen." Lauren couldn't keep the envy out of her tone. Amber had it all. Looks, smarts, muscles, and golden feathers.

Nona looked sideways at her. "Not all beauty is the same."

A nice sentiment, she supposed. She shrugged and went about hunting for something to call a butt rest. Rain came in from the broken windows high above her. Irritated by the splashes and nervous about the Gierdes on their collective asses, she summoned armor to stay dry. It made her feel an ounce better. She found a chair, but it was bolted to the concrete. With only a brief thought for vandalism in the already vandalized place, she cut the bolts and took the chair to a spot closer to the office. She flopped into it. Immediately, a yawn erupted and her head started bobbing.

"She been out long?" A voice asked.

"A few minutes." Someone replied.

Voices? Who was out? What? Oh, had Gierdes shown up? That was nice. Gierdes?! Lauren snapped up, armor on, spear poised, breath coming in harsh pants.

"Whoa, Ren. Calm your tits, girl."

She swung toward the voice. Amber was there with her hands up. "Amber?"

"That'd be me." Amber smiled softly. "No Gierdes yet. You can put your weapon away."

Slowly, she took in Nona and wide-eyed Trevor, the dusty factory, the sound of rain beating against the metal roof. Royce waved from where he was crouched some distance away, camera out, safe and sound. Lauren closed her eyes, took a breath, and dismissed her magic. She slumped back into the chair.

Another yawn stretched out.

"She's gotten less sleep than me, I think." Nona said. A sympathetic yawn overtook her. "What I wouldn't give for a solid eight hours."

"Set yourself an hour alarm, Ren. Grab a nap." Amber suggested. "Even a team in town wouldn't get here for at least another hour. We both know that the team after you is probably back in Indiana if that cop reported seeing you. Otherwise, they're on their way to Iowa."

Half-closed eyes fumbled to bring up the clock on her phone, to set that alarm, then almost dropped it on the ground. The phone barely made it into her pocket before her eyes fully closed once more.

⚬

Booming thunder rattled Lauren awake. Lightning chewed across the sky, making the factory's shadows dance a broken jig. Gierdes could already be here. They'd never have heard their approach over the storm. Lauren scowled at the shadows, considered poking into them. Her alarm jangled its mocking tune until trembling fingers swiped it into silence.

"Balls." She breathed, swiped a hand over her face, swore at the scabs she pulled. Dropping her hand, she yawned and swore again as that pulled the scabs too. She felt like she hadn't slept at all. Where was Nona?

Only a few yards away. She was talking to Trevor about something. Up above, Lauren saw the faint red glow of Amber's lamp. A form moved across it, probably one of them pacing. No Gierdes yet. Amber was a better lookout than Lauren. She was better at everything than Lauren. That was why she had an incredible spouse and successful life.

Sighing, Lauren rose and stretched, waved a greeting to Nona, and decided to walk a perimeter check. Bugs skittered. Glass crunched. A few mice squeaked angrily at being disturbed. Nothing and no one jumped out and tried to kill her though. When she got back to the lamp, nothing had changed. She yawned and dropped back into her chair.

<hr>

Waiting for a fight that could go horribly wrong was officially Lauren's least favorite activity. Maybe not *the* worst. Watching Nona slowly turn into a human popsicle was definitely the worst. This was a close second.

From where Nona was sitting on a chunk of broken machinery, watching Trevor draw on the concrete wall with a marker that had appeared in his hands, she frowned and turned to look at Lauren. Flushing, Lauren dropped her gaze. How long had she been staring at them? Thinking about how fiercely she needed to protect them, wondering if she would feel this protective of any other mother and son in this situation. Her flush grew hotter as she considered the answer.

She looked at the office thirty feet up, where shattered windows overlooked the factory floor. Amber and Royce were there. Amber would drop down when the Gierdes showed up, thinking they'd cornered Lauren. Until then, Lauren, Nona, and Trevor were bait. Helpless bait.

Growling, Lauren summoned her spear and began simple training exercises. Amber wanted her to rest and conserve her energy, but Lauren couldn't rest, couldn't sleep, and couldn't keep still anymore. She needed the exercise to keep from thinking.

"Mom?" Trevor asked. "Are lokref superheroes?"

A surprised giggle came out of Nona. "I don't know if they all are, but Lauren is."

"Yea!" came his agreement. "That's what I thought."

Did he think superheroes always murdered unarmed people? Or was he okay with it? Or did he not really get it? How fast would Nona run when she could?

Her thoughts froze when her nose seized up and exploded in a cannon-shot of a sneeze. Then another and another and three more that left her lightheaded and woozy. Stupid allergies. She wiped her nose on a sleeve and wished for her summer allergy meds.

"Wow, Lauren! You sneeze a lot!" Trevor giggled.

"Yea," muttered back. Stupid allergies. She returned to her anxious watch, flicking her sight from window to window, down the hall, watching the sun's light retreat farther and farther until only flashlight and lamp kept the shadows at bay.

Shattered glass crunched under heavy feet and abruptly the abandoned building was full of yelling lokref, armor gleaming and weapons glinting, rushing at Lauren as a solid unit. She barely had her shield up when Amber dropped from above and broke the formation, taking on three of them at once, leaving two to Lauren.

Lauren's tired brain couldn't help the little snicker that always bubbled up whenever she saw a group of lokref in armor. They looked like they belonged at a hokey renaissance festival or a comic con. That usual amusement wasn't enough to prevent the adrenaline that flooded her at the sight of the leader. Not only was the lokref gigantic, tall and built like a bulldozer, but his armor was right out of a Japanese horror movie.

Scene-stealing, ancient samurai armor complete with blood-red demon mask. Huge tusks jutted out from a mouth grinning death at her.

An amplified howl curdled her blood as he hurtled right at Lauren. She shrieked and barely got her shield up in time to block the gargantuan sword that crashed against it. Aftershocks zinged down her arms, through her shoulders, and across her back.

The massive thing was already coming back around. Taking it with the shield was not an option; those zings would quickly turn painful. She ducked the swing, exchanged shield for spear and spun into attack. Another lokref attacked her flank, and the world devolved into dodging, feinting, jumping, spinning, and trying not to die.

She was struggling to breathe, to see through the sweat dripping in her eyes, when the awful realization occurred that she could barely fend the two lokref off, let alone launch a counterattack or help Amber or protect N–

Nona. Lauren risked a glance and took a hard kick to the stomach for it. She hit the ground hard and gasped. She tried to rise and run to Nona, but the two lokref on her refused to let her pass.

"Nona!" she wanted to yell. She didn't have the breath for it. Poor Nona was huddled in a corner, Trevor tucked behind, terror plain in every line of her.

Fear shifted to panic as one of the lokref that Amber kicked aside decided to give up that fight and stalked toward Nona instead. No! Lauren managed a whirling blow that swept the feet out from under the shorter lokref. She leapt over them, intending to rush to Nona's side. The demon armor blocked her path.

She dodged the sword, missed her counter, and was forced farther from Nona. Dammit! Another dodge, another miss, another push back. The lokref advancing on Nona conjured a massive battle axe, a weapon even more monstrous than the one thrusting at her.

There was nowhere for Nona to run, no way she could fend the Gierdes off. Lauren howled her frustration. She had to protect Nona! If only she could get over there! Lauren heaved at the lokref in front of her, but he parried and remained firmly in her face.

"Nona!" Absolute panic and terror rushed through Lauren. Nona needed help! What was the point of all this if she couldn't protect Nona? She had magic, dammit. *Magic*! If only she could give Nona her shield! She had to give Nona her shield.

The axe swung.

An ear-splitting *clang* vibrated through the air, and the world stopped. The lokref fighting Lauren paused to stare. Everyone else did as well.

Lauren's shield was hovering between Nona and the axe. Nona slowly blinked at it, reached out, and grasped it with both hands. Tingles went through Lauren. She shivered and stared, yet the shield didn't vanish. The axe-wielder was already swinging again. The weapon crashed into the shield, nearly crushed Nona to the ground, yet didn't kill her.

"What's happening?" The demon samurai in front of her demanded.

Lauren's heart pounded as she watched Nona stagger to her feet, shield in hand. She wobbled for a moment. Her frame stiffened, courage and determination hardening her. She stood bravely before the axe-wielder.

The axe lowered. Its owner turned to his commander. "Sir?"

Bright blue eyes appeared where the helm of Lauren's opponent was. A familiar face looked at her. Senior Knight Wells. Strong, well-liked, smart, and fair-minded. A good knight. He stared at the shield *still* in

Nona's hands. "We were told you two weren't bonded, that you'd broken the law."

"Awfully convenient, huh?" Amber barked into the heavy air. Her silver armor glinted in the lamplight.

Wells turned to her. "Why isn't their registration on file, Knight Garrett?"

"Because Ren probably forgot to mail it in." Amber sighed.

Registration? Bonded? What was Amber saying? "But w-"

"Or maybe it got conveniently lost." Amber spoke over her. "Have you ever heard of a lokref sharing her magic like that with someone she's not bonded to?" She waved at Nona, who was *still holding Lauren's shield.*

Air was getting pretty thin in her lungs.

"No," muttered Wells. His brow wrinkled in discomfort. "But our orders..."

"What exactly were your orders, Knight Wells?" demanded Amber. "To apprehend or dispose?"

Wells frowned.

"You ever notice how much Meisenger *really* doesn't like dark feathers?" Amber went on. "Lauren didn't have an enemy in the world until her wings showed up, then suddenly everyone hated her, suddenly Meisenger took a particular interest in her."

The lokref shifted uneasily.

Nona's gaze darted around. She edged toward Royce, one hand on Trevor's arm, keeping him behind, the other kept the shield up.

"And now here we are, Gierdes being sent to hunt down a bonded pair for doing what exactly? Trying to live their lives?" Amber huffed. "This is bullshit, Knight Wells, and you know it."

"I've never seen someone break nullen cuffs before." A lokref grumbled, not quietly.

"Me either."

"I didn't sign up to kill lokref, especially ones who haven't broken the law."

Lauren shivered.

Wells pointed his sword at Lauren. "You're bonded to her?"

She wanted to be. The thought made her flush. She'd never been more glad for her dark helm.

"Trent." Wells demanded an answer. "Are you bonded to Nona Hummel?"

"I..." she gulped. Shit-balls-fuck!

Amber was giving her a fucking-lie-already-look. Nona was silently begging her to do something. And Trevor… he was busy staring at all the armored lokref.

"Yes." Lauren lied.

"Bullshit!" Axe-wielder banished his weapon.

"Gelding!" Wells yelled. "What are you doing putting your weapon up?"

Gelding threw his arms out. "Screw this, Wells. I'm not going to kill bonded lokref that haven't done anything wrong. And you aren't planning on it either. The internet was quiet about lokref until Tibbits kidnapped a bondmate!"

Wells stared for another moment, then he too banished his weapon and armor. "Get the fucking paperwork in, Trent."

The whole team released their magic, leaving jeans and sneakers where bulletproof armor had just been.

"Better yet, I'll help you file it. That way I can honestly say I made sure the law was followed."

Lauren stared. "You will?"

He looked distinctly uncomfortable. "More than just this operation has had a bad smell to it," was said quietly. Louder, "Pack up. Ramsey, you and I will escort these fine people home. The rest of you, return to station."

"Sir?" A broad-shouldered man questioned.

"In case Tibbits thinks we failed our mission and sends another team. We'll be there to make sure there isn't more miscommunication."

Muttering and casting looks, dark and intrigued, at Lauren's group, most of the team headed out into the storm. Wells and another man, who must be Ramsey, stood muttering quietly by the exit.

"That's it?" Nona wondered. "Just like that, they're leaving us alone?"

Lauren looked at Nona, got distracted by the shield. How? How had she given Nona her shield? Her magic hummed bright and fierce at the connection.

"Looks like they are." Amber crossed her arms.

"Oh. Well." Nona lifted the shield. "This is getting a bit heavy. Lauren, can you…"

Her magic hissed. She couldn't banish it, not until she physically retrieved it. Nona scooped up her kid and squeezed him close.

"Mommy!" He objected.

Nona let him slide back to the ground and looked at Lauren. "What now?"

Um. Lauren struggled with a lead tongue.

"Why don't we go back to our hotel?" Royce suggested. "We can get cleaned up, order some pizza, get some sleep. Then we can drive up to Lauren's place tomorrow?"

She nodded, grateful.

Amber slung arms around Royce and kissed him soundly. His hands trembled for a moment before fisting into her shirt. She could relate. Post-adrenaline shivers were starting in her too.

Warmth along her side drew her attention. When had Nona gotten so close? How terrorized was she? Wh-

"That was awesome!" Trevor whooped. "Lauren, how'd you do that? Can I hold it too?"

Could he *hold* it? He was *excited*? What kind of planet did this kid live on?

"Is this kid serious?" Amber demanded from around Royce's shoulder.

"You know, I kinda get where he's coming from." Royce coughed out a laugh. "Magic, action, *and* his mom being a badass. What's not to get excited about?"

"And you took pictures the whole time, didn't you?" Lauren almost said out loud. She caught herself with only a strangled noise escaping.

Amber raised an eyebrow, but Nona spoke first. "Thank you."

"What?"

A smile graced her frazzled features. "You saved us again."

Not that she had any idea *how*. "Um." She made an awkward motion with her shoulders. "Yea."

Nona shifted closer, pressing their arms together, and leaned down. Lips touched Lauren's cheek. Lauren froze, and the lips lingered. Her body followed the lips when they finally retreated. Cheeks pink, Nona straightened.

"Are we going to Lauren's house first?" Trevor bounced on his toes.

"We'll drive up in the morning." Nona told him.

"Cool!"

"Trent." Wells spoke. "We noticed only one car out there. Can the five of you fit in it or would you rather share our SUV?"

They could, technically. They had. It wasn't comfortable. The back of the little coupe wasn't made for tall people. Stretching out in the SUV was tempting, yet it was a Gierdes' vehicle, driven by Gierdes.

Warmth from Nona continued to spread across Lauren through their touching arms. Nona and Trevor were alive. Amber and Royce were safe. The Gierdes had dropped arms and armor. No one was fighting. Her eyelids drooped.

"Why don't we table that idea for later? I'm not comfortable with it right now." Nona said.

"Yea." Good idea. Delay decisions until after sleep. Lauren yawned, stretching her jaw wide, making it and her ears pop. Her body listed toward Nona, her head wanting to drop to her inviting shoulder.

"Okay." Wells nodded. "We'll follow behind." He gestured at the exit. "Lead the way."

Amber took point, but not before giving Lauren and Nona a victorious smile. Or was that a smirk? Well, she had come up with all the good ideas. She deserved to smirk about them. They dashed from door to door, trying not to get totally drenched. Shoulders damp, they squeezed into Amber's car, and endured the cramped half hour trip in silence.

The hotel was cheap, small, and most of its rooms were booked despite being on the edge of town. There was some convention nearby taking up all the double rooms. Ramsey and Wells didn't seem perturbed by having to share a king bed. Lauren was simply ready to plow face-first into a mattress and stay horizontal for the next week until she realized that she had to share with Nona.

Wells faced them, his hands fiddling with the key card. His room was right next door. Amber's was down the hall. "One of us will be awake and on guard at all times." His gaze drifted across them. "Please don't find a way to be alone and noisy. I don't want to hear that." He turned and strode to his door. A quick swipe of his key and the two Gierdes vanished.

Amber laughed. "Come on, Royce. I don't care who hears us." She tossed a grin over her shoulder, winked at Nona, grinned wider at Lauren's scowl.

What were they smiling about… oh. Heat blossomed up her neck. Everyone thought she and Nona were a couple. Even Amber, though she should know better. Or was Amber pushing Lauren to try a relationship? Did she not see how *not* gay Nona was? How badly Nona deserved someone who wouldn't constantly put her and Trevor's life in danger? Someone who had their life together, who had a decent future ahead of them?

"It's okay." Nona spoke quietly. "I'll just get an extra blanket and sleep on the floor. Not much worse than backpacking."

"Is the bed small?" Trevor asked.

Nona pushed open the door. "Not small, but three people won't be comfortable."

"This is our room?" Trevor stared. "That bed is huge!"

Compared to her tiny bed at home, yea. She spied an armchair, the fabric faded, wood heavily scuffed. She dropped her bag and dropped onto the thin cushion. The springs squawked, yet didn't poke through the fabric. She sighed, let her eyes shut, and jerked at a touch on her arm.

Nona was there, a contrite expression on her tired face. "Sorry. I know you're exhausted, but I wanted to ask what you want for dinner before you fell asleep and the restaurants close."

"Uh?" Lauren couldn't think. "Anything but cabbage. I hate cabbage."

"Sure thing. Why don't you lay down? It has to be more comfortable than a chair?" Nona tugged and maneuvered Lauren from chair to bed. The moment she hit the pillow, she was out.

Nona set her empty Chinese food carton aside and frowned at Lauren's prone form. The woman hadn't even twitched when the food had arrived, barely grunted when Trevor tried shaking her awake. Poor thing. She'd sacrificed so much to protect them! Her safety, her job, her future, her integrity. Granted, she might have a job when she got home. Not likely. Her boss letting her off the hook the first time was a huge surprise! How many bosses wouldn't fire someone for a no-call, no-show? Especially a second time?

Lauren would have to get a new job, would have to lie to the Gierdes for the rest of her life, might never bond with anyone because of it. She was beaten and bloody. She'd have scars to lie about for years. She'd known all of that from the beginning, that she might have to sacrifice everything, yet she'd done what she did anyway.

Cheese and rice, Lauren was incredible. She was so selfless, brave, and strong! The idle crush Nona had been nursing was full blown now, but Lauren deserved more than some awkward mountain woman. She deserved a queen, a woman as strong and courageous as herself, a woman who could give her everything.

But… Nona chewed her lip, twisted fingers into her sweater. But Nona wanted her. She was selfish like that. And being with Nona wasn't that bad. She had a whole slew of good qualities! She was physically fit, not ugly, could do all the domestic stuff like cooking and cleaning, and was definitely smart. She had her own house and business, could give Lauren access to empty skies. She could tell her she was gorgeous and wonderful every day. She…

Had a whole truckload of baggage, a kid, a mortgage, a horrible ex, a job that took her away for sometimes weeks at a time, a problem with Lauren's messy room. Wow. That was something she worried about? The stacks of papers and scattered mail on Lauren's floor? And what about how Lauren would react to Nona's sexuality? Not everyone was as small-minded and hateful as Duncan, yet what if Lauren was too?

She shuddered thinking about it.

"Mom, I'm done." Trevor was folding up his carton. He'd eaten maybe half. "I'll put the rest in the fridge with Lauren's." He did that, went to the bathroom, brushed his teeth, and slipped under the covers.

Nona's heart fluttered. Holy macaroni. She stared at the adorable sight of her son tucking close to their hero. She stared until her food grew cold and yawns overtook her. The bed had plenty of room for her. She gave the unwelcoming floor a glance, decided to hell with it, and crawled into the bed. Trevor tucked between them, Nona allowed herself the delightful fantasy of doing this often in the future. The three of them. Together.

City light streamed into Meisenger's office, cast a glare on his phone, made him snarl and get up to yank the curtains closed. He was expecting a status report from Tibbits soon. It better be a good report. He couldn't afford yet another new phone. He touched the bandage across his palm, angrily yanked his attention from it, and paced his oak-paneled office.

The moment Tibbits' call came through, he slammed the accept button and glared at her face on the screen. "Is it done?"

"Sir." Tibbits greeted. "No."

"What?!" he howled. "What happened?"

"The team retreated without capturing or eliminating either target."

"Why?" growled out.

Tibbits swallowed. "Trent gave Hummel her shield, from the other side of the battlefield."

What? How?

"They claim they're bonded."

"When?"

Tibbits hesitated. "Sir, I'm not certain if they're bluffing or not, but the team believed it. Wells is personally escorting them to Trent's home in Iowa and plans to help them file their registration."

The phone shattered against the far wall. Dammit! Damn the black-wing!

Chapter Twenty-one

Family

An elbow jarred Lauren awake. It drove the breath from her, made her jump clean out of bed, and thud hard to the floor. Up and down her body, pain throbbed protest. From her face to toes, there was something that hurt, and raising her hand to her tender face brought a waft of stench that made everything worse.

"What the…"

She sniffed at her hands. Oh. Oh it was that awful slop she'd fallen in yesterday. Yesterday. Groggy eyes blinked around the shadowy room. Yellow light snuck in through shabby curtains, exposing more than one moth-eaten hole. A hint of old carpet and mildew graced her sinuses as her brain cycled through senses. Cheap hotel. Right. The rest of yesterday's events came to her, and she stood with a suppressed groan.

On the other side of the bed, the clock glowed 3:37AM. Too early. She needed more sleep. There was a small body in her spot on the bed now. And the other side held another, longer, curvier. Hadn't Nona's plan been to sleep on the floor? Lauren looked at the corner where a blanket was laid out sans Nona. Why? Had something scared her?

Unless she wanted to wake the woman up, she'd have to wait for answers. In the meantime, her bladder was awake, and after dealing with that, her stomach woke with an angry growl. Nona'd ordered food, hadn't she? Where was it? She muffled a crow of victory when she found it in the mini-fridge. Eat it cold or use the microwave? She gave the sleepers a considering glance. Not here. Shoes and hoodie were thrown on, and she snuck out. Near the lobby, there was a little common room that had a table and a couple ragged armchairs, a microwave, toaster, and coffee pot.

The front office kid gave her a friendly wave from behind a big textbook. Notebooks, pens, and highlighters surrounded him. What was he studying? Her stomach bugled for her attention. Okay, okay. Feed the beast, talk to the stranger later. If she couldn't go back to sleep.

Food was tossed in and buttons were poked. Her foot tapped an impatient beat as she willed the microwave to zap faster. An eternity later, it dinged. Hot food in hand, she flopped into an old armchair, dug in with a flimsy plastic fork, and moaned at the fresh garlic zing. Nice. She'd been expecting cheap shit like the hotel, but Nona had found a decent restaurant. Damn, what would it be like to have Nona in her life every day? To have Nona to go to when… No. Stop it. Nona would be returning home to Colorado.

They could talk on the phone if Nona wanted, probably should make a few calls to keep up appearances. Meisenger must be foaming at the mouth by now. At the repeated failure to snuff her life out. He'd take any excuse to try again.

The grim detour her thoughts were taking killed her appetite. Doggedly, she managed to finish and sat there with her dark thoughts and imagined nightmares until she focused on the coffee pot. Could she get back to sleep? Her eyes felt like concrete blocks, heavy and gritty, and she couldn't keep her eyelids up. But behind them, the previous days lurked. Blood and Gierdes, the threat against Nona and Trevor, the cold future ahead…

Nope. It was much too loud behind closed eyes. She brewed a pot of coffee and soaked in her first cup sitting in the empty room. The second one poured, the emptiness of the room got to her; she needed company, didn't want the company of a stranger, and went back to her room, slipped in, and sighed at the company of familiar people. The urge to crawl in and cuddle with her companions got even stronger. So did the fear of rejection.

She ended up grabbing the blanket off the floor and sitting in the chair, wrapping the blanket around herself, and crying into her coffee.

Morning eventually came and outside noises began to filter in. At six, shortly before Nona had planned to rise, she got in the shower to hide her puffy eyes and make an attempt at scrubbing off the rotting meat stench. She scrubbed until her skin was raw and the water turned cold. Even then, the rank odor lingered. Dammit. What was it people talked about to get rid of skunk? Tomato juice? She needed a bath in tomato juice. There was complimentary hotel lotion. It smelled like oranges. Maybe it would help.

She toweled herself down, slathered on lotion, wrinkled her nose at the fake oranges dancing in rot, sighed, and threw on clothes. The bathroom was given up to Nona, and she went to her phone in search of answers about tomato juice. It took a full minute for the search page to load. A minute after clicking a promising link, and it still hadn't loaded more than the site's banner. Stupid farm country! She missed the city and its decent data access. Ugh!

She was about to throw her useless phone at the wall when a touch on her arm had her eeping, jumping, and almost punching Nona.

Her hand zipped back. "Sorry. I called your name, but you were super focused on your phone."

Oh. "Um. Yea. Signal here is shit. I can't get this webpage to open." Lauren grumbled.

Nona's lips pursed, her head canted. "Looking for help sleeping?"

"What?"

"I heard you get up in the middle of the night." Her hand moved as though to touch Lauren again. "You never came back to bed."

"Why were you in the bed?" She turned it back around on her. "Thought you wanted the floor?"

Nona looked away, seemed to fold in on herself. "I was lonely, and the bed was big enough."

Oh. Yea. She could understand that. She nodded and looked back at her stubborn phone. An error popped up. *Server timeout. Unable to connect.* Dammit.

Nona's hand moved, this time making contact with Lauren's arm. "Lauren?"

She looked up. Her breath stuttered at the tender expression she saw, the vulnerability in Nona's eyes. "Y-yea?" She swallowed.

"I..." Nona bit her lip. Her eyes closed, and she sighed. "Could we stay with you a few days? I can get an air mattress and stay in the basement. I could use a few days to sleep and gather myself, so could Trevor. He'll need some coaching about how not to talk about... what happened."

"Of course! Is he okay?"

"He'll be talking about your shield and that fight for weeks. I'm not sure if it'll hit him later or not about what could really have happened."

Lauren felt the fingers on her arm fiddling with the hoodie's seam. "I'm worried about his reaction to being apart from you too soon."

From being away from her? But she was the problem! "What? Shouldn't he want to be as far as possible from me? I'm just a problem magnet."

The hand squeezed. "You're his hero, Lauren. You're my hero," came quieter. "We aren't ready to be far from your protection yet."

She gaped until a text from Amber blipped. She stared at the screen without reading it. Another text blipped.

Wake up. Let me in.

Lauren unlocked the door to find Amber waiting. She didn't say anything, pushed past Lauren, turned the TV on, nodded at the news anchor that popped up, put the volume at just below too loud, then faced them. "You should let them see you being affectionate." She spoke quietly.

"Being what?" Lauren balked.

Amber rolled her eyes. "Look like a couple, touch and hold hands and shit."

"What?!" Disbelief coughed out. No. No. No. No!

"It'll be more believable," came her calm rejoinder.

"What will be more believable?" Trevor asked. He turned off the bathroom light and jumped to the bed.

How had this day gotten worse? She'd rather be fighting Wells again!

"That Lauren isn't always a grouch." Amber smiled.

"Rude." She was a perfectly nice person when her life wasn't a living hell. "And you know damn well that not everyone who bonds is dating. We don't need to put on a show."

"I do, but Nona isn't a rich CEO or princess or mob boss paying you for lifetime protection." Amber deadpanned. "What other reason are they going to believe for *you* bonding her?"

"Why do you need to do that?" Trevor asked from where he was lounging on the bed.

From behind him, Nona mouthed *I'm sorry.* "Just until the paperwork is in, pumpkin."

Amber grimaced, probably chastising herself for being careless around the kid, just like Lauren was. Dumbass. One wrong question from Trevor could blow this whole thing up! It *could still get worse.* So much worse if Wells found out they were lying.

Trevor frowned at them, up at his mom. "Is Lauren coming to live with us?"

"No, she's not."

"But she's family now, isn't she?"

"Well..." Nona looked lost.

He switched to frowning at Lauren. "You said if you bonded with Mommy, you'd be family. If you aren't family now, that means you lied to the scary men. Why did you lie? Don't you want to be family?" Tears were in his eyes now. "Aren't we good enough?"

Good enough? Her heart tried to claw out of her chest to go hug him. "You are more than good enough, Snowman. All I want to do is protect you. That's what family does, they protect each other." For the rest of her life. Unless some miracle happened, and Xuande's Law was abolished. Then Trevor and Nona would be free of her and her problems. That talk about her being their hero was nonsense. A real hero didn't let her problems hurt her friends.

He sniffled, and tears spilled over, tracing lines down his cheeks. "You didn't lie?"

"No." She shook her head. "No, Snowman. We're family now."

He suddenly flew off the bed to throw himself at her, latching arms around her waist, and crying into her shirt. Knocking at the door only tightened his hold. Amber was closest, and she peeked through the eyehole first. *Wells*, was mouthed back.

"Don't worry, Trev." Nona's tone was gentle. She moved close enough to put an arm around his shoulders and kiss his hair, to put her other arm around Lauren's waist, though she didn't and the lack made Lauren wish harder than ever that life was different. "We'll have plenty of time to talk about this at Lauren's house. We'll finish our vacation there."

"Do I get to tell Aunt Lee how Lauren is family now?" He perked up.

Nona made a noise in the back of her throat. "We'll talk about that too."

"But we are family now?" He pressed.

"Yes, we are." Nona said softly, firmly. So close, her eyes were intense, vividly bright and full of determination. "And we'll protect each other."

"Okay."

Amber opened the door. On the other side, Wells raised a hand in greeting. "I didn't think you were still sleeping as loud as you have that TV, but I wanted to make sure you were up anyway. I'd like to be on the road in an hour. The sooner we get this over with, the better."

He gestured across the road. "There's an IHOP over there if you want pancakes. We're going."

Nope. Not her thing and also, IHOP was gross.

"Pancakes?" Trevor chirped. "I want pancakes!"

"Sure, pumpkin. We can do pancakes. We are on vacation, after all." Nona smiled bright enough to show her dimple. She glanced at Lauren.

"Okay." She could eat an omelette or something. IHOP couldn't screw up eggs and sausage that badly.

Amber started laughing. "About what I said earlier? Forget it. There's no need." And she kept laughing as she walked out the door.

Wells gave Amber a look, shook his head, and held the door in obvious invitation.

"What's that supposed to mean?" Nona muttered.

Not a clue. Lauren shrugged. "Come on, Snowman, let's go get you pancakes."

The restaurant was slightly more pleasant than the dingy examples back home. Better owner or management or something. It inspired her to order extra servings of eggs and sausage and nearly ordered another. She sucked down three cups of coffee and paid before Nona could touch the receipt. Pit stops in the restaurant toilet, then again at the hotel, and the vehicles were loaded up.

The idea of being crammed into the back of the coupe for more than thirty minutes eventually decided Lauren on getting into Wells' SUV. She expected a similar line of thought drove Nona or she wouldn't be poring over their bags, making sure she had everything she or Trevor could possibly need for the remainder of the trip.

"Text me when they're gone and we'll drop your car off." Amber whispered.

Lauren nodded into the hug. She had the spare phone that Amber had given her last night stuffed in her back pocket. She'd called Keith from the restaurant's bathroom and told him how she'd managed to find a way out of her problem, that Amber would be coming by to give him money for the car she'd destroyed -as well as the location of where she'd dumped it, in case he wanted to sell the rest for parts or be prepared for if cops called about it- and pick up Lauren's car. Best best-friend ever.

That Amber was going to make things right with Keith and Jeannie and would be bringing Lauren's car home was a huge weight off her shoulders. She had enough to deal with. She needed to replace Nona and Trevor's phones, find a new job, probably sell her Acura, a thousand other things, *and* call her parents to tell them she'd bonded with Nona. Balls! Lying to Mom and Dad about something that important made her want to vomit, but it was way too dangerous to let them know the truth. They didn't need the responsibility or the danger that came with knowing it.

At least the weather matched her mood. It was raining again. A cold drizzle that warned of the frigid months ahead. Lauren glanced at the feather poking out of Nona's hair. The black and scarlet feather.

It was common enough for lokref to give their bondmates a feather. It couldn't carry the promise, didn't need to, not with the bond, yet it was symbolic. The tradition dated back centuries. A displayed feather was like a ring, even more powerful for a lokref. Other lokref would see the feather and know that they were bonded. Or that they were safe to talk to about magical matters.

Nona must have felt her gaze. She looked up from the pad of paper she was writing on. It was hotel stationary. She'd been working at it when Lauren had stumbled from the bathroom. Figuring out what to tell her friends and family about her disappearance. They must all be worried sick. Poor Nona. Stuck in this shitty situation.

Lauren attempted a smile. It must not have been as sick as she felt since Nona smiled back, a pretty, soft expression that made her eyes glitter. Lauren jerked away before she fell into those eyes. Stupid green sinkholes.

She went back to the landscape, the fields and cows and occasional town. What was it like to live a normal life? Not have magical problems on top of the already difficult mundane ones like paying bills and being gay?

"Bathroom break!" Broke into her thoughts. Half-asleep doze. Her eyes fluttered open, and she yawned, angering her injuries as she groaned upright from her slump against the door. Ibuprofen was not cutting it. Did Jeff have any painkillers left from when he broke his collarbone last year?

Bright lights of a gas station poked through the gloom, made her blink and curse the dense, grey clouds above. Rain pounding on metal drowned out nearly everything until she was in the fluorescent buzz of the store. She found her way to the refreshingly clean restroom and relieved herself. A woman washing her hands squeaked at Lauren's appearance. Another walked in after the squeaker hustled out, carefully perused Lauren's face, glanced at the door.

"I saw who you came in with. They look like hard men." The woman said quietly. "Do you need help?"

Help? Yea, she did. She needed an entirely new life.

"It's okay to ask for help if you need it." The woman didn't move closer, didn't block the door, and offered only a calm smile. "I work as a counselor at the local shelter."

Oh. Oh! She thought Lauren was an abuse victim. Close, but nothing for a human counselor. What if she was lokref? Lauren gave her another lookover. There was a pearly white feather hanging from a bracelet.

"Nice feather. Mine are all black. No one's a big fan of them." Lauren said.

"You're lokref."

She nodded.

A fresh perusal was given her. She reached into her purse, pulled out a business card, and handed it to Lauren. "Dr. Amanda Fawkes."

"Lauren." She took the card and shook her hand. "Lauren Trent."

"Oh Mylanta. Oh." Dr. Fawkes' mouth fished. "You're, you're *her.*" She sucked in air, blinked rapidly, and gathered herself. "I saw the video. Those injuries make sense now." She frowned. "How did you get out of nullen cuffs? They were nullen, weren't they? Did your bondmate call you? Is that why you aren't in jail now? You were obeying the call? Surely they can't hold that against you. But if those were nullen cuffs you broke out of, why were you being arrested and why are you walking free now?"

The barrage of questions had her reeling. How to answer? Not the truth. What?

The door opened again, admitting Nona and Trevor.

"Lauren," Trevor whined, drawing out the vowels. "How much longer til we get to your house? I'm tired of…" He noticed Dr. Fawkes and bit his lip.

"Go on, Trev." Nona ushered him into a stall, though her eyes were on Lauren. "Go pee." She brushed close, whispered softly, "You okay?"

Not in the slightest. Lauren shrugged. Brow creased, Nona cast a glance at the woman, a clear question. Lauren shook her head. Nona gave Lauren another perusal before slipping into a stall.

"It was nice meeting you, Ms. Trent." Dr. Fawkes smiled politely. "You have my card if you need anything."

"Thanks. I, uh, I will." Lauren gave an awkward wave.

She nodded, left, and the moment the door shut, Nona's stall opened. "Who was that?" was whispered quiet enough that Trevor might not hear it over his gurgling pee.

Lauren's response was equally quiet. "She works in a women's shelter. She thought I was an abuse victim when she first saw me."

"You *have* been abused," came an angry hiss. The fury of it stunned Lauren rigid. Nona's cheeks were blotchy red, and her eyes blazed. "You've been beaten, manipulated, and threatened. Over nothing!"

Trevor pushed his stall open and went to the sink. He gave them a funny look. Nona snapped her jaws together. Silently, she turned to the sink and washed her hands with too much vigor. She made overly cheerful talk about lemon bars she'd bake later to cheer everyone up. With dry hands, Trevor took hold of both theirs and pulled them outside.

Where had that anger come from? Nona chewed her pen, peeked over at Lauren, who was fast asleep again. At the mere glance, she felt her cheeks heating. Ah. Okay. Her crush on Lauren had officially crossed the border from mild attachment to falling in love. Falling in love! She didn't even know if Lauren was single or interested! Cheese and rice.

Another peek. She had evidence that Lauren found her attractive. Or at least that Lauren thought her eyes were pretty. Lauren had never spoken of a girlfriend or anyone she had a thing for. Not that they'd had much opportunity to discuss anything except topics relevant to staying alive or finding Trevor. What kind of woman was Lauren looking for? Was she looking? Was all that flirting back on the trail in Colorado a regular thing for her? Did she flirt without knowing it? Had it even been flirting?

Focus, woman. Thinking about Lauren wasn't why there was a pen and paper in hand. She needed to figure out something safe to tell Lee, her mom, and everyone else who would've been freaking out over the past few days. She'd had car trouble. They all knew that. She'd stopped in Des Moines, struck a deal with a mechanic, and borrowed a vehicle. She should have arrived at Becky's two days ago. If Becky or Lee had called the police to report her missing, would the police have said that they were already looking? That they had a report that Lauren Trent had kidnapped her and Trevor?

If they had, how would Nona play that off? Blame Duncan? Say that he'd gotten jealous or angry that Nona was flirting with Lauren? How he could have learned about Lauren was another problem. Both her and Trevor's phones had broken, been stolen, that she hadn't remembered anyone's phone number, so when she'd had to stay a few days somewhere, she couldn't call anyone? Lee would slap her for lying. Nona had her sister's, mom's, and a dozen other numbers memorized.

No one would believe half the truth. Who would kidnap Nona Hummel? Aside from Duncan's mother? Even breathing about kidnapping would lead to talk of who to blame, where to send police, of lawyers and jail time and a mountain of stress.

What if she got Lauren to expose lokref? There was already that video of her escaping Gierdes. If they exposed magic, the commandant would probably discover that Lauren really wasn't bonded to Nona. What would happen then?

She wanted to scream in frustration! Being around Lauren was fraught with trouble. What would an actual relationship with her be like? Worse?

Better?

Focus! She would call Lee as soon as she was back in Des Moines. Or text her. Yes. Text her. A lame apology about how some trouble came up. Lee would immediately call and scream at her. It c-

"No!" Lauren barked, shooting upright, her shield materializing, sending Nona's pen flying, making Wells jerk the wheel. She blinked and looked around. "Wha..." She focused on Nona, and her breath caught. "Oh." Her frame slumped, the shield vanished, and she scrubbed at her face, flinched. "Sorry. I was, uh, dreaming."

"Shit!" Wells growled.

Lauren's arm twitched, as though about to flip him the bird, but she shook her head and set her gaze out the window.

"It's okay, Lauren." Trevor was reaching out. When she turned her gaze to him, he pat her arm. "Just a bad dream."

Lauren looked ready to fly away. Or wrap him up in a hug and never let go. Her hands played with her hoodie pocket. "Yea. Just a bad dream," didn't sound like she believed it, especially not with how her eyes darted to the Gierdes up front.

His gaze followed, and he stuck his tongue out at Wells. Nona choked on whether to chastise or applaud. They fell into a discussion of what they would do once they were out of the car, and Nona returned to romantic thoughts. Should she tell Lauren that she was interested in a relationship? Absolutely!

She nearly laughed aloud at how quickly she decided on that. Her stifled noise got a glance from Lauren, but no questions. Her lips were quirked at Trevor's enthusiasm over exploring the corn fields. Sweet peaches and cream, she had nice lips. Were they always that kissable looking?

She tore her eyes away before she got caught. Wait. Didn't she want to get caught now? Wasn't that the point? Amber had suggested making a show of flirting. Nona was more than happy to oblige. Lauren was reticent, probably because she was an awkward muffin like that. This was only complicating matters. Lauren would think any flirting that Nona was doing was for the Gierdes' benefit. Nona would have to be blunt and say *exactly* what she wanted.

Her heart galloped at the following thought of how Lauren would react. Would she be thrilled, disgusted, angered? Was she against the idea of romance altogether? Was that why Lauren hated the idea of fake flirting? Her single bed at home, was that because Lauren only did one night stands at hotels, because she'd chosen a life of solitude? The urge to scream boiled in her throat, and she had to cough to clear it.

How much further? Another two hours? Not screaming, not professing her attraction, she somehow made herself focus and decide what to say to her family and friends.

Chapter Twenty-two

Paperwork

There was a single, relieved groan as Wells parked in Lauren's driveway. The occupants tumbled out and sucked in deep lungfuls of brisk, clean air. Someone had farted for most of the last hour. Nona suspected Trevor. Or the stone-faced Ramsey.

"Hey, T-"

The sound of wood cracking on wood snapped everyone into rigid poses, whirled them toward the sight of a man rushing out of the side of the garage. He had shoulders the size of Utah and carried a sledgehammer almost as big. Around him bolted two huge, angry, barking dogs that had Nona sweeping Trevor behind her and wishing for an ice axe.

"Max! Bubba!" Lauren grinned. "Hey, buddies!" Their barking switched from threatening to excited, and their tails windmilled hard enough their butts did a silly side to side dance. Trevor laughed and squirmed out of her grasp to join Lauren getting licked by the excited beasts.

"Ren?"

"Yea, h-"

"Ren!" Another voice called out, and a woman in pale pink scrubs ran from garage to Lauren. She swept her into a tight embrace, kissing her cheeks, crying, demanding answers, asking what the hell had happened, who the hell were these people, and why the hell had Lauren worried everyone?

Was this woman why Lauren chafed at fake flirting? A girlfriend she hadn't mentioned? The thought hit her guts like an avalanche.

"Ren, what the hell?" The man holding the hammer demanded.

"We apologize." Wells' tone was contrite, with a professional firmness to it that surprised Nona. "Ms. Trent and Ms. Hummel accidentally got involved in a situation we had to protect them from. Now that it's safe, we've brought them home."

"A situation?" The woman demanded.

"Yes, ma'am. Agent Wells, FBI." He flashed an official-looking badge. "My partner, Agent Ramsey." His face didn't change as he flashed his own badge. "We're here to escort your friends home and help Ms. Trent fill out some paperwork." He held up a hand as Grace's mouth opened and the hammer shifted again. "I can't discuss the situation and neither can your friends, so please don't ask. It's a confidential case."

He ushered them to the door as Trevor tugged on her shirt. "Mom? What's FBI?"

"A type of police, pumpkin. I think he's going to help us explain where we've been so Lauren's friends don't ask questions we can't answer." Nona glanced at their retreating backs. "Remember that lokref and everything that's happened the past few days is a secret. We only talk about it with Lauren or each other. No one else unless Lauren says it's okay."

"A secret. I remember."

She hoped so. Trevor's personality didn't make him prone to gossip. He told his auntie almost everything though. Nona needed to prepare for that eventuality. In the meantime, she smiled at Lauren, who was holding the door open, and hustled Trevor inside the house. "FBI?" she breathed by Lauren.

"I should have remembered. Sorry." Lauren whispered as she turned to let the door close. "He'll spin a believable pedestrian story. It helps keep the lokref secret." Her expression lightened, and she spoke louder, "Come on, I'll introduce you to my roommates."

Pedestrians? Was Lauren being condescending? She didn't sound like it, but what else could it mean? Answers didn't reveal themselves before she was being introduced to Grace and Jeff.

"Oh, Lauren's told me so much about you!" gushed out. Nona felt a bright smile curve as she held out her hand. "You both seem like amazing people. The house is gorgeous, Jeff. And Grace, I love your decor. I'm Nona. My son Trevor."

Confused eyes glanced at Lauren as the roommates accepted Nona's introduction. "Thank you." Jeff spoke first. "I'm pretty proud of what I built." Pleasure lit his face, framing a gorgeous smile and extremely white teeth. Were all of Lauren's friends painfully attractive? Was it a side effect of her own perfect packaging?

Grace's smile seemed more a habit than intended friendliness. Her lovely honey-brown eyes weren't aggressive though, merely wary. She softened to bend down for Trevor. "Hi, Trevor." Her tone was gentle, her offered hand non-threatening. "It's a pleasure to meet you."

He glanced at Lauren first, much to Nona's swooning surprise. "Hi." He accepted the hand. "You live with Ren?"

"Yes, though some days her dirty laundry makes me regret it."

Lauren rolled her eyes.

Trevor grinned. "Mom's laundry stinks too, especially after she comes home from work in the summer."

Embarrassment blasted her neck and face as chuckles danced around her.

"I don't know why you single me out." Lauren complained. "Jeff's is as bad as mine."

"He never let his build up in his room until it was so bad I suffocated."

"That was one time!"

"You didn't do laundry for a month, you skeezy lump. And then you left your nasty laundry mountain in your room when you went to visit your parents for a week. When the power went out during that storm, it went from bad to fermented vomit air!"

"It was summer, and there was a tornado. It wrecked a power station." Jeff supplied. "We didn't get power back for a few days."

"Between the heat and the stench, I had to get a hotel room." Grace scowled.

Jeff grinned wider. "I donated what was left in the freezer to the fire station and slept on a cot in my work trailer."

"Is this how the story about the incense started?" Nona asked.

"Yes!" Grace gestured widely. "I burned a few sticks of incense to cover up the garbage heap, and she flipped out."

Nona tried to stifle her laughter behind a hand. Lauren glared at her. It made her snort, and the dam broke, laughter billowing out, triggering Trevor's and the roommates'. Lauren's glare lost its heat. She rolled her eyes, sighed, and moved toward the kitchen door. "I'm going to get a drink. If anyone wants to do something other than tease me, they can come too."

Trevor bounded after, asking about juice.

Wells spun a crazy story about a classified investigation the trio had stumbled into. They'd been taken into protective custody for a few days until they could be safely brought home. There were non-disclosure agreements and a lot of legal jargon thrown around until Jeff and Grace went glassy-eyed and Nona started yawning. Grace got up to leave for work. Jeff stayed, saying his foreman was competent, could handle a day without the boss.

They got the bond registration off the internet. Subconsciously, Nona'd expected some big mystical event like a raven appearing in a puff of smoke with a papyrus roll sealed by arcane symbols that needed a complex ceremony and blood to open. Or at least having to wait for mail delivery. Lauren's twist of her head and sudden smirk said she heard Nona's surprised noises. She pulled the papers off Jeff's printer with a flourish and presented them.

"We stopped demanding signatures in blood a century ago. Sorry to disappoint." She handed over a simple black pen.

"I'm sure you're not, you scamp." Nona returned.

Lauren laughed.

There was a lot more than expected. Four papers were blocks of legalese spelling out how they were bonded by blood and magic. Another explained her rights as a bonded pedestrian under Gierdes law, a pedestrian being a non-lokref person - oh, that's what it meant. The last few were a copy of Xuande's Law of Quiet. All needed to be signed and dated by both of them.

The Gierdes told them to keep a copy of the registration in a secure place and said they'd take care of the police hunt for Lauren. They helped Nona make video calls to her horrified, yet relieved friends. Her mother took it too calmly; experience said she was going to explode on Nona later when they were alone.

"There's no way I can keep the actual truth from my sister. Trevor tells her everything." Nona whispered, glad that Lauren had distracted Trevor and Jeff with games out back with the dogs. The clouds were gloomy and awful, but weren't dropping rain here and making everything a muddy mess. Laughter and barking drifted in through the closed windows.

"She is your immediate family, who lives with you." Wells said. He gestured at the signed papers. "It is allowed under the law." Warning darkened his eyes. "But she will be subject to the law if she knows."

A shiver went through her. "I understand."

Nona thumbed Lee's number into the phone and told the voicemail that she and Trevor were safe and alive; she was sorry about the lack of contact, and she would tell her everything when she came home in a few days. And yes, she'd already called their mother. And yes, she was acting like a timebomb, and she didn't look forward to the explosion.

"What about Lauren's job?"

Wells sighed. "That would require more paperwork. We could get it under normal circumstances."

"Under normal circumstances, we wouldn't even be here." Ramsey muttered.

"But the commandant won't sign off on it. He says Trent did it to herself when she failed to submit the proper paperwork in a timely fashion. She's free to tell the same story we've given today, but without anything to back it up."

"That asshole!" seared through Nona's teeth.

The men chose silence, though Ramsey nodded.

She couldn't sit still any longer. She raged from her chair, went to stalk out the door and vent to Lauren, but stopped with hand on handle. Lauren's roommates wouldn't understand. Trevor didn't need to see his mom this way. She glanced at her watch; 12:14. Lunchtime. She went to the fridge and cupboards, pulled out ingredients for her go-to stirfry. The roommates must have gone shopping for veggies the moment they'd gotten home. Everything was fresh and crisp and begging to be eaten.

"Staying for lunch?"

They looked at each other. Wells shrugged. "We'd be delighted."

"Good. You can help prepare it. Ramsey, wash vegetables. Wells, find the rice. I think I saw it in that bottom cupboard."

They looked at each other again, this time Ramsey letting a grin crack his fixed expression. "Yes, ma'am."

It was fun with them helping. Both had amiable stories about cooking and Ramsey's knife skills were impressive. He turned carrots into beautiful slices of perfectly even, orange ovals. Napa cabbage, onions, mushrooms, they all got the same quick, efficient treatment. Wells looked at the package of chicken in his hands, snorted, and traded Ramsey for the ginger root. He made a big deal out of peeling and grating it while they laughed.

The scent of cooking food drew the others in before it was quite finished, Trevor racing in first to use the bathroom. Lauren inhaling and joking about how Nona could stick around. Jeff laughed and agreed. The dogs danced at the outskirts of the kitchen and whined.

"Since when don't you two go charging for scraps?" Jeff pat their bellies. He frowned, shrugged. "Come on. Lunch. Kennels."

The dogs barked and raced up the stairs.

"Is it a lokref thing? Animals acting like that?" Nona dropped her voice low.

Lauren picked up a towel to dry her hands. "Yep. Took months for Bubba and Max to get used to me."

"Animals can sense our magic in a way people can't." Wells added.

"I disagree with that theory." Ramsey shook his head. "People can sense it. Animals have the better sense to be wary of it and stay away."

Lauren shrugged and started pulling plates from the cupboard. A large table in the next room got them, made Nona wonder again about whether the roommates had guests. Trevor returned, his hands glistening with damp, took a look at what Lauren was doing and asked where the silverware was. Lauren showed him and proceeded to get glasses, chuckling when Trevor followed behind, dropping forks and knives beside every plate.

Holy macaroni, if she didn't tell Lauren how much she wanted her soon, she was going to explode.

"Might want to turn the stove off." Ramsey poked at her.

She whirled and pulled the food off the heat as the first tinge of scorch hit her nose. Ramsey chuckled. A moment later, Wells did too.

"Mom, why are you red?"

"It's hot in front of the stove, pumpkin. Is the table set?"

"Yea! I helped Lauren get it ready!"

"Wow." Jeff reappeared. "Good smelling food I didn't have to cook *and* a set table. Is this really my house?"

"Ass. I cook great food all the time. So does Grace."

"Grace, yes. You?" His mammoth shoulders rolled. "Maybe."

"Just because I refused to cook cabbage on St. Patrick's Day doesn't mean I'm not an epic cook! Cabbage is nasty!"

Jeff stared her down for a moment. "Okay. You're a great cook. But," his tone was dry. "You're a destroyer of traditions."

"Exc–"

"Okay, you two." Nona stepped between them, steaming pan in hand. "Lunch time."

Chairs got butts, plates got food, and glasses got beverages. Talk wandered from cooking to cooking shows to reality TV to whether cop shows got it right. Wells and Ramsey maneuvered through cop talk smoothly while Lauren fidgeted and Nona kept her thoughts to herself. Jeff must have felt the tension because he began asking Nona pointed questions about her profession. She dove into the topic with relish, feeling herself relax, seeing it mirrored in Lauren, even Trevor. Both of them began adding to the conversation, and the remainder of lunch finished with laughter.

"That was fantastic!" Wells pat his stomach and melted into his chair, a wholly content smile on his face.

"It really was. Thank you, Nona." Jeff flashed a grin handsome and charming enough to heat Nona's neck.

"It was just a simple stir-fry." She waved it off.

"Simple, my ass. I usually only tolerate Napa cabbage since it's not *exactly* cabbage, but this? This was amazing." Lauren beamed, and Nona had to grab her chair to keep from kissing her right then and there.

"Thank you," she wheezed.

"I wouldn't complain if all our missions ended up with good food." Ramsey added.

Wells' smile shifted, darkened, was shaken off. "Speaking of mission ends: we should be going." He stood, Ramsey following. "Thank you for lunch."

"And thank you for taking care of us." Nona stood as well, holding out a hand. "You didn't have to go to the trouble."

He shook his head and grasped her hand. "I did. And I'd do it again. Come on, partner. We've got paperwork waiting for us."

Ramsey accepted her hand, then Lauren's and Jeff's. "Take care of yourselves."

Lauren walked them outside while Jeff and Nona started clearing the table. She returned and pulled dirty dishes from Nona's hands. "We got this. Grab a beer, relax."

"Bu-"

Jeff held up a hand. "You cooked. Ren and I can clean. Seriously. Relax."

"I'll help!" Trevor bounced to Lauren's side. "I can put dishes away."

Along with her heart, she melted back into her chair, accepted the cold beer pressed to her hand and watched the trio clean, throw soap suds, and laugh together. She was yawning by the time they were done.

A large air mattress was pulled out of a closet and settled in the basement. Sheets and blankets covered it, and Nona went down with Trevor for an afternoon nap. She woke up alone. And hungry. Yawning, she fumbled for her watch and was surprised to see it was after five. Quick trip to the bathroom later, she went upstairs to find a full house. Amber and Royce were there, along with a marvelous smelling pile of takeout containers.

"Good nap?" Lauren asked.

"Yea." She yawned. "Guess I needed it."

Dark rings under Lauren's eyes tightened. "Me too. I got an hour in before a ni-" she coughed. "Before I woke up."

Nightmares. The urge to hug Lauren and kiss those nightmares away flared bright in her chest.

"Anyway. Food."

Enchiladas, tamales, and fajitas were being dished onto plates. Lauren dumped a big brown bag into a bigger brown bowl. Chips mounded and skittered over the side anyway.

"Have I mentioned you are a queen? A goddess?" Lauren gushed around a mouthful of chips, batting her lashes at Amber.

Amber snorted. "Not nearly enough. Keep going. No, don't, not while your mouth is full, you heathen.""Hey!" Royce stuck his lower lip out comically far. "I'm the one who thought of enchiladas. Don't I get some credit?"

Lauren hummed and shoved another salsa-covered chip in her mouth.

His spouse eyed him. "Some. Maybe."

Hands came together in a praying motion. "And what, dear goddess, do I have to say or do to receive thine praise?"

Her mouth opened. Her eyes glanced at Trevor. She snorted. "Perhaps, had you gotten me churros, I would be obligated to dole out praise. Alas."

Royce's expression shifted from entreating to smug. "One moment." He darted out the door and back, one hand hidden behind him. He waited for his audience's attention before bringing another paper bag into view, opening it, and displaying its contents for all.

"Royce, husband, *this* is why I married you." Amber cooed at the mound of churros in his hand. "All may praise my husband, for he is thoughtful and grand!"

Giggles circled the room, followed by more nonsense teasing. The atmosphere of a party felt like it could have lasted long into the night, but Royce started yawning, then Amber and Lauren. Jeff had to take the dogs for a walk. Trevor wanted to watch cartoons.

"We got a room at the Hilton downtown." Amber said. "Royce deserves some real pampering. We'll be in town for a couple days getting massages and eating steak."

"Isn't my wife the best?" Royce cooed, clutching at his heart.

Amber seemed like a wonderful person. She got extra points for being an insanely good friend to Lauren. But it was more the beautiful relationship Nona saw between Amber and Royce she truly admired and envied.

"We'll see you tomorrow, Ren." Amber was hugging Lauren. "And you, Nona." Her embrace was cheerful and unexpected. She looked like she wanted to say something as she withdrew, but she pressed her lips together and stepped back. "And you, Trevor!"

He threw himself into her hug, then waved with his whole arm as she and Royce left the house. Not a second later, he jumped to the couch and turned the TV on.

"Hey, mister. This isn't our house, and I didn't say we *would* watch cartoons." Nona reprimanded.

Petulance lifted the remote, turned the TV off. "Mom, can we watch cartoons? Please?"

"Jeff, Lauren, is it alright if w–"

"Yea, go ahead." Jeff yawned and moved to the stairs. "I'm going to bed. Being lazy today was exhausting."

A yawn mirrored itself on Lauren, but she went to the couch, put her feet up on the coffee table, and elbowed Trevor. "What cartoons are we watching? That Finn guy again?"

"I was thinking of watching classics."

"Classics?"

"Yea." He nodded as Nona joined them on Lauren's other side. "Like *Pokemon* or *Thundercats*."

She remembered watching *Thundercats* as a kid.

"Aren't those 90s cartoons? You sure they're old enough to be called classics?"

"Yep." He clicked the TV back to life.

Lauren leaned to Nona and whispered. "Your kid is calling us old."

She chuckled. "Yes. Yes he is. But he's eight, and I'm closer to thirty than twenty."

Lauren made a noise in the back of her throat. "Oh, and by the way, I took painkillers. I will probably pass out and snore like a chainsaw soon."

"That's fine. We'll put the volume higher."

"Good to know you care."

She shrugged.

"Bitch," was hissed.

She bumped her shoulder, and they set to giggling, was shushed by Trevor, which set them off more, and finished with them flopping against each other and gasping for air.

"You're surprisingly comfy for someone so bony." Lauren hummed as she snuggled into Nona's side.

Her breath caught, choking up any retort she might have made. A moment of boldness draped her arm around Lauren's middle. The woman stiffened, and Nona almost withdrew, didn't, and was rewarded with a grunt and sleepy mutter as Lauren relaxed.

"Goodnight."

Trevor glanced over and went back to his cartoons. She tried to follow, but all of her senses were completely focused on the feel of Lauren tucked into her. Warm, soft, firm, t- No. Nona, don't be a letch. She scolded herself, took a deep breath, and got lost in the scent of Lauren's hair. Vanilla and citrus. Shampoo? Lotion? She took another, luxurious breath. Wow.

Explosions on the TV drew her gaze for about 30 seconds. Lauren made a noise, wiggled, and acquired Nona's undivided attention until her own eyes drooped, and she succumbed to sleep.

◆

She snorted awake at the sound of a door closing, fumbled at the weight of a body draped on her, and in the light of the TV, discovered Lauren. On her other side, Trevor was snoring lightly. Nona flushed remembering the first moments of Lauren cuddling with her.

"Who the hell passed out in front of the TV this time?" a woman grumbled as she kicked off shoes.

"Sorry. We didn't mean to." Nona replied when she realized the woman was the third roommate. The woman she still wasn't certain if Lauren was romantically involved with.

Grace stopped, stared. "Holy shit. I did *not* see this coming."

"Wha's happening?" mumbled out of a yawning Lauren.

"What's next, mud wrestling?"

Lauren sat up, squinted. "What time is it?"

"Almost midnight."

"You're home late."

"I'm home right on time. I'm on third shift this week." Though she sounded irritated, Grace was smiling.

"Long day?"

"Yes. And I desperately need a shower. I had three separate patients puke on me tonight."

"Nasty."

"Yes, well, it's the job. And yet, my laundry has never stunk up the house."

Lauren groaned and flopped back. "Fuck off."

"That has never been in the cards, besides, Ren, you have guests." And with that, Grace flounced away.

"Is she angry?" Nona hissed.

Lauren lolled her head over to sigh. "I don't think so? I think she's being a pest because you're the first person I've brought to visit other than my parents. And you're a woman."

"Because you like girls?" Trevor asked. Had he been awake for all of that?

Lauren palmed her face. "Yea. Friends like to harass friends about their love lives. Or lack thereof," finished in a mangled whisper.

Nona's hopes soared at the almost admission of Lauren being single.

Lauren jumped up, stretched. "Don't know about you, but I'd rather sleep in a bed. Goodnight."

"Yea," came out of Nona as she imagined sharing a bed with Lauren. She pouted at the sight of Lauren going up to her room alone. Tomorrow. She was going to tell Lauren about her Alaska-sized crush on her tomorrow. For now, bed. She ushered Trevor to the bathroom, followed after, did her business, brushed her teeth, and changed into pajamas.

"Hey, Mom?"

She set her pile of dirty clothes on the floor and looked at him. He wore a serious, thoughtful expression, normal for him, yet the use of 'Mom' over 'Mommy' was new. When did he suddenly grow up? "Yes, Trevor?"

"I just wanted to let you know I'm okay with it if you like Ren."

Her jaw should have bounced against the basement floor with how far it dropped. "What?" croaked out.

"You like her, don't you?"

She picked her jaw up and plopped to the bed. "I do. Lauren is a wonderful person."

"Yea. She makes you smile, and she treats me like I matter." He pat her hand. "And I think what Dad says about gay people is stupid. Just because he's scared of people who are different doesn't mean he should say bad things about them."

Her emotions couldn't find a balance between rage at Duncan's selfishness and joy at Trevor's maturity. They wobbled like a child's top, making her head spin, and her heart race. She chose joy and scooped Trevor into a tight hug. "Cheese and rice, you're a great kid, pumpkin!"

His little arms squeezed, but he pushed back quickly. "Mom! I'm not done." She wanted to keep holding him until he could never forget how much she loved him. "Mom!"

"Okay, okay. What else?"

"Do you like girls *and* boys?"

Her heart jumped into her throat. She considered deflecting, lying, or twisting the truth. No. The truth, no matter how hard it was for people to accept. "Yes. I do."

He nodded, once, his hair flopping forward. "Okay." He puffed at his bangs. "Can I get a haircut tomorrow? I don't like it long."

She could use a trim too, she supposed. "I'll find us a salon."

"Can I get it dyed purple like Ren's? She's so cool. Did you see her fight? She was all bam, pow, take that!"

His dad would have an aneurysm if she let him dye it. Her mother probably would too. Other kids would tease him for it being purple. They'd tease him for having a not-heterosexual mother too. "I don't think I'm ready to answer that right now. Let's talk about it tomorrow."

He squinted, then nodded. "Okay. Tomorrow. We can hug again now."

Affection and adoration making a whole fireworks display in her heart, she wrapped around him, kissed his head, cried. "I love you, Trevor."

"Love you too, Mom."

Chapter Twenty-three

Cookies

"Having trouble, shrimp?" came Nona's teasing words. From across the kitchen, she grinned at Lauren's struggle.

"No." Lauren grumbled.

"Looks like you need help."

"Dammit, woman. I'm fine." Lauren shot back. Whose dumb ass put the new peanut butter on the top shelf? Her fingertips could touch the jar, but it kept slipping further away with every attempt to grab it.

An arm reached over hers to grab the evasive peanut butter. "Must you be so damn tall?"

Face so close that her warm breath tickled Lauren's ear, Nona chuckled. It shot lightning right to Lauren's core and turned her knees to jelly. She had to grab the counter for support, and Nona paused long enough, was close enough that Lauren was suddenly certain Nona was leaning in to kiss her. "I'm afraid you'll have to deal with it, shrimp." Words, no lips.

Lauren whimpered.

Nona's brow arched. "Are you alright?"

Still too close. Smelled too good. "Um..."

"Lauren?"

Why were her eyes that damn green? How was she supposed to think about anything except how intense the color was this close? The way she was blushing was only making them greener, and damn, was she getting closer?

"Mom?"

That intense stare shifted off her, and she sagged.

"Yes, Trev?"

"Mom, did you find crunchy peanut butter? I want crunchy peanut butter." While Trevor continued on about crunchy peanut butter, Amber smirked at Lauren from across the room. What? Lauren scowled, and Amber grinned wider. Beside her, Royce's grin was just as smug. Assholes. They could make their own damn snacks.

Lauren let Nona make hers and Trevor's sandwiches before slathering her slices of bread with the peanut butter and peach jam. She chewed irritably while Amber and Royce whispered to each other and laughed. What were they so damn amused about?

Peanut butter washed down with a cup of coffee, Lauren decided to go outside for fresh air. The sun's arc was already dipping to the south, and the air was brisk. Maybe she should take a walk.

"Hey, Ren!" Trevor bounced out of the house. "After we go home, you'll come visit us, right?

Automatic refusal died in her throat. Why not? There was no reason to hide having a connection to Nona anymore. There were a lot of reasons for Lauren to visit the mountains. Nice weather. Incredible, empty skies to play in. Nona.

Lauren fiddled with her pocket seam. Nona. Just her name made Lauren's heart rev. She was so nice, so cute, so amazing! So much everything! Ugh. And Lauren wanted her. She shivered.

"Ren?" He tugged on her hand.

"Um."

Nona wouldn't do the terrible things to her that Whitney had. Lauren was suddenly, absolutely certain of that fact. Yet she came with her own set of problems. One was the matter of Nona's sexuality; was Lauren even on her radar? What if Nona was painfully straight? Falling for a straight girl was the worst. Her first crush had been straight and dating the most popular boy in school. It was stomach churning to want the impossible.

"Trev," entered Nona's voice. Leaves crunched under her feet. "Could Lauren and I talk alone for a few minutes?"

"But she hasn't promised to visit yet!"

Nona's expression was odd. Her smile was somewhere between sad and hopeful. "We'll talk about that. Why don't you go see what Amber has for you?"

His head canted like a puppy. "Amber?"

"Yes, pumpkin." Nona ruffled his hair as he jogged toward the house. She met Lauren's uncertain eye. "Will you walk with me?"

She glanced at Trevor, who was halfway up the porch, wide eyes on the opening door. Amber stepped out with a small container in her hand.

"Cookies," sighed Nona. "Right after a peanut butter sandwich."

Amber tossed eyebrows at Lauren. Her chin bobbed at Nona before returning her attention to Trevor, effectively distracting him.

Balls! What did Nona want to talk about badly enough to wrangle Amber into it? Groaning, Lauren started walking. Fast. She charged off the lawn, down the sidewalk, and around the corner. Her skin prickled in the light breeze, reminding her that she was in a tshirt when everyone else was wearing sweaters and jackets. People would stare.

Grimacing, she aimed for the wooded area on the other side of the walking trail. It was popular for the area, yet still saw less traffic than the street. She charged along it, frowning at a pile of dog poop left by some lazy jerk despite the free bags the homeowners association kept stocked at the trailhead. Why would a–

"Something in particular you're running away from?" Nona seemed out of breath despite the fact she could billygoat nearly vertical surfaces at high altitudes without even breaking a sweat.

Lauren braked her frantic pace, forced herself to stroll. "Not really." Liar.

"Oh." Nona turned and smiled at the trees, commented on the bright colors.

Yea. They were pretty. Lauren shrugged, and talk died. The trees thinned and stopped at a hard line where farmland began. Short, yellow stalks of harvested crop spread out as far as she could see. "What do you need to talk about so bad you got Amber to distract Trevor for you?" Lauren finally demanded.

Nona jerked at the sharp tone. "Cheese." Her eyes met Lauren's, darted off. "I…" Bright pink was spotting across her cheeks. What was *she* so nervous about? Was it what Trevor was asking?

"I won't visit if it makes you uncomfortable." Lauren whispered, "Or even try to keep in contact.""No!" Nona cried out. She heaved a breath, the pink darkening and spreading. "Oh, sweetie. That's not it at all."

She felt her own flush build at Nona calling her 'sweetie'. She'd said it before, but this time felt… *softer*. "Then what is it?" nearly choked her.

"It's the exact opposite." Nona's hands fluttered. "I like your company. I…" she seemed to gulp for air. "I like you, Lauren," rasped quietly enough that the light breeze nearly drowned her out. Hands balled into her sweater. "I like you so much that I wish we didn't live so far apart, and I could ask you out on a date."

Date? Nona liked her? Wanted to date her? Her brain broke in a thousand different directions, and her mouth fell open.

"It's not that surprising, is it?" Nona wheezed. Her poor sweater was a wrung mess. "I know I'm not pretty," a hand waved at her scars before returning to mangle her sweater. "And I've never been with a woman, but I think you're super cute. And…"

Anything else she said was lost behind the thought, 'Not pretty?' "Are you shitting me?"

The hands stopped. Stunned, absolutely *gorgeous*, eyes flared at her. "No?" Uncertainty made her shrivel.

"You're fucking hot!"

Slowly, Nona's lips peaked into a smile. "You think so?"

"Yes! Balls, woman. I get distracted every time I look at your eyes. Or your butt. And you always smell good, like painfully good." Except when she couldn't shower. "Okay, not always, not out camping…"

Their gazes met.

As one, they exploded into giggles. It took a while, but they eventually sobered. Nona toed at the leaves. "It doesn't bother you that I don't have any experience with women?"

Lauren shrugged. "It's not like my experience with them has been great."

"Is…" Leaves tumbled in a gust, danced around Nona's shoes. "Did someone hurt you?"

Hurt was a mild way to put it. "Yea."

"I'm sorry, Lauren. You don't deserve to be hurt."

Yea. She frowned at the leaves.

"Lauren?"

She quit trying to make the leaves combust with her glare. "Hm?"

Nona's chin ducked as her blush returned. "Is it okay that I want to kiss you?"

Kiss her? Nona's lips were awfully nice. What would it be like to kiss her? To hold her close? To explore her…

There was pressure on her arm. "Lauren?" Sweet-looking lips formed her name.

"Huh?"

The pressure trailed down, formed into fingers that caught her own, softly twined around them. "You're really cute when you're flustered."

Nona smiled. She took a step closer, and the scent of her shampoo teased Lauren before the breeze took it away.

Lauren's chin lifted of its own accord, and her lips twitched.

Lovely green thinned to rings as Nona stared down at her. "Is it… Lauren," her words were husky and dry. Her head tilted down, but didn't close the distance. "Can I?" waited on her.

"Uh huh," puffed out as her calves flexed and lifted her up. Lips met. Bright and electric, tingles spread out from the contact, making her shudder and wobble. Luckily, there was a strong, inviting body there to catch her. Crash into.

And suddenly they were both falling to the ground, Nona first, with a surprised, "Oof!" Lauren on top of her.

"Oh shit! Nona! Nona, are you okay?" Lauren scrambled to get off, looking anxiously for anything broken because of her fat ass. Her fat, unreasonably girly ass. She'd nearly fainted like a dumbass in a movie!

"Hnn," groaned painfully.

"I'm so sorry." What a loser she was. Nona was going to realize what a mistake she'd made with Lauren and…

"I'm okay." Nona wheezed as she sat up. A shit-eating grin spread across her face. "I think I really like being the taller one." She giggled. "I'll actually catch you next time now I know you're a fainter."

Really? She stared. "You want to catch this fat ass?"Confusion tilted Nona's expression, was quickly overrode by disbelief. "Fat? Cheese and rice, Lauren! I thought you were crazy attractive under a thousand layers of winter gear. In that tshirt, you're," her eyes did a quick once-over. Air was quickly sucked in and blown out. "Wow."

Really? She still couldn't believe it. She knew she was sexy thirty pounds ago – twenty now, she had lost *some* weight – before she'd eaten her way through her post–Whitney depression.

Leaves crunched, twigs snapped. Nona was scooting closer. "Sweetie. You are gorgeous, would still be gorgeous with another fifty pounds of flesh on you. If anyone calls you fat or ugly, they're an asshole and a liar."

Tingles buzzed out from the sudden warmth in her chest. A smile pulled at her cheeks. "Thanks." Was it okay to kiss her again? She was so close.

"Any time," replied in a low, husky tone. Nona leaned in.

"Is this why you have an ex-husband?" Lauren's mouth didn't ask her head for permission to talk. "Because you're gay?"

Nona's head jerked back. Her expression tightened into a frown. "No." She fixed her eyes on the empty field.

What the balls, Ren? You dumbass! "Sorry, I..." was a dumbass. Why bring up an ex when they were about to kiss? She screamed at herself.

Nona began to speak. Quietly, as though afraid Lauren might hear. "I don't identify as gay. I still think some men are attractive." Or afraid Lauren would run? "Duncan couldn't handle that my sexuality didn't revolve solely around him. Our marriage was happy until I came out to him. I thought he would understand that even though I loved him, was happy with him, wasn't looking for anything but him, I found some women attractive." Her fists curled. "He didn't."

Seriously? A happy marriage with perfect Nona and the asshole freaks out because she admits she's not entirely straight? "What an asshole."

Sad green eyes flicked to her. There was a wall there, ready to go up, to push Lauren out if she was an asshole too.

"I, uh, I'm monogamous, and if you are too, cool." Monogamy? That's what came out of her? "Um! Not that I'm insinuating you have to be my girlfriend right the fuck now. Uh, but if that's a possibility, I um..." She groaned up at the treetops.

"You really don't care that I want to see Chippendales dance *and* sit here and kiss you?" Nona boggled at her.

Her face scrunched at the idea of all that naked man flesh on stage, all that swinging ew. "As long as I don't have to go see them with you."

Delight was a second sun on Nona's face. "Cheese, I didn't think you'd get any better!" She launched herself at Lauren, knocking her to the ground, pinning her there with lips and hands and the weight of her body.

It was some time before they made their way back, holding hands like the lovesick fools they were.

Tibbits smiled at the copy of Trent and Hummel's bonding registration. Despite Meisenger's distrust, Tibbits respected Trent, her courage, generosity, and determination. The woman would have made a fine knight, if it wasn't for Meisenger's fear of her black feathers. A nail tapped on the table. A second nail joined.

Both hands lifted and set to work rattling her keyboard. She needed to know. Why? Why was there this fear of dark feathers? If they were so dangerous, why wasn't the knowledge public? She'd need to be careful, collect little tidbits here and there. Emails were sent, requests for info left on certain websites, and a few phone numbers saved.

She even contacted a weaver she knew. Meisenger might have burned all his bridges, but she hadn't. Yawning at the late hour, she nodded in satisfaction and walked away from her desk. Answers or leads would be in her inbox soon. She only had to wait.

Chapter Twenty-four

Magic Doesn't Exist

House, head, and heart too full to process, Lauren made apologies after an early dinner and escaped for a few hours. She spent most of that time driving around with no objective and no real memory of where she'd been. Eventually, she stopped in front of a familiar grocery store when her stomach gurgled.

"I hear you," she muttered at the beast and went in hunt of a snack.

Her brain was only half on the topic despite her stomach's continued grumblings. She bumped into a man's cart, almost knocked a display over, and ended up staring at the frozen dinners.

What she really needed was time to wrap her head around the sharp changes the last few days had taken. Gierdes letting them go. Officially filing a bonding registration. Kissing Nona. Remembered shivers vibrated along her spine, lips, and hands, made her smile and fidget. Wow.

"Ren?"

She turned at her nickname. Steve was there, his expression one of shock and horror.

"Fucking hell, Ren! Where have you been? What happened to you?"

"Um." She had a story ready, the fake one Wells had cooked up. Another lie. Steve didn't deserve lies.

"I was fucking livid when I saw that video. I thought you were out there pulling pranks instead of coming to work, but shit. Your face." He waved at her arms. "These bandages. What the hell happened?"

She squirmed, her hands bunching in the fabric of her pockets. She was so damn tired of lying! "Um…"

Intense eyes scoured her. "Last time you disappeared, I read every newspaper I could find, looking for you." His voice was low, a whisper, but it was as intense as his gaze. "There was a lost kid in Colorado. His mom was that trail guide you got trapped in that blizzard with. That same cutie who came into the shop last week." His breath was ragged. Her own matched it. "Then that video came out... The comments were on fire about magic and people called lawkef. Wh-"

"Lokref," was her automatic correction. Horrified, she bit her lip.

His eyes bugged. Another shopper drew close, her cart squeaking. The young woman mumbled an apology as she squeezed past to the ice cream section.

Steve looked at her, then Lauren, the lack of groceries in either of their hands. "You eaten yet? I could go for pizza. On me."

Lauren nodded.

"Great. I'll have it delivered to my place." He thumbed at his phone as they stormed to the exit. "Two pizzas. Meat lovers and a supreme. Good?"

She managed another nod. They passed through the exit, headed across the parking lot, stopped at his Jeep.

"Where's your car?" He worried.

Um. She scanned the lot. Two aisles over. She scanned it again, this time looking for Tibbits or another Gierdes. "It's fine."

He danced from foot to foot. "Good." He opened his door, and she went around to the passenger side.

Awkward, heavy tension filled what air the pungent man-scent didn't already permeate. An old fast-food bag crinkled under her feet. Every few seconds, she felt Steve look at her. She studiously watched the road, her mind running a thousand miles an hour, her heart racing almost as fast. What was she doing? What was she going to say? She was so caught up in trying to find a way out of this mess she didn't notice they'd stopped until Steve's garage door was rolling up in front of them.

"We don't exist," blurted out. Slammed brakes made her seatbelt lock up, her body jerk, and every injury howl in protest.

"What?" Steve demanded.

"Lokref don't exist. And if you try asking about them, someone will show up to kill you."

Uncertainty bulged at her. "What?" squeaked again.

"Magic isn't real, that video was a hoax, and you should fire me," spewed out.

He blinked at her for a long minute. Fingers creaked on the steering wheel. "What?" He whispered.

The garage yawned at them. Down the street, a dog barked at a passing bicycle. Steve's huge eyes flicked to the mirror. He took a deep breath and eased the Jeep into the garage. The door's motor hummed, let the door slowly slide down.

He turned the engine off, and they sat there listening to the moving parts creak and clunk as they cooled and settled.

"I'm not going to fire you." Steve announced quietly.

"What?" was her turn to demand.

He frowned at the steering wheel. "There's always been something about you. John's fucked up rottweiler growls at everyone except you. Shit. All dogs act funny around you." He scratched at his chin. "You're never cold. Ever. Not even that bad cold stretch last January didn't bother you. Fucking negative twenty for three days, and you're the only one who didn't bitch about it."

"Magic doesn't exist," was her weak response.

He fully turned in his seat to face her. He stared until the garage's light timed out and left them in darkness. "A few months ago, a buddy of mine was telling me stories about shit he'd seen as a firefighter. One in particular stuck out. Couple of dumbasses crashed during a race, then beat each other up after."

Oh. Fuck.

"The weirdest part was that one was a gangster with a gun. There were bullet holes everywhere except in the other driver, who barely had a scratch on her. He ended up in ICU with a broken face, broken ribs, broken arm, *and* internal bleeding. The woman's car had crashed head-on into a building."

He took a breath. "What was *really* weird was how the engine block was in the car's cabin, should have pinned her, crushed her chest, killed her instantly. But, the driver's seat was mangled, and the steering column was on the floor. On the fucking floor because it'd been sliced clean in half!"

She shouldn't have gotten in the Jeep.

"How the hell did you survive that, Ren?"

Some days, she wished she hadn't. At least then she'd be free of all this bullshit. "People who ask the questions you're asking end up dead, Steve. They tried to kill me. They *keep* trying to kill me."

His breath was heavy, ragged as a rusted muffler. "Fuck, Ren."

"You need to fire me," was all she had to say to that.

He continued to sit there, chest heaving with his struggle until his phone beeped. She could read the message when he opened it. Pizza was cooked and on the way. Fifteen minutes. "God dammit." His tone was dejected, exhausted.

She cringed. "Sorry."

"I don't understand!"

Guilt filled her throat. "It's better that you don't."

"Fine. You're fired." The Jeep's interior blazed with sudden brightness as he opened the door. "Now, let's go in. I'll mix us up some Jack and Cokes, and we can start looking at old beaters you can fix up and sell."

Important Terms

- Lokref: people born with magic in their blood. They're able to summon magical armor, weapon(s), and wings.
- Gierdes: a force that polices the magical community. It has a presence on every continent, headed by commandants.
- Pedestrians: people who don't have magic and therefor can't fly; used by lokref.
- Scarecrows: slang for Gierdes; used by weavers.
- Shadows: an ancient enemy not seen for millenia.
- Skugg: traitor who works with the shadows.
- Slug: slur for people unable to fly; used by lokref.
- Weavers: people who can control magic.

Acknowledgements

Who couldn't I have done this without? My parents. Those long-suffering souls who've supported all of my craziest adventures. My work fam who put up with me constantly filling the quiet moments going on and on about books, especially Linnae, who not only read those awful early drafts, but gave me invaluable feedback.

My fanfiction readers. Yes, I have humble beginnings. Those wonderful readers and reviewers showed me how much other people wanted to read what I had to write. They helped improve my craft and cheered my publishing journey on as well!

Every excited voice that learns I'm an author. Yea, we shouldn't rely too much on the opinions of strangers, but damn it's still validating to hear a random cishet woman exclaim their interest in my very gay writing.

My oh so excellent GoFundMe donors who made hiring a professional cover artist a reality! Amanda, Mithu, Lexie and Suetta, Bill and Su-jin, Mom and Dad, and many others. Thank you, thank you, thank you!

All the authortube creators, writing bloggers, and writer podcasters that I spent (still spend) crazy long hours learning from and relating to.

Friends who may never read any of my work, yet still cheer me on, because friends fucking do that.

Thank you.

About the Author

This sassy, quirky, lesbian wordsmith was born and raised in the American Midwest. She's prone to "opes" and hour-long goodbyes. Please don't hold it against her.

She's got obnoxious, fluffy writing companions who know *exactly* when she's busiest writing or gaming and insist on scritches and snuggles. Right now!

She spends her days nerding, wandering, and beavering as whim dictates. Sometimes even writing. Okay, maybe she works at dirty nine-to-five to pay to the bills, but someday, all her hours will be her own to, oh look, something shiny!

Before You Go

Like what you read? Please leave a review wherever you bought this book!

Want to follow progress on the next book, behold some gay shenaningans?
Follow me on <u>Twitter</u> (@jenthewordsmith)
Join me on Tiktok (@jmbarrows)
Check out my website (jmbarrows.com)

www.ingramcontent.com/pod-product-compliance
Lightning Source LLC
Chambersburg PA
CBHW021130190726
48288CB00008B/2593